Famous In Cedarville

Famous In Cedarville

Erica Wright

The following is a work of fiction. Names, characters, places, events and incidents are either the product of the author's imagination or used in an entirely fictitious manner. Any resemblance to actual persons, living or dead, is entirely coincidental.

ISBN 978-1-947993-72-3

eISBN: 978-1-947993-85-3

Library of Congress Control Number: 2019948495

First hardcover edition October 2019 by Polis Books, LLC

221 River St., 9th Fl., #9070

Hoboken, NJ 07030

www.PolisBooks.com

POLIS BOOKS

Also by Erica Wright

The Red Chameleon
The Granite Moth
The Blue Kingfisher

In memory of Larry and Nancy Edwards

CHAPTER 1

FADE IN:

INT. HOTEL BALLROOM - NIGHT

Well-heeled ladies and gentlemen waltz to "Love's Own Sweet Song."

DISSOLVE TO:

ABIGAIL, an uninvited guest, pulls a silver pistol from her satin handbag.

CLIVE, a former bigwig who bet on the wrong horse, grabs her arm.

> CLIVE
>
> If you're going to kill me, I recommend a quiet corner. A deserted balcony, maybe, where I can plead with the moon for mercy.

1

ABIGAIL

The moon's not much on mercy these
days. You go ask.

CLIVE

Best wait 'til morning then. See what
the sun has to say about all of this.

ABIGAIL

You need guts for that sort of
mission. I left mine back home.

CLIVE

At least tell me you didn't leave
your name there, too. You got a name,
don't you?

from *Midnight Millionaire* (1939)
Written by Bucky Carruthers and Hope Lancaster
Directed by Jonathan S. Ferguson

Samson got the call because he skipped church most Sundays,
not because he had any experience with removing a body. Still, when
the Meeker brothers asked for a favor, you found your coat. He let his
old pickup warm for ten minutes before putting it into gear, so he was
the last to arrive on the hill. The other men watched him approach, their

expressions hard to read. The town had gotten used to him over the years, but he was nobody's first choice.

"She still inside then?" Samson asked, stretching his long legs to the gravel driveway. He left the keys in the ignition and slammed the door shut behind him. The locks had stopped working years ago, but the truck wasn't worth stealing, more rust than even scrap metal these days.

Grunts greeted him in response, and only Cully Barnes shook his hand. Samson hoped the four of them would be enough. Cully was built like a steam engine, but going on seventy, his gray hair meeting his beard in a sort of dog fight. Jamie Meeker and his younger brother Leejon were stick-thin and already buzzed at 10 a.m. Must be nice, Samson thought, stomping his boots against the frozen ground. A deep breath burned as the air slipped into his lungs. Samson hadn't touched a drop of alcohol since he got married, more than ten years back now.

The group turned toward the house, clambering up the rotting steps. The place used to be a showstopper, or so all the locals said. Samson had never seen inside, and part of him thrilled at the prospect despite their grim task. He'd gotten into antiques as a hobby, but now it seemed more like a calling. He placed his hand on a pillar as he passed, noting the strong oak, sturdy despite the termite damage. Yes, it had good bones, and Samson wondered who would inherit the three-story Victorian.

The front door wouldn't budge, but Leejon found a cracked window and pushed it up far enough to squeeze through and then let everyone else in. They moved quickly, glad to be out of the cold. A staircase greeted them, six feet wide and ascending to a large pane of stained glass, pale winter light making the dust shimmer and dance. The place felt like it hadn't been disturbed in years, that they were trespassing on holy ground, but Samson knew he was just being superstitious. He'd gotten that way lately. They had a job to do, and they would get through it.

"Damn shame," Cully said, and Samson pulled his attention to the sitting room, which was packed with newspapers and magazines, the kind of hazard you hate to see anywhere, but especially in a town with a volunteer fire department that got called mainly for drunk teenagers taking a curve too fast on Sable Road up near the high school. Good men, but not exactly known for their fast response time.

The smell wasn't as bad as Samson anticipated, more earthy than rancid, and they headed toward the back bedroom where, they'd been told, Cedarville's only celebrity had slept for years, rarely venturing farther than her front porch. Samson had seen a few of her movies. They were mostly B-quality, and Barbara Lace was never the lead actress, lucky to have a few lines and a tailored dress. Sure, she'd been a looker, but lacked the box office appeal of a Rita Hayworth, though the two were rumored to have entertained the troops together in 1944. If rumors were rivers, they would flood Cedarville, though. Samson only believed what he saw with his own eyes.

He glanced at the Meekers and Cully, assuming they'd never heard of Rita Hayworth or Ingrid Bergman or Dorothy Dandridge. Maybe Marilyn. That was all right. He'd come to accept his neighbors' unimaginative range of interests, admiring, even, their predictability. He doubted the men had ever suffered from anxiety, a morning feeling of dread simply because countless days stretched between now and the end. He'd wished for death so many times that the sight of Ms. Lace's bloated face didn't shock him at first.

Samson stopped at her bedroom door for a moment, peering in. She looked far from at peace, though her eyes were closed. Her dry lips were parted, her teeth almost bared in a grimace. The hand clutching her quilt confirmed an anguish in her fi nal mo ments, a n d Samson looked away, unconcerned about what the men might think of him. A queasiness settled in his stomach, and he coughed into his sleeve. He'd shown up, hadn't he? And he would see this thing through.

Cully crossed to the window, putting his shoulder against the frame to force it loose from the paint. With a shudder, it creaked up, and icy air whipped into the room, blowing Ms. Lace's white hair across the pillow. Samson took a grateful breath and stepped into the room. He thought someone should take Ms. Lace's bony wrist between his fingers to check for a pulse, but it would have been a formality at best.

"How I'd like to go, sure enough," said Jamie.

"How's that?"

"My own damn bed. Middle of the night."

Samson didn't respond, thinking about how many days the actress might have been lying there before someone noticed that her lamp stayed on, dusk to dawn. Before someone noticed that something might be wrong. The call went to an answering machine, of course, Clark Bishop more a police officer in name than anything else. He got sent out less frequently than the fire department, even though he drew a paycheck. Sheriff Bishop knew how to write a speeding ticket, and that was about the highest compliment Samson felt comfortable sharing.

Cully picked up a corner of the blanket, folding it across the dead body, then repeated the gesture at her head and feet. When she was fully wrapped, each man took a corner, assuming their roles as makeshift pallbearers without need of any instruction. Some tasks are instinctual. They lifted their burden, Samson cringing as the body slid toward his side. Then they headed back toward the foyer and through the front door.

The quilt bothered Samson, a Lancaster blue made—he guessed—in the 1870s and in collectible condition. The kind of heirloom that should have been passed down. The kind of heirloom that could pay off somebody's credit card debt. He tried not to, out of respect for the woman he carried, but he couldn't help wondering who would get the sideboard he'd glimpsed or the red bergère chair in the hallway. If it all went to auction, could he afford a few pieces? Were the kitchen drawers full of Rococo silverware? He forced himself to pay attention to the job he was performing.

They were careful going down the steps, watching for black ice. The hearse could be seen creeping toward them, and they shifted their weight from foot to foot, unwilling to put the blanket down on the driveway, but ready to hand over their responsibilities all the same. It was going on noon and First Baptist would be getting out, the parishioners sure to gawk at them and stop their cars before going home. Samson didn't much care for being gawked at. 53 Chritton Lane was remote, but not quite remote enough for a place short on news.

It was the kind of town where you couldn't rightly refuse a favor. With a thousand residents, Cedarville would fall apart if anyone learned to say no outright. You could age out, hoping a teenager would step into your place, wouldn't decide to abandon his boredom for college or a job. Always a gamble, trying to keep the young people around. And everyone knows you never bet against the house.

Mr. Pitterson shuffled out of his vehicle, Cully mumbling "Christ" at his appearance. The undertaker looked more phantom than human, looked every inch of his eighty-eight years.

"Hello there, Mr. P.," called Samson, raising his voice so the old man could hear him.

"Hello there, son. You holding up?"

Mr. Pitterson opened the back door, and the younger men surged forward, lowering the body onto the clean white sheet waiting for them. They stepped back, wiping their hands self-consciously. Even Cully looked a little pale, and he'd done two tours in Vietnam.

"I sure do appreciate y'all," Mr. Pitterson said.

Samson knew that the hospital a town over took care of transportation on most occasions. Mr. Pitterson and his son waiting for him back at the mortuary weren't up to removals anymore. Eli Pitterson,

Jr., had cracked three vertebrae at a graveside service last summer and now hunched slightly. They should have both retired, but there wasn't anyone around to take their place. When one of the other funeral homes in the county went belly up, the Pittersons took on more than they could really manage from neighboring towns. Three or four unlucky souls per week, embalmed or cremated. Not to mention the services with programs to print, a piano to tune, paperwork to fill out. People joked that you better double-check your loved one's faces before lowering them into the ground. But Samson didn't care for that sort of talk.

"Kap's fifteen now," Jamie said, bringing up his youngest brother. "If you need some part-time help."

Samson doubted the cocky teen he'd seen around the square would take kindly to that suggestion, but then again work was work. The assembly plant up in Tewson was on an unofficial hiring freeze.

Mr. Pitterson nodded in response. "I'll keep that in mind. I truly will."

Samson glanced back at the house, its patched roof sharp against the white sky. Something seemed to flash in an upper window, but when it disappeared, Samson shook himself. Nothing but a trick of the light. He'd gotten used to seeing things from the corner of his eye, gotten used to turning a second too late.

"Will you be contacting her family?" Samson asked as Mr. Pitterson climbed into the driver's seat. He sat on top of a Nashville phonebook, so that his small frame could see over the dash.

"If I can find any."

The Meeker brothers were already in their truck, nodding good-bye to Cully, who turned to walk back to his place a mile or so in the distance. Samson offered him a ride, but Cully declined, lighting a hand-rolled cigarette and ambling away. After the hearse pulled onto the road, the only sound for miles was the wind and the periodic call of crows. The quiet kept Samson in Cedarville. Without any distractions, he could still hear his wife's voice sometimes, not as a whisper but clear as day. She might have been calling him from across the nearby field, telling him to come home. He looked there just in case, then he walked back into Barbara Lace's abandoned house, checking to make sure he wasn't watched. He shut the door behind him and let his eyes adjust to the dim light.

The oil portrait of Ms. Lace was a fair representation, painted sometime in the '60s, Samson speculated. A depiction of a mature, handsome woman with carefully plucked brows, lined lips, and shoulder-length curled hair. The colors were muted grays and greens, as if she were emerging from a forest, dressed to the nines. Pearl earrings and a pearl necklace made her look like a politician's wife, but her expression seemed tough, fierce even. Independent and no man's sidekick. While it was the most striking object in the foyer, Samson stopped to look at the framed photographs as well, recognizing Ms. Lace smiling alongside the incomparable Isadora Alvarez, a true Hollywood legend. The women must have been in their thirties, youthful and unstoppable, smiling at the lucky person holding a camera. It wasn't a paparazzi shot, but it was casual. A party, maybe, or somebody's wedding.

Samson fought an urge to take the photo off the wall and tuck it into his jacket. He thrilled at the prospect of exploring every nook and cranny of the place, soaking in the history. In the den, there were movie posters behind acrylic, and he knew a few of the titles. *All the Guests* and *Wild in Montana*, a western from the '70s. The place was generally neat, but a couple of shelves overflowed with souvenirs—cocktail napkins from the Ritz, poker chips from a Las Vegas casino, a couple of yellowed scripts, one written by Ms. Lace herself. There was a prop crown that looked heavy, but lifted easily in Samson's hands, the rhinestones still sparkling after decades of neglect. A couple of stuffed teddy bears, the kind a lover might pick up if he forgot about Valentine's Day. Samson stopped feeling nervous about getting caught as he took the stairs two at a time. He had wanted to see Barbara Lace's old house ever since his wife told him about its folklore. Always practical, she objected to his use of the description "folklore." *She's flesh and blood, same as the rest of us.*

But Barbara Sussennox had a history that was anything but typical. At eighteen, she hocked her engagement ring and bought a plane ticket to Los Angeles. She checked into a cruddy hotel, and nobody heard from her for ninety-seven days. Her abandoned betrothed insisted she'd been kidnapped, but the police never pursued that theory, preferring the simpler explanation that she'd been hysterical, and wasn't a hysterical woman likely to abandon her societal duty? Her parents were a wreck, but her neighbors in Cedarville? They said she should have known better, that she deserved whatever happened to her for treating them all so poorly. But what should have been a cautionary tale ended with a twist. Barbara Sussennox—now reborn as Barbara Lace—could be seen on the silver screen, carrying a champagne glass through a crowded ballroom. "Pardon me," she'd called to Humphrey Bogart, her brunette pageboy sparkling in the chandelier light. One line, but one line counted. A bona fide speaking role in a movie. By Cedarville standards? She was a star.

And stars are forgiven for their sins, Samson thought as he reached the stained glass window, more appropriate for a church than a residence. It depicted an angel in indigo robes looking skyward. Gabriel maybe, or Azrael. Samson didn't know much about angels. From a distance, the scene was beautiful, but up close? Up close, the eyes were on different levels, and the hands were more like paddles than flesh. The figure looked almost melted, and Samson hoped for better finds on the dark second story. He didn't dare switch on a lamp, worried that whichever neighbor had reported the first time would call in a burglary.

There was light through the windows, though, and Samson

turned left into what must have once been the master bedroom, when Barbara was still able to navigate stairs. There was a door to what might have been a servant's quarters in a different century. An enormous four-poster bed with a mint-green canopy stood in the center of the room, not touching any walls. Samson moved closer, rubbing his hand along the frame appreciably, and he let out a low whistle. The piece was in good condition, so he doubted he could get much of a deal. Still, off the top of his head, he knew three buyers who would be interested and grateful for a favor. He'd ring them when he got home.

The velvet comforter had moth holes, and after a moment's hesitation, he pulled it off, coughing as dust filled the room. A similar sound came from inside the next room, and Samson froze. Had he imagined the sound? His eyes burned from the filth he'd uncovered, and he wasn't surprised when his voice shook.

"Who's there? I don't mean any harm."

He wasn't sure if that was a true statement, but no answer greeted him either way. Instead, the house settled back into its tomb silence, and Samson fought all of his instincts to flee, forcing his boots toward the servant's door, which he flung open before he lost his nerve. He hoped that he would see a forgotten pet, some sort of ratty lapdog perhaps grateful for discovery, but instead there was a woman, her face streaked with tears, her arms cradling a 1910s-era Winchester rifle. An antique, sure enough, but old or not, it could still blast a hole through a man.

"Easy," Samson said, holding out his hands as he would to a skittish horse. "Easy."

The woman laughed, more of a bark, and peered down the sight. At this distance, there was no way for him to run or hide. For a brief, sweet moment, he welcomed the situation. At last, he thought, and such a tidy solution. Then, after months of depression, adrenaline took over, his heart racing, urging him to react, to survive.

"What do you want?" he asked, wondering if he might be able to launch himself out a window and survive the fall.

"I want," the woman began carefully, a considerable pause between each word, "I want to be left alone."

"Now that's a request I can surely grant a lady," Samson said, taking a step back.

The woman lowered the barrel by a few inches, and Samson got a better view of her face. Lined but luminous, an almost unearthly white at odds with the sun-damaged faces he usually encountered. Her eyes were wide, the color indistinguishable in the low light, but decidedly red-rimmed and puffy. She was an apparition, wild like a banshee in her grief or madness. Samson didn't truck with ghosts—at least not this kind—and retreated farther, afraid to be in her crosshairs again. He had no thoughts other than escape.

"I could take you captive instead," she said. "Trespasser."

The word came out as a hiss and stung because it was true. What was she, though, if the woman belonged here? Samson tried to get his muddled thoughts in order. Who was the intruder? Had she broken in or had he?

"Forgive us our trespasses as we forgive those who trespass against us," Samson said.

"I'm not from these parts," the woman said, her otherworldly voice taking on a distinct note of disdain.

Without knowing how he managed the distance, Samson found himself outside of the bedrooms and on the landing, stairs looming nearby. When he stepped to the right, his heel slipped off into nothing, making him yelp. The sound startled the woman, and she raised the gun again as Samson stumbled, his knees slamming into the hardwood floor. Pain ripped through him, and when stood up, his leg ached in protest. No

11

longer a young man, he thought, as if he had all the time in the world. He turned, limping down the steps, hoping rather than believing that the woman wouldn't pursue him. Flinging open the front door, he tried to run to his truck, satisfied that he seemed to be moving a little faster at least. Not fast enough, though, to escape the sound of a rifle shot ripping through the air, scattering the assembled crows.

CHAPTER 2

CUT TO:

Sunbathers relax by a swimming pool, reading magazines and sipping cocktails.

THE STEPS

NORMA clinks her glass with a manicured nail to get everyone's attention.

NORMA

To our favorite friend, stealer of hearts, knower of best clubs and worst restaurants, a rich woman's saint and poor man's devil in a blue velvet tuxedo, the last of the bon vivants! Let's hope at least—

A WOMAN
(from outside the frame)
Hear, hear!

NORMA

```
You've got fans, my love. And you
can live without anything
else.
```

from *All the Guests* (1941)
Written by Bucky Carruthers and Blane Pruitt
Directed by Tyson Banks

The sole member of the Cedarville police force eyed Samson suspiciously and leaned against the side of his trailer, a single-wide that served as both his office and his home. The official station on the downtown square didn't see much action. Bishop's patrol car was parked out front and badly in need of a wash. A new bumper wouldn't have hurt either, or at least a paint job to cover the key scratches left by bored teenagers. As the only official authority figure in town, Clark Bishop was an easy mark for contempt. Never mind that he'd never actually reported any kids for underaged drinking or half-assed graffiti attempts. Samson tried to give the man a little understanding—tried to sympathize even—but Bishop's bad attitude went beyond put-upon and into hostile. He seemed angry at Samson for reporting an unhinged woman at 53 Chritton Lane. Samson resisted using the word "suicide," though he couldn't help wondering where the round had gone if it hadn't gone into his back.

"A girl, you say? Up at the Lace estate?"

Locals always referred to Barbara Lace's house as an estate, though it was only an oversized Victorian that had seen better days.

"A woman, yes. Out of her mind."

Bishop spat a wad of tobacco onto the ground, then squinted at it as if trying to make a decision, like reading tea leaves. He nodded once and looked back up, his face twisted as if he'd bitten into mold.

"You under some stress these days, Sammy?"

If Samson were transplanted to Manhattan or Chicago, he would have been called "rugged." His wrinkles were deep-set at forty-three, his hands calloused from his work, refinishing furniture. He dressed like everyone else—jeans and sweatshirts, the occasional flannel and aftershave if he had to dress up for, say, a niece's dance recital in the town over, the one with a grocery store and fast food joints. Still, the citizens of Cedarville had greeted him with suspicion for years, considered him a little womanly for their liking. He could talk a blue streak when he got going, always ready with an anecdote or a joke. His fussing with antiques bothered them as well, at first. Worst of all, he was tall and thin with no hint of paunch. His wife, on the other hand, had looked like she could wrestle a sow because she could. Farm-raised then farm owner, she had arms that could cart hay bales or turn a calf tangled up backward inside its mother. God, Samson had loved her.

Nobody had ever told him that marriage could be like that, waking up each day surprised that tenderness could be so ferocious, like a feral cat taking comfort by the hearth, deciding to stay. After she passed, his friends—such as he had made—urged him to leave. But there was still something of his wife left in their home, and until she vanished completely, he'd keep looking for her in every closet and on every surface, loyal and hopeless.

"It's not some damn stress," Samson said, cussing to show he was serious. *Fucking stress* would have made more of an impact, but that wasn't a word he used very often and always seemed forced when he tried. He'd never gone with language harder than the occasional hell after his marriage. "There's a lady up there, roaming around like she owns the place."

"And what were you doing exactly?"

Samson took an irritated intake of breath, exhaling through his nostrils like he'd been taught. Bishop's stomach stretched his uniform, and he hadn't shaved for days. Samson knew the sheriff just wanted to get back to lunch, likely a casserole one of the biddies had dropped off, assuming that a divorced man wasn't capable of taking care of his most basic needs. Or maybe they hoped he would reform, turn an eye toward one of them after their husbands passed. Never too early to start planning, Samson supposed. He felt calm enough to respond.

"Ah, you know me and the Meekers were clearing out Barbara Lace this morning. May she rest in peace."

Bishop had probably been called, too, but he could beg out of most unpleasant tasks, saying he was on duty. Samson thought that was all the more reason for him to help, but he held his tongue, thinking he should have called 911 and let the dispatcher take over. It wouldn't have been any slower than arguing with this man to do his job.

Bishop grunted, knocking his knuckles against the plastic siding of his house, then straightened his holster.

"The others'll back you up on this?"

Samson explained that he'd gone back inside because he thought he'd heard something, and Bishop raised an eyebrow. He wasn't a dumb man—lazy but not dumb.

The drive back to the Lace house took all of five minutes, but the stretch had never seemed longer. Samson kept second-guessing himself, wondering if he should have left well enough alone. What if he got them both killed? Bishop didn't use his firearm for much more than shooting rats at the dump on Saturday nights. If he'd been trained, that training was a couple decades in the rearview mirror.

A first-floor light was on when they pulled up, and the men approached with more confidence than they felt, at least one of them. By the time Bishop rang the doorbell, Samson was sweating despite the chill. He could feel a drop run down his spine and into his pants. The crows watched from a safe distance in the trees, remembering everything. When the door swung open, Samson would have been less surprised by a mummy. The woman he'd met before stood in her bare feet, but was dressed in a tailored beige suit, her previously wild hair pulled into a neat chignon. Her skin remained the ethereal pale, but with red lipstick, the effect was glamorous rather than ghostly. She could have been an extra in one of Lace's films.

"Your beast?" Bishop asked, glancing at Samson and enjoying himself.

"Pardon?" the woman responded, wrinkling her brow. "How can I help you, gentlemen?"

Samson didn't know his lines. He couldn't tell if she was pretending that they'd never met or simply playing her cards close to her chest. He remained silent as he tried to reconcile the professional image before him with the woman who'd threatened him a mere half hour earlier. His confusion turned to self-doubt then frustration in a flash as he realized how this scene would unfold. Bishop reprimanding him and laughing about him later over beers with his childhood pals.

"Sorry to disturb you, ma'am," Bishop began, clearing his throat. "We had a report of a break-in following the, um, extraction of the body. May she rest in peace."

Samson thought Bishop might be mocking him, but he kept his attention on the woman, whose eyes pooled immediately—conveniently—with tears. She turned her head away, composing herself. Part of him felt rotten about it, but he studied her profile, looking for signs of genuine grief. He recognized them, but he didn't believe them. Waiting for Bishop to push her seemed like his only choice, and he stuck his hands in his pockets, rocking back on his heels. The motion caught the woman's attention, and the corners of her mouth quirked.

"I'm afraid," she said, coughing when the words came out in a low quaver. "I'm afraid that your colleague startled me, Officer."

"Sheriff," Bishop corrected her, and Samson managed not to roll his eyes. Sheriff of a one-horse town didn't mean much.

"Oh! My apologies, Sheriff. Your schedule must be so busy, and here you are dealing with a lark. Your colleague startled me earlier as I was going through Miss Lace's personal effects. She was quite particular about what she wanted kept from her adoring fans."

Samson balked at "fans." Barbara Lace was all but forgotten. Her death might warrant an obituary in *The Tennessean*, but camera crews were unlikely to descend on Cedarville. Still, it was possible the old woman had delusions of grandeur. Doubt started to creep back into Samson's understanding of the situation. Had the woman waited upstairs while he and the other men completed their mission? It was strange at the very least, if not illegal. She could have at least unlocked the door for them.

"I'm sorry I scared you, ma'am. That wasn't my intention. I'd thought you would have made yourself known before we removed her."

"And I'd thought you would have shown more respect for private property."

The woman placed a hand on her delicate hip, and Bishop chuckled, enjoying himself after all.

"All a misunderstanding then. How long you staying for, Miss...?"

"Callista Weathers. Executive assistant. And I'll be here for as long as it takes to sort the estate."

Bishop seemed satisfied by that answer, expressing his

18

condolences and tipping his felt hat. Samson tried to glance further into the house, but Callista blocked his view. He could hear the sheriff's boots crunch the gravel behind him, and he turned reluctantly, trying to forget his unease. He hadn't always been a superstitious man, but his gut churned in a kind of warning. What harm could a person do in an unoccupied house anyway, he tried to rationalize.

"You just going to take her word for all that?" Samson had climbed into the passenger seat of the patrol car, accidentally kicking empty Diet Coke cans littering the floorboard. The upholstery smelled sickly sweet, a combination of cologne, sweat, and crushed candy bars.

"For all what, Sammy? If you think there's some big conspiracy surrounding an old lady's death, you need to get out more. Hell, you need to get out more regardless before you turn full-on loon. You know what happens to crazies around here?"

Samson didn't answer, thinking the whole town was stark-raving mad and seemed to limp along just fine. Bishop turned his body to back down the driveway, and Callista waved at Samson, her fingers moving up and down as if playing scales on a piano. For a moment, she seemed like an apparition again, something from one of his frequent nightmares, an unassuming face turning into a pit of fire, then back again, blinking in and out of focus. Finally, just a woman in a doorway, waving good-bye.

Bishop and Samson never spent much time together. Bishop was local through and through, had a group of high school friends he could call if he needed help with a case of Bud Light. Everyone knew Samson didn't drink, and most resented him for it. Only happy people didn't drink, they figured, and who really had a right to be happy? After the funeral, Samson didn't leave his house much, accepting the casserole dishes that appeared on his doorstep as if they belonged there. The church ladies switched to disposable pans when they realized they weren't going to see their dishes again. They pictured a sink of dirty plates and roaches, but in reality, he hand washed everything he received at first, stacking them on the kitchen table. For a while, he'd even kept track of who belonged to the blue bowl and who had the 8x12. He put Post-it notes on everything, an organized haze. He lost track somewhere along the way, though, and couldn't seem to care about politeness anymore.

Samson, who had always been so quick with a compliment. Samson, who had his own monogrammed thank-you notes and dropped off Ms. Bellwether's newspaper on her porch so the delivery boy didn't have to bike up the town's biggest butte. Samson, who wouldn't ever dream of interrupting an elder or complaining about a crying baby. Who warmed up his wife's truck for her in the winter and picked flowers for her in the spring. Who volunteered for the dunking booth at the annual school fundraiser and never minded when rabbits ate the corn he'd planted along the fencerow. Gentle, funny, polite Samson Delaware didn't return a single goddamn piece of dinnerware.

The utilities office sat on the square between the boarded up general store and the only restaurant in town. Samson could smell chicken drying in grease as he pulled out his water bill and a blank check. He doubted the place would ever embrace a credit card machine, but he didn't like to use his American Express anyway, figuring there'd be an emergency soon enough. Brigit smiled as he approached the Formica counter, her bright pink lips parting to reveal two rows of even teeth. She must have reapplied when she saw him pull up. Pretty, but the woman made him cringe. At thirty-six, she was the only single one among her friends, and her determination to change her status was more depressing than inspiring. Samson knew the smile wasn't only for him, but for anyone left, and he counted now among that merry band of eligibles. He had never wanted to belong to a group less.

"How's the day treating you, Brigit?"

"No complaints. Honey's got a new litter if you're interested."

Honey was an Irish setter, as sweet as caramel with the biggest brown eyes Samson had ever seen on a dog. Every couple of years Brigit would breed her or her sister, Sugar, to make some extra money. She'd replace her curtains or put up a swing, some improvement visible from the road if anyone ventured down there.

"More of a mutt man myself. Though Honey sure is a beauty."

Brigit leaned forward conspiratorially, letting the top of her breasts show above her scoop-neck sweater. He tried not to glance down and failed.

"She is, isn't she? Don't know why this county's so horse crazy when dogs are around."

"Easier clean-up, too."

Brigit took Samson's bill, nodding. "Well, there's a runt if you change your mind. Fifteen pounds, but strong enough. Would do you good."

Her face softened, and Samson wished he couldn't see the sincerity, the real pain she felt for his real pain. He preferred the fakes these days, and there were plenty around.

"Well," he said, stepping backward and trying to change the subject. "Shame about Barbara Lace."

Samson watched Brigit's thin fingers write on his receipt. She didn't look up as she responded.

"Guess *Entertainment Weekly* will skip Cedarville this year."

Samson laughed, and Brigit glanced up at him to wink. She surprised him, her easy shifts in mood. The drab office didn't suit her, and the town would lose when she finally wised up and left them all. He hoped that was sooner rather than later. She stood up to hand him the receipt.

"Anything else I can help you with?"

A couple of days had passed since Samson's run-in with Callista Weathers, but he remained unhappy with her explanation. It seemed odd that he'd never seen her around town before. One recluse could be excused, but two? Wouldn't Callista have needed to run errands for her boss?

"Did Ms. Lace pay her bill in person like us commoners?"

"Oh no, never saw her. Her checks were always in the night box and always on time. I never had any reason to pester her."

"Never? What about her assistant?"

Brigit shook her head, and Samson thanked her, heading toward the exit. His hand was on the doorknob when Brigit called him back.

"Wait, I remember a woman in here once. She sort of stuck out, you know? A suit in summer. Heels."

Samson's heart sped up, though he couldn't say why exactly. That bit of information didn't prove anything.

"How'd she act?"

"Act?" Brigit asked, and Samson thought for a moment that she wouldn't answer. "Snooty is as snooty does. Her check had roses on it. I remember because I asked where I could get some, and she said, get this, not around here. Can you believe that? Like we don't have everything we need. And then some."

Brigit put her hands on her trim waist, and Samson's eyes dwelled on the silver belt buckle shaped like a dog's head. The eyes glared out, rubies or imitations most likely.

"Nice belt," Samson said, stopping himself from asking to see the receipt. Brigit would have probably shown him, and he had no intention of getting the woman fired, not even for her own good. And what would it have told him anyway? That Ms. Lace paid her bills, same as regular folks. Well, not quite the same. Nobody else around town had a tony assistant.

"You know Aunt Sylvie—been dying for twenty years now? Won't stop hiding the heirlooms? This one's mine, though. She gave it to me. Clear title."

When Samson left, his thoughts swung between Brigit and Callista Weathers, the memories pleasant and frustrated, respectively. He wanted them both gone from Cedarville for wholly different reasons. Cedarville wasn't the kind of place to keep secrets, and he wondered how long until everyone would know he'd been prowling around the Lace house. They'd laugh, then forget about his transgressions. There were benefits to being the town eccentric. Throw in a little grief, and neighbors would excuse nearly anything.

He slowed to a stop at the railroad tracks, watching the arm drop in front of him. Putting his truck in park, he eased his foot off the brake and waited as empty train cars crawled past, Maersk and Southern mostly. The Nashville to Chattanooga route once bustled, and Cedarville revolved around the now decorative depot. Days gone by, and Samson had never seen them. A car pulled up behind him, and he stuck his arm out the window to wave at Cully, on his way home from his plant job in the nearest city. Samson wasn't surprised when Cully climbed out and headed his way. It looked like the train was going to take its sweet time. Samson had grown accustomed to waiting and found himself amused by the impatience of people who'd grown up here. Time to think, he figured.

"Nothing to be done," he said when Cully got to his window.

"You're right, you're right sure enough. Still."

"Still," Samson agreed.

Cully's face was covered in gray dirt, and he smelled of sweat and onions. Samson didn't hurry him off, though. The silence was companionable, and Samson was in the habit of appreciating anyone who wanted to be companionable. The man was quiet, flinching when the train brakes squealed.

"Thirty-three," Cully said finally.

Samson didn't correct him, even though he'd counted thirty-seven cars himself. He was glad that it was a single train. Cedarville had a side track where trains could pass, one of the few in the state, and it could halt traffic for at least fifteen minutes. Caught by the trains was an acceptable reason for being late. It wasn't the sort of thing you could lie about anyway, the rhythmic chug of wheels heard from miles away.

Cully drummed his knuckles against the truck's hood, heading back to his own abandoned vehicle.

"Auction's Saturday," he yelled over his shoulder. "Thought you'd want to know."

Samson thanked him, grateful that Cully hadn't mentioned his snooping, though that was clearly why he'd brought up the auction. Cully probably thought some old piece of furniture had caught his eye, and he wasn't far off. Samson had no intention of missing a chance to see what the Lace estate offered, even if the auction seemed a little rushed.

His mind busy with ottomans and grandfather clocks, he didn't notice the wooden box at first, tilted but upright on the side track. When it finally caught his attention, Samson shivered the way he always did when an object was out of place. He must have been staring because Cully honked, and Samson jumped in his seat. Then he pulled forward and off to the shoulder so he could investigate. It's probably nothing, he thought, debris from a boxcar. Cully paused while he passed, rolling down his window to make sure everything was okay.

"I got a tow hook if you need one," Cully said. "That hunk of metal finally give out on you?"

Samson's truck looked rough, no doubt about it, but Cully's

ribbing didn't bother him. Nobody was driving anything fresh off the lot.

"You know me. I can't resist a diamond in the rough," Samson said, gesturing toward whatever rested near the train tracks.

Cully shook his head and drove on, leaving Samson feeling foolish. When he stepped down to the ground, he felt even sillier, telling himself again that it was would be picked up by somebody who lived nearby, no need to trouble himself. Something compelled him to keep going, though, and he checked to make sure no trains were coming. On closer inspection, he discovered it was an open jewelry box, plain on the outside but ornate inside with carved poetry around the rim and plush pink fabric. He lifted it into his hands, amazed that the wood was so clean. There was hardly any dirt and no visible tears, though the fabric was coming loose in a corner. He inserted a finger underneath and pulled, inadequately surprised by the slim letter tucked inside, his own name staring back at him: For Samson Delaware.

CHAPTER 3

A romantic comedy about a fast-talking journalist and the shiftless neighbor who mistakes her for an heiress. When the reporter travels to Niagara Falls for her sister's wedding, the neighbor follows, convinced that she's the woman for him. Will their love survive the train trip when the truth's revealed?

> pitch for *The Leopard Apartment* (1945)
> Written by Blane Pruitt and Barbara Lace
> Never filmed

Before dawn, Samson slid his tired feet into some boots and slipped out of his house. Tree frogs bleated in the distance, but otherwise the quiet was all-consuming, a pressure that warned him against the darkness. But it wasn't fully dark, and he could make out the outline of a dog or a wolf in the overgrown field. The animal didn't concern him. He'd sold off his wife's livestock and given away her pets, unable to care for them through the fog of grief. The bright red bee boxes that had brought them both such joy stood empty, their silhouettes more like broken robots than habitats. Sometimes Samson missed the barn cat. Popcorn but Samson had called him Polo, a more dignified name for the explorer. Mostly, though, Samson missed his wife's loud voice, how she'd call to him, "Finally up, Sleeping Beauty?" He'd grin, thinking 6 a.m. was early enough. Enough time to finish whatever he wanted to finish and still cook dinner for the two of them, roast chicken and asparagus or pasta primavera. A hearty soup on the stove in January.

The far-off animal sensed his presence, moving back into the trees, and Samson stepped toward his shed, not bothering with any outside lights. There was about five thousand dollars' worth of inventory in the space, but who would think to raid such a forlorn spot? How would they make off with an armoire anyway?

His latest acquisition leaned up against a wall, waiting for his attention. The table didn't look like much yet, but it would. Samson ran his finger along an edge, whistling when he got to the painted-over engravings. He planned to unearth those markings by the afternoon, and the thought of such a slow, deliberate undertaking calmed him. The letter in his pocket would remain ignored a little longer. It could hardly contain good news. Cracking his knuckles, he switched on the electric tea kettle and the radio before sitting down with his tools. Some he'd purchased—the putty knives and sandpaper—but others he'd invented himself with tape, cotton swabs, and lengths of bark. On this day he whittled an elm branch to a fine point before dipping it into turpentine. He breathed deeply, hoping the fumes would make him forget everything except for the wood underneath his fingers. It worked for a while, and Samson was surprised when he felt sweat drip down his brow. He pulled off his sweatshirt and threw it into a corner.

Sitting up hours later, he noticed the untouched hot water and the full sun shining through the windows. With all the morning dew burned away, the yard looked too earthly, too real. He guessed the time was going on noon and grunted in satisfaction, pleased by his favorite magic trick, the one that made time bearable again. When he stood up, his knees popped in protest, and he rubbed his back, wishing the pain away.

An old, pristine black Cadillac pulled into his gravel driveway, and he sighed, not sure if he had the patience to deal with Mrs. Answood. She had been the first to accept him in Cedarville, and he was grateful, but she was also hard-nosed and unsentimental. In her eyes, he'd mourned for quite long enough. Her cane emerged first, followed by Italian leather loafers in a men's size ten. When the woman herself got out, she unfurled to her full height of six feet, two inches and used a manicured hand to pat down her already immaculate helmet of gray hair. If any customer could barter him out of house and home, it was Mrs. Answood, former high school history teacher and wife to the late mayor of Cedarville. Her money came from horses, or so everyone said. Samson didn't pry. Both her size and her age intimidated him, but it was too late to hide. Instead he went on the offensive, flinging open the door and faking cheerfulness that used to be second nature. He felt like an unprepared understudy for the role of Samson Delaware, the audience inevitably disappointed by such a forced performance.

"Why Colleen Answood, if you're not a vision this fine day. Is that a Tahari suit I spy? Custom-tailored?"

"Mr. Delaware, a gentleman should not pretend to know a drip about ladies' fashion."

Samson let her maneuver toward him, knowing from experience that an offer to help would not be met with gratitude.

"The glamorous do love their secrets."

When Mrs. Answood got close enough, she did little to hide

her evaluation, clucking her tongue at Samson's thin frame.

"Wasting away to nothing," she said, shuffling by him and invading his private space. "Well, I've seen the chest, but what's that beauty there?"

The table did look nice, at least the parts he had scraped and cleaned. When he smiled at Mrs. Answood this time, his jaw relaxed, and he rattled off what he knew about the piece's provenance. A walnut inlaid card table with genuine—though damaged—leather interior, circa 1885, passed from family to family until forgotten in an attic. He'd picked it up at a yard sale outside of Birmingham. The story was a familiar one, yet Samson still delighted in recounting the steps that led an antique to him. Little frustrated him more than a missing decade in a piece's history. He'd rather a chipped drawer than a timeline gap. A drawer could be fixed.

"An attic. You've stumbled across the very reason for my visit, Mr. Delaware."

"Keeping unknown treasures in yours, I presume. You'll show me one of these days."

"You've sold me all my treasures. You know them better than I do. No, I'm on an entirely different mission."

Samson pulled out two folding chairs, knowing the woman would insist on standing unless he also sat. He wiped them off with the cleanest rag he could find, then lowered his long frame onto the seat, gesturing for his guest to join him. Mrs. Answood sat primly at first, then slid back to rest her whole body on the small chair like a ship settling into its slip.

"I'd like your advice on Baby's auction. Barbara, I suppose she'd wished to be called after all this time." Mrs. Answood paused, seeming lost in thought. When she continued, her voice was brisk. "What's worth a bid and how high, that sort of thing."

Samson had never heard Mrs. Answood call anyone except her late husband by their Christian name, and his interest was piqued. Baby was an undignified nickname, but he'd heard worse.

For a town of gossips, they were steadfastly tight-lipped about their most famous resident. There was an unspoken agreement of some sort, to respect her privacy. If she wanted to be a recluse, she got to be a recluse. A few reporters had shown up over the years, especially when she'd first returned. They wanted untold tales about her more famous friends like Rita or Isadora. But Ms. Lace stayed behind locked doors, and Cedarville folks shrugged or scowled when asked questions. There may have been a prank or two, a dead opossum in somebody's floorboard, that sort of thing. The reporters would leave, and after a few years, nobody bothered.

"You were friends with Ms. Lace?" he asked.

"Friends?" she said. "I'd hardly call us friends. She fancied Hank her beau for some time, but he came to his senses, and she flitted off to Hollywood. That was that."

Mrs. Answood made a bird motion with her left hand, drawing his attention to the plain gold wedding band. Samson remembered attending Mr. Answood's funeral, at least eight years in the past. Mrs. Answood seemed to be implying that her husband had once been engaged to Ms. Lace. It fit with the rumors he'd heard, but he pressed the matter all the same.

"Ms. Lace and Mr. Answood dated? Well, he traded up, that's for sure."

Mrs. Answood's expression softened, and Samson suspected that she was remembering a young Hank before he ran for mayor of Cedarville, a position he held for forty-six years until gout made his office days too difficult. There weren't a lot of people clambering for the position, even if the duties were few and far between. A couple of ceremonial appearances. A budget that paid a few salaries and tried to keep the fountain turned on, April through September.

"What was she like back then?"

"Oh, wild to the bone. Pretty, of course, but wild. She would slip out of her bedroom window and take off with some boy from Clarkton or Maines. An older crowd. Drinking and you know." Mrs. Answood paused before continuing in a quieter tone. "Nothing much compared to the young ones now, I suppose. But something of a scandal at our high school. She couldn't leave Cedarville fast enough."

"Maybe I could learn something from her," Samson said.

"Maybe you could," Mrs. Answood replied, reaching for her cane and starting to rise. "But we both know you won't."

January 15, 1983

Dear Samson Delaware,

Belated congratulations on your nuptials. I met your wife once at a fundraiser for restoring the depot and found her to be a sturdy, sensible girl. A good match, I mean, though I don't express myself well anymore.

Would she like this jewelry box, do you think? She doesn't seem like the type for ornamentation, but I don't have any use for it. And the poetry's nice. Elizabeth Bishop, I think, going on about some maps. I've traveled enough for ten lifetimes.

May you be blessed and happy.

Regards,
Barbara Sussennox

The letter was a curiosity, to say the least. Composed on a typewriter and signed—Samson couldn't be sure of its authenticity. And yet, what reason was there to doubt that Barbara Lace had once met his wife and been impressed enough to think of sending a wedding present? Albeit a year late. His wife had been decidedly impressive. But why address the gift to him, and why did Ms. Lace change her mind? The more pressing question, of course, was why the box had been left for him at all. Samson hated to indulge in conspiracies, but he had no doubt that someone had seen him waiting for the train to pass and decided to drop this for him to find.

The thought of being watched made him shiver, and even though he was inside his own house, he glanced behind him before setting the box down and opening it again. He tugged up the corner of the pink sateen and restored the letter, then ran his fingers along the lines of poetry. Though pretty, Samson wouldn't call the box an antique. It seemed to be a mass-produced object from the mid-1970s.

Much like this tie, he thought, his fingers fumbling to make a respectable knot. He kept his eyes down to avoid his reflection in the mirror. He knew the sad, hollow eyes that would greet him, and Samson had no patience for this unrecognizable version of himself. But he didn't miss the young, livelier version either, the one quick with a compliment or a joke, quick to laugh. He didn't miss him, because he forced himself not to dwell on those happier days.

The drive into town calmed his nerves, but Samson stayed alert, maneuvering what could safely be called a crowd for Cedarville before finding a parking spot. The event would be well attended with buyers traveling up from Atlanta and down from Nashville. The short notice would only deter a handful of interested parties.

The auction house had descended on the town. There was no other word for the hawk-like team as they invaded the only bed-and-breakfast, staked off an acre of territory, and devoured the possessions of Cedarville's most recently departed citizen. The six additional people made the town seem bustling. Not only were there six new mouths to feed at the diner, but there were a dozen more tongues than usual wagging there. One lone reporter, Kit Forrester, came for a morning or two, but was met with platitudes, every man, woman, and child understanding the unwritten code to give nothing away. Most had never met Barbara Lace, but she still belonged to them. Folks complained about the circus, sure, but liked the explosion of activity. They talked at the gas station about how glad they would be to see the buzzards go, then asked their family whether there might be anything they could bid on. Something little, you understand. A token of sorts. Maybe a hairpin or some bookends.

Saturday morning found residents in front of Ms. Lace's house, armed with five pages of single-spaced, typed print, a catalogue of every chair and every rug. An impressive feat to accomplish in a single week. It was as close to a festival as Cedarville could get, and Samson was unsurprised to see children darting through the legs of adults. The air still held a chill, but a bright sun made anything seem possible, even in late winter. As his neighbors scowled or pretended to scowl, Samson admitted to himself that he was in his element. He was relaxed despite the jewelry box, which he'd stored in his shed, not wanting to keep it inside his house in case it was cursed. Others might object to this rush, the parceling off of a soul's worldly goods. But the ritual appealed to Samson, the history in each listed item, the story of an encyclopedia set and the biography of a chandelier. Objects with more permanence than humans. We make things that last even when we can't stay behind ourselves.

Mrs. Answood squeezed Samson's arm, reminding him that he was her escort and personal expert. A prize. She'd been easy enough to spot when he arrived, and the two of them made quite a pair. Both hovering around six feet tall, both widowed, one all but erased by his grief, the other grown more solid over the years. Samson knew what her house—and budget—could hold, and he'd advised her against the larger pieces. They'd surely be snatched by the serious collectors. Instead, he directed Mrs. Answood's attention to a Georgian tea table and a pair of Quaker chairs, though personally, he wanted to see the Arne Vodder sideboard.

Music City Auction House managed the parceling off of estates throughout Tennessee and up into Kentucky. They had a reputation for being particular but fair, making what was a confusing process for many families easier to bear. Professional to the nth degree, they also had a sizable bottom line, growing their profits annually at a rate most small businesses could only dream about. Samson had purchased a few pieces from them over the years, slipping their receipts and form letters into a filing cabinet his wife suggested he keep in the shed. It was a rusted old thing, but it served his needs. The rest of the decorating, excepting a few comfort pieces, she had left to Samson's better eye. The place looked magazine-ready, though his wife would have objected to a photographer in their living room. Or cackled, delighted by the absurdity of a farmhouse flaunted in such a way. There were eggs to gather and bees to tend.

"This way, Mrs. Answood," Samson said, leading his charge to the registration booth where they both could obtain their paddles. A man who once outbid him on a working Underwood typewriter in pristine condition nodded at Samson. But Samson wanted to avoid shop talk and be left alone, so he ducked his head and stepped up to the folding table.

"Hiding from someone?" Brigit asked. Samson should have expected to see her there. The utilities office manager had volunteered for or worked every T-ball game and fundraiser. She'd sold him popcorn and raffle tickets, candy apples and coupon books. He owed her five dollars for a car wash gift certificate he'd never redeemed. That day, Brigit had her long hair pulled into a loose bun, several strands refusing the more professional style. Chapstick replaced her usual bright lips, and Samson wondered if the auction team had coached or at least provided guidelines of some sort. He glanced around at the other temporary employees, and they looked equally subdued.

"The usual riffraff," Samson responded.

"Oh, I know the type. I can't get far enough away from those lamp lovers either. And the armchair fans? I'd rather not even mention them. Heathens, the lot of them."

"Stay clear of the dining set crowd for the love of all that's holy."

Brigit crossed Samson's name off the list and gestured toward Mrs. Answood, who was standing a polite distance away.

"Colleen, too?"

"You go too far, miss. Better not let the dragon hear you call her by her Christian name."

"But dragon's all right?"

Samson put his hand to his heart before answering, noticing that the auction had improved his mood considerably.

"A grand and noble creature, if I've ever seen one. I'd be a dragon if I could."

"I bet you would. Tell Colleen to come see me for her number."

"My dragon's a little rusty, but I'll try."

"My knight." Brigit grinned at him, and he realized that he'd gone too far, enjoying the banter that the woman might mistake for flirting.

"I'll tell her," he said, tacking his number under an arm and turning away a bit too abruptly to be considered polite. Mrs. Answood watched him, her watery eyes still sharp as lasers. He repeated what he'd been told, and her tranquil response surprised him. Mrs. Answood wasn't the kind of person to be summoned.

35

"Best see what my grandniece wants. She's been up to something since the day she was born, if you ask me."

"Grandniece?" Samson asked, surprised he'd never been told about the connection before. He could make family trees for nearly everyone around and felt reasonably confident that skeletons didn't stay in their closets very long. Not that anyone would mistake Brigit for a skeleton, he reminded himself, watching another healthy strand of her dark hair work itself loose and fall into her face. When Mrs. Answood sat down next to her and seemed to settle in for a long chat, Samson wandered toward the property's backyard, hoping—if he were honest with himself—for another look inside.

Someone had mowed the grass, but the grounds were still bleak, more brown than green. The trees loomed over him, their gnarled branches bending precariously toward the roof. A strong storm could smash a hole through the shingles, and Samson knew what would happen next. An abandoned property like this? First the kudzu would creep up the walls and then inside, followed by rat snakes and squirrels. Kids would throw rocks through the windows and five months later? A year? Some forgotten electrical wire would come alive in the night, and a blaze would take the whole house out. Down to the scorched earth.

Samson would have settled for a clean pane of glass, but a side door swung open when he turned the knob. The kitchen was stripped bare, every cabinet open, every drawer empty. What the Music City Auction House couldn't list would be sold in bulk to flea markets or pawnshops, then the dregs would be donated. The team had removed even the appliances, exposing cords and outlets. It seemed like an overreach, an unnecessary step that would make selling the house even more challenging. Buyers weren't lining up for a three-story Victorian in a town with no job prospects. The space left behind was bare and ugly. Samson couldn't picture Barbara Lace fixing her tea there. Or cocktail, he corrected himself, remembering how Mrs. Answood had called her wild. Whatever that meant.

After she returned to Cedarville following forty-plus years in Hollywood, she led a quiet life, playing the recluse with Oscar-worthy intensity. She'd show up somewhere once or twice a year—the high school graduation, say, or a summer barbecue—but mostly she kept to herself. A committed bachelorette for the ages. Was she lonely? Samson wondered as he stepped into her den, checking first to make sure he was alone and that the curtains were pulled shut. They'd set up the area as a donation room, and stacks of casual clothes and worn-out towels were piled in corners. A box of knickknacks caught his eye, and he bent down to sort through cracked porcelain figurines and decks of playing cards. Blank postcards for Madrid and Capri were faded and curled at the edges. Enviable, really, that adventurous spirit. This woman had lived, had stories for days. Samson smiled a little, thinking of a young Ms. Lace on a yacht off the coast of Italy or flirting with Glenn Ford over a late-night card game. Shopping with Isadora Alvarez. If you could turn the volume up on life, Ms. Lace lived at a ten. Always a step or two away from being recognized, from paparazzi and stalkers. In Samson's view, the best kind of Hollywood career.

The photos that had once lined the foyer were stacked in a corner, and he hoped they weren't being tossed. After a moment's hesitation, he took the one of Ms. Alvarez and Ms. Lace out of its frame and slipped it underneath his coat. He didn't recognize many of the other faces, though he assumed they were well-known figures in their day. The men were impeccably dressed in three-piece suits, but they looked relaxed, hands in their pockets, sunglasses hiding their eyes. Ms. Lace hadn't displayed any of the slick studio-produced photographs popular in the '40s and '50s, and Samson liked her the better for it.

He reached for a jigsaw puzzle box that was split down the side and noticed a small, loose floorboard underneath. The plank came up easily in his hands, but he slammed it back down when he heard footsteps approaching, the crisp click of heels on a hardwood floor. What would happen if he was caught again? Sheriff Bishop might not look the other way. He scrambled up, desperate for a place—any place—to hide.

A scan of the room quickly showed him that there were no promising options. The boxes weren't stacked high enough, and he'd never make it to a window. His heart pounding, he tried to keep his wits about him, knowing that a full-blown panic attack would leave him shaking in the middle of the floor, not exactly inconspicuous. He shut his eyes tight against the black spots clouding his vision, and the heels clicked closer like a clock counting down to his execution.

CHAPTER 4

FADE IN:

EXT. A BEACH IN MAINE - NIGHT

A woman stumbles over rocks toward the water, pulling a thin cardigan against her body. The moon calls to her death.

                                                    CUT TO:

MARKSON, watching from a nearby cliff. He waits until the waves are lapping at her skirt before rushing toward her. When he grabs her arm, the woman turns, stunned and angry.

                          MARKSON
          Not like this, Sarah Jane. In the
          middle of the night with nobody to
          watch you drown.

UNNAMED WOMAN

I haven't been Sarah Jane in years.
Maybe ever.

MARKSON

Remember when we stole a bottle of
rum from that awful gas station and
drove all night to Philadelphia?

UNNAMED WOMAN

You mistake me for someone else. You
mistake too much.

from *The Neighbors* (1946)
Written by Bucky Carruthers and Hope Lancaster
Directed by Jonathan S. Ferguson

In a better frame of mind, say a couple of years in the past, Samson would have laughed at being caught red-handed. He would have tried to charm whoever came into view, and dollars to donuts, would have succeeded. Instead, he listened to the steps come closer then pause, out of sight but plenty close enough to hear him if he so much as cleared his throat. Samson tried to calm his breathing, taking air into his lungs steadily, as he considered removing his boots and creeping toward the back door. The screen would give him away, though, its guaranteed creak better than a home alarm system. He was good and truly stuck, relying on luck that the woman would return the way she came. While he didn't dare try to peek, Samson assumed it was Callista Weathers, Ms. Lace's personal assistant. He hoped her Winchester rifle had been tagged and catalogued.

A Bing Crosby tune began playing outside, making him jump half out of his skin. The tones of the classic song were more glaring than dulcet because of the high volume and poor quality. The speakers crackled in protest. Someone had decided that music would inspire nostalgia and loosen wallets. True, he could almost conjure a different sort of crowd in his imagination, one with three-piece suits and fur stoles. Cigars instead of the chewing tobacco favored by his neighbors. The music wasn't a terrible idea, and it provided him some much needed cover.

He ducked back into the kitchen and slid up against the wall where a refrigerator once stood. His racing heartbeat annoyed him. He was a guest at the auction, someone likely to make several bids even, and he was snooping at worst. A bit too curious, but not criminal. And yet he couldn't get his fear of being caught under control. If anyone found him hiding, he would look as guilty as he felt. When had he lost his nerve? He pressed himself even more firmly against the wall when a second pair of shoes joined the first, and they both entered the living room he had vacated seconds before.

"Are we about ready then, Gabriel?" Callista called over the song.

"Almost," a man answered. "Another five minutes."

"Always another five minutes with you."

"And always impatience from you. These sorts of events take finesse."

The man drawled and made finesse sound like fine-ness. Callista made an ugly noise, her heels moving closer to the kitchen, then turning around. "Finesse? For this overgrown yard sale?"

"If you'll take a look at the catalogue, I think you'll agree—"

"I don't need to see descriptions of this stuff. I've lived this stuff."

"We've prepared for this day, and I suspect you're suffering from

41

a bit of nerves. Scotch? I've got a good year."

The two voices fell into silence as Samson tried to understand what he was hearing. Could the man's voice belong to Gabriel Correa? Samson hadn't seen him around, but this was a big enough event for the Music City Auction House owner to make an appearance. Samson was most startled by the familiar tone of Callista Weathers, the loathing that she spat into each word. These two weren't exactly friends.

When a floorboard popped nearby, Samson's right hand darted to his heart. And that's how Mrs. Answood found him as she opened the back door and shuffled into the kitchen, scowling first at its forlorn state then at her antiques dealer trying unsuccessfully to disappear into the paisley wallpaper. She pursed her lips and shook her head before heading toward the den and calling out "Hallo there!" in a falsely cheerful manner.

"Hallo," she called again when she reached the doorframe. She was five inches from Samson, but pretended that he didn't exist. "Hall—oh, my dear. Pardon me for interrupting. I've found someone in charge at last. You must be in charge with that smart dress. I was instructed that the only available toilette was a plastic rectangular contraption outside, but I'm too old and too feeble for such accommodations."

Samson bit back a laugh at Mrs. Answood characterizing herself as "feeble."

"Of course, ma'am," Callista responded after a stunned pause, her voice losing any signs of frustration. Mrs. Answood stepped out of the kitchen. Samson waited for three sets of footsteps to move in the opposite direction, then tiptoed back the way he had entered, rushing into the bright, crisp day outside. He took a few big, grateful breaths, then tried to make his gait look casual as he headed toward the makeshift chairs around front. They were mostly filled, and he chose a standing spot in the back, not trusting himself to bid on anything yet anyway.

Why, he wondered, did the house seem to call to him? As if it wanted someone to know its secrets. That sounded like an excuse, even coming from his own head.

He had already memorized the item order, but he read through the list again, deciphering his own invented shorthand. An asterisk for curious, a star for yes. The underlinings and initials made sense only to him, although someone could have guessed that "OP" meant "overpriced." Quite a few items boasted that designation, and Samson concluded that Gabriel Correa was banking on notoriety to drive up prices. He'd never met the owner, but his photograph stared amiably from every mailer. A handsome older man who'd built himself a successful business. Smart, had to be.

"Samson Delaware?"

He heard his name in an assertive but cracked voice, and he turned to find a woman around his age in jeans, T-shirt, and blazer. She needed a coat, but didn't look bothered by the cold. Her short auburn hair had streaks of white, and her eyes found his from behind a pair of wire-rimmed glasses. Somehow he knew who the woman was, though he'd never seen her before. Kit Forrester. The reporter everyone had been dodging.

"Samson Delaware? I was told you're the man I need to see."

"That would be a first."

"I'm covering Barbara Lace's untimely passing for *The Hollywood Sun*, and I'd like to ask you a few questions about the auction."

"Untimely?"

"She was only seventy-three."

Samson's uneasiness increased. He knew the woman was hunting for something, but he didn't know what. He didn't trust himself not to blunder into some secret he didn't know was a secret.

"Oh, I'm not sure how much help I'd be. I'm just a furniture repairman."

"Antiques expert."

Samson made himself chuckle, and even to his ears, the sound was hollow.

"You're a long way from home. How does our humble town compare to Los Angeles?"

Kit stared at Samson long enough to make him uncomfortable again, then she smiled a bit as if amused by him. "Why don't you tell me what items are most valuable. Surely there's no harm in that?"

Samson considered her request, then relaxed, mentioning a couple of pieces he'd marked "OP." Kit took notes in a small green journal, encouraging him to reflect on Ms. Lace's taste if he wouldn't comment on her life. Samson figured it would be a boring story if actually published, and he was glad when Kit wandered off to pester someone else.

After another Bing Crosby song ended, "Pennies from Heaven" crackled on, and Samson shifted his weight from leg to leg. A few folks said something to him as they passed by, and he tried to match their uninterested cadence. When he saw Mrs. Answood appear, he waved her over, chagrined and prepared to repent. He dusted off the chair he'd been saving and helped her settle, propping up her cane and tucking her embroidered purse underneath her legs.

"On top of everything, you're a saint," Samson began, laying on his accent thick.

"Tell me again, Mr. Delaware, when my items are up."

"Of course, Mrs. Answood."

The old woman shifted in her chair, trying to find a comfortable position on the metal. "What's that? You'll need to bend closer so I can hear above the racket."

Samson crouched down next to Mrs. Answood, resting his

forearms on his knees. "I said, of course, Mrs. Answood. Anything for you."

She leaned even closer, and he expected a reprimand. A rap on the knuckles would have been appropriate, but instead she grew still before whispering.

"There's something not right about that girl, Ms. Weathers she calls herself."

"What makes you say that?"

"Don't get coy with me, son. I wasn't the one hiding from her."

Samson stood back up, and they both turned their attention to the front porch, where an auctioneer gestured toward an ornate cuckoo clock and reviewed its finer points—German Black Forest with an authentication certificate and working hourly performances. Excellent condition. It was a beauty, sure enough, but Samson preferred unlicked find. He was also distracted, glad that Mrs. Answood shared his unease about Callista Weathers but unsure what that meant, if anything. They didn't like the woman, but so what? She'd be gone soon enough. Samson zoned out as he considered why Mrs. Answood had taken his side. Her tone was above gossip. Not a warning either, but more like a call to arms, the way a wife might mention to her husband that their toilet was leaking. Well, not his wife.

She would have fixed the problem herself, comfortable with having married a man who would get emotional carrying out a mouse caught in a trap. He trapped spiders in jars and released them far from the house. Did she appreciate her gentle groom? God, he hoped so. He hoped that she had loved him as much as he had adored her. He hoped the memories hadn't been altered by tragedy, dodged and burned until they were soft as kittens. And yet, who would correct him if he were wrong? What was the harm?

"You asked about Barbara's crowd," Mrs. Answood said. Samson bent his body toward hers again to better hear. "I'll tell you, if she has friends left, they're mostly in Hollywood. They're not known to us."

A movement inside the Lace house caught his eye, and he watched Callista peer out. Nobody else seemed worried about her moon face staring at them, but Samson shuddered, thinking her maroon shift dress made sense. Red for danger, and Mrs. Answood—he realized now—was granting him permission to pursue his suspicions. The presence of Callista in town screamed at him, something off about her story, about herself. He would treat her like any other discovery, he decided, a puzzle only he could solve. Not because he was more clever or more cunning, but because he was the only one interested. And because Samson Delaware had always been a patient man.

He waited for the auctioneer to finish his chant before excusing himself. Samson scrawled two stars on Mrs. Answood's papers, then squeezed through the crowd, abandoning the fire grate and iron coatrack that he had wanted. He had a new goal, a new target, and she was lurking behind the scenes. Logical or not, he knew that she was an intruder, a coyote among the cattle. Samson didn't pause to consider what that made him as he stalked closer to the window, staying on the periphery so as not to call attention to himself. He found a spot under a large oak tree that shaded him from view but allowed him to peer inside the house from time to time. He watched people, his blood thrumming, feeling more alive and alert than he had in years. Vigilante or voyeur, depending on the light.

CHAPTER 5

A psychological thriller about a blind seamstress and the man who sits on her fire escape at night to watch her sleep. But what if a bigger danger lurks inside?

    pitch for *Vigil* (1949)
    Written by Blane Pruitt and Barbara Lace
    Never filmed

The glare from the microfiche reader made Samson's head hurt, but he still considered himself lucky that the closest library had so many newspapers, journals, and records archived. Not everything, of course. The place had a small staff—a smattering of volunteers, a couple of part-timers, and only one credentialed research librarian—but they'd done a respectable job over the years. He figured out that Callista Weathers grew up 700 miles from Hollywood in an unincorporated speck on the map called Shining Creek. At eighteen, she pursued English at San Jose State University, and at twenty-two Los Angeles beckoned. Before long, she settled into a salaried position at MGM Studios where she went from answering general calls to answering the vice president's calls in a little under six months.

Samson congratulated himself on another find as he paid two cents to print the roster of MGM employees in 1973. Callista was employed from 1972 until 1987, five years after Barbara Lace moved back to Cedarville. Callista hadn't moved with Ms. Lace—the young woman's presence would have made more of an impression on his neighbors. Yet, she'd been there in the background somehow for more than a decade, helping or waiting for her moment to pounce. Samson's biggest question was when exactly she had arrived. Her current address was easy to find in the white pages. She rented an apartment in a different town, one closer to a mall and grocery stores. That part wasn't unusual; there weren't any apartments nearby. But if she drove into Cedarville every day, people would recognize her car at least.

Samson took a minute to stretch, grateful that the glass-walled technology room was separated from the stacks. He could see out, but felt cocooned, safe from interruption. He selected the print option for Gunner Weathers's obituary. Callista's father had died in 1979 from surgical complications and was survived by his only daughter. Was she an orphan now? His parents had passed, too, and Samson had thought he understood grief until he lost his wife. It wasn't the dull ache that textbooks warned against. Not even the guilt, every cross word and lost opportunity, the fact that he hadn't noticed when she first got sick. It was crows eating his liver every day, then beginning again each morning.

To be honest, he was proud of the little county library turning up employment records and an obituary if nothing else. They'd made the most of their recent grant. While documents about Callista were scarce, there were several referencing Barbara Lace. Six profiles from the local, a few mentions in national places like the *Los Angeles Times* and Washington Post. He scanned articles from *Variety*, wishing there were more back issues, and printed off several grainy photographs. Ms. Lace had written a film, *Signs of the Children*, that had never been released. He thought of the script he'd noticed in her living room and how disappointing it must have been to never see her movies onscreen. Samson even found a byline or two by Kit Forrester and wondered why she'd bother with the death of an all-but-forgotten actress. Maybe she missed the gentler scandals of a bygone era. Or maybe she knew something he didn't. Vanderbilt University would have more, but he hated to make the trip to Nashville before he knew what he needed. Perhaps proof that Callista wasn't who she said she was. Proof that she was the trespasser, not him.

His favorite story highlighted a visit that Ms. Lace made to Macotte High School in 1977. A sort of victory lap accompanied by her friend Isadora Alvarez, who caused quite a stir. The two pulled into town in a limousine that had trouble navigating the one-lane roads and hidden driveways. The vehicle alone made sure that nobody missed the pair of actresses. And while they didn't eat at whatever restaurant was around back then, they did accept a key to the city from Mayor Answood at a ceremony on the square. Women wore their Sunday best, but their cotton dresses were nothing compared to the silk finery of their guests. And the jewelry! Ms. Lace and Ms. Alvarez showboated, and everyone loved them for it. They loved Barbara because they could claim her, and they loved Isadora because she was a star.

Samson printed out the article, wanting to take a closer look at the photographs. There had been two men with them, one clearly a chauffeur, the other's role more ambiguous. Shaking out his cramped legs, Samson approached the copy machine, muttering under his breath when he saw that the tray was empty. When he opened the paper drawer to find the jam, everything looked normal. Crouching down, he swept his hand underneath to see if the papers had fallen, but only found dust. Samson was still hunched awkwardly on the ground when a librarian approached, humming softly to herself. They had introduced themselves to each other before, but Samson couldn't recall her name and began with apologies.

"Sorry to disturb you, ma'am, but there seems to be something wrong with the copier. Maybe my requests aren't sending from the machine?"

The woman seemed to doubt his story. "Worked fine a few minutes ago. I saw a woman scoop up her work before she left. You about done here? We're closing up."

Samson jerked his head toward the exit, although he knew he wouldn't see anyone. He'd been working alone all afternoon, watching parents and children come and go, but never spotting another living soul in the technology room. Had someone taken his work on purpose?

"Was she pale and thin? About yay height?" he asked, holding his hand up to his throat.

The librarian squinted at him, then took a step back. "As I say, we're closing, Mr. Delaware. Let me know if you want to check something out."

She turned her back on him, but glanced over her shoulder a couple of times before returning to her post at the circulation desk. Samson often made people nervous these days, but there wasn't much he could do about his new talent. It was as if grief had changed his DNA, and there was no going back. It had grown dark outside, and the lamps cast shadows onto the desks, stacks, and floors. The place had overhead fluorescents, but they were rarely used, just for cleaning really.

The drive back to Cedarville should have lifted his spirits. The cloudless sky stretched in all directions, and although the trees were still bare, their tips glowed red in his headlights, promising spring. It was warm enough to crack a window if he left the heat running. But his lost work was a frustrating coincidence at best, a sign of trouble ahead at worst. Lord knows, he didn't go looking for bother.

"Trouble sure is sweet on you, though," his wife had told him once when a wasp stung him on the nose. She'd tended the wound with loose tobacco and gentle hands. Later, when the two of them lay beside each other, she'd laughed, a booming sound that filled every part of him with joy, even his swollen face. Samson refused to admit that he looked funny, but she was right, as always. He was a funny-looking man before the insect attacked him, and he'd be a funny-looking man after. He'd never cared.

When he turned toward the train tracks, he thought back to the jewelry box and Barbara Lace's letter speaking to him from beyond the grave. Speaking pleasantries rather than fire and brimstone, but speaking all the same. Their reappearance felt important, but also like a practical joke, nothing more and nothing else. A little push to unnerve him. There was also a thought he kept repressing, one trying ferociously to claw its way to the front part of his brain—did madness start like this? A sliver of obsession that turns into a ravine, tempting for its promise of abyss, of losing yourself.

He'd read a book or two on mourning. They kept showing up in his mailbox, gifts from well-meaning neighbors, some bought new and some dusted off. They puzzled him, surprising him on his nightstand or next to the toilet like silverfish too cunning to be caught. There was a lot of advice about choices, focusing on positive memories instead of dwelling on absence, making yourself participate in familiar activities, asking for help, and—his least favorite phrase—moving on. What did that even mean? Going someplace else? He didn't think it was a coincidence that the same language was used for dying. They've passed, they've gone, they've moved on.

His house looked inviting from a distance, its cheerful yellow door and shutters. Up close, the roof needed some new shingles and the yard needed grass seed. The driveway could've used a few loads of gravel, and the fields had been reclaimed by nature. His wife's wooden bee boxes stood empty and would, he hated to admit, remain so. He sat in his truck, staring at them, wondering when mold had crept along their sides. Five little empires, abandoned.

With a low growl, he tumbled out, stomping toward his shed. The hacksaw waited for him, and he yanked it from the wall hook. His breathing sounded rough to his own ears, but there was nobody around to care. He approached the first box with fury, bending down for one last look at the rusted nails and ripped mesh screen. As soon as the blade bit into the pine, a feeling of peace washed over him, and he completed his grim task without a break.

CHAPTER 6

Tinseltown sparkled even more than usual last night as A-listers gathered for the premiere of Jonathan S. Ferguson's latest, *Forbidden Drive*, a suspenseful drama starring Tipper Kent and Isadora Alvarez. The champagne flowed, and the cameras flashed, catching Miss Alvarez's lush lashes flirting with her co-star. Steel your hearts, ladies! Those rumors of an off-screen romance just might be true after all.

—Peter Campbell, *Variety*, July 2, 1952

Coyotes yipped in the distance, and Samson tightened his grip on the saw. The field behind Barbara Lace's house was overgrown, and he knew nobody would notice him in the tall thistle. The night had turned cloudy, but the moon emerged from time to time, bathing the stalks in silvery light. They looked like battle-weary soldiers keeping vigil. Samson shifted his weight from leg to leg, but he hardly noticed their growing stiffness. He craved action, wanted to do something—anything—to make sense of the past few days. He'd chosen this lonely mission, and it suited him.

The windows were dark except for one, and he watched Callista Weathers walk past every so often. An insomniac, like himself. She wore a long-sleeved nightgown and carried papers with her on each pass. It was hard to tell if she was packing or organizing, but the routine continued for hours. Fleeing, perhaps, he thought, escaping at first light. Or fending off ghosts. Samson could relate, and yet his doubts about her grew. You don't pace at midnight if you're at peace.

A flash to his right jerked his attention away, and he turned toward the lightning, counting one Mississippi two Mississippi three Mississippi until the thunder arrived. The storm was close, but not close enough to send him home. When he turned back toward the house, the windows were all dark, and he crept up to the ground level. The auction crowds had left the yard more dirt than grass, and he scuffed his boot prints away as he made them, hiding any evidence. His heart beat unsteadily, but he kept going, only stopping when he could get a full view of the den. All the furniture was gone, but the donation items sat untouched, and he scanned the room quickly to make sure nobody was there. He could have used the window Leejon had opened when they were sent for Ms. Lace's body, but he didn't want to risk being seen from the road. The backyard seemed safer.

Looking around to make sure he was still alone, he wedged his saw between the frame and the window, feeling old paint pop loose as he slid the blade down. The window creaked open an inch when he pushed. He paused, sure the pulleys would squeal as he lifted. For a moment, he considered abandoning his quest, but he shoved those thoughts away. The noise was as loud as he expected, and after making a space big enough for his body, he hid behind a tree and waited. He'd grown accustomed to standing still, and ten minutes passed quickly. He removed his boots, returned to his entry, and slipped inside.

After Samson's eyes adjusted to the dark, he could see piles of books and a few trash bags full of clothes. The place looked cursed, a life reduced to disposable possessions. The photographs were still stacked in a corner, and he wondered if anyone had noticed that he'd taken one. Stealing had been surprisingly easy. He made his way to the loose floorboard he'd noticed when he was last in this room. He pressed on one end, and the plank lifted. He slid it to the side, releasing a musty, pine odor. At first, the hiding space looked empty, and he almost laughed at his foolishness. The cubbyhole was bigger than it first appeared, though, and he stuck his arm to the back, pleased when his fingers touched a stack of papers, a bundle of photographs, and a single film reel. He pulled his prizes out and tucked them into the bag he'd brought in case he found anything.

Moving even more quickly, he slid the board back into its place and started to retreat. Thunder rumbled nearby, so close this time that he almost didn't hear the scream. He whipped toward the sound, knowing he'd been discovered, but nobody was there. He froze, confused and panicked, until another shriek came from the second story, and he hesitated. When he remembered the night, he'd dwell on that detail, his hesitation. The woman sounded distraught, but he couldn't save her from a nightmare. He'd never be able to explain why he was there. The next scream was cut off by a gunshot, and Samson leapt from his trance, bounding up the stairs two at a time and running toward the sounds.

He paused on the landing, disoriented by the dark and wondering which direction to turn. But there was light seeping out below one doorframe, and he groped his way toward it. When he flung open the door, he didn't understand the scene in front of him. Callista Weathers was on her knees, facing the bed as if in prayer. The blanket in front of her was splattered in blood, and her head leaned against the wall. When he took a step, her body collapsed, what was left of her face slamming into the hardwood floor. The bullet had ripped through her left eye and exited out of her skull. Dizzy with adrenaline, Samson crouched down beside her and lifted her wrist, mechanically searching for a pulse that would never come again.

"Jesus, Samson."

"I know."

"Do you? 'Cause I'm starting to think you may be a smoke short of a pack."

Samson didn't like coffee, but he took a sip of the cup in front of him for something to do. Bishop moved restlessly around what passed as an interrogation room, adjusting his belt and wiping his eyes. It was 6 a.m., and the cop wasn't pleased about being woken up. His emergencies tended toward car crashes, not murder. And certainly not murder called in by one of his own who just happened to be breaking and entering.

"And with a hacksaw," he shouted.

There were a dozen or so cops from the county, a whole team back at the mansion who had taped off the room and started snapping photographs. Someone from the TBI had already arrived from Nashville. Lord only knew where the agent would stay with the only real bed and breakfast filled by the auction house staff. Bishop would have to ask around for a spare room.

Samson stared at Bishop, wishing he didn't know so many private details about the sheriff's life. Bishop's ambitions started small and got smaller. At eighteen, he'd wanted a paycheck and a little respect. He hadn't been a bully in high school despite his size, and he'd been popular enough. A fullback with a couple of nice plays his senior year. He passed his classes, and one or two teachers might remember his name. A wife, he thought that had seemed possible. Like not asking for too much.

Someone a little bit pretty who liked his jokes. Children so that his mother could be a grandmother. Then Rachel bit into him and wouldn't let up. An accidental pregnancy, a shotgun wedding, a few good years, then divorce and child support. He hadn't seen much of his youngest lately. Bishop could have been thinking about his son's red hair as he stared at Samson, then remembered why they were there and wasn't happy about it.

"Jesus, Samson."

"I know."

Bishop had thought to do a little good for his community. Now his greatest ambition was sleeping through the night. He prayed for accidents to be outside the city limits, and mostly he got his wish. If someone came through Cedarville after midnight, that stranger was lost and creeping, worried about whether there was enough fuel in the tank to make it back to the exit. The local gas station kept bank hours, more or less.

Samson could see Bishop's indecision and let it fester. If he said anything, the officer might decide he'd rather side with his fellow professionals than with his eccentric neighbor. Samson knew Bishop believed his story, but that didn't mean he would walk free. What would he do in the cop's shoes? Samson couldn't rightly say and took another sip of the coffee, grimacing and hoping he wouldn't have to use the toilet in Cedarville's lone holding cell.

Bishop sighed and sat down in the remaining chair so that the two men faced each other, both tired from the late—or early—hour and from the hands they'd been dealt.

"Could you say you was telling the value of the remaining items? What do you call it, consulting?"

Samson waited until he was sure he understood that he was being offered a way out.

"Appraising? In the middle of the night?"

Bishop shrugged, rubbing his eyes again. "I know you didn't kill

57

that lady, but God bless this is a cluster. Here's what I say—let folks think what they want. We're not so old we don't have a couple of rides left in us. Hell, maybe you were sleeping with her."

"I wasn't."

"But you could have been. You got something better?"

Samson shook his head, assuming he'd feel relief later, maybe even gratitude. At the moment, he couldn't stop seeing blood, baffled by how he'd missed someone else in the house. He'd been watching for hours, and except for Callista pacing, the house had been completely still.

"Get on home then. This will all start again in a few hours."

Samson stood, shaking out his left foot, which had fallen asleep. "Fanny's got a room," he said. "Used to rent it out every spring 'round graduation."

Bishop responded with one curt nod.

"Maybe the agent will get out of town sooner than later."

"You're not worried about a killer on the loose?"

Bishop looked Samson up and down before responding. "Callista Weathers was an outsider killed by an outsider. Whoever did this is long gone and don't have shit to do with us."

Samson walked out into the dawn, its cruel brightness making his eyes water. He probably shouldn't have been driving, but there was nobody to come get him and nobody to stop him. The talk would start soon enough anyway. Best not to let anyone see his truck at the station. A wave of loneliness crashed into Samson, and he held his stomach and then the driver's side door as he heaved, coffee burning its way up his esophagus. He slid down to the pavement, his back to his truck, his vision black and painful. The world felt tilted, as if he'd slide off if he tried to ever stand again. When the feeling passed, he got himself home, opting to sleep on the couch so he wouldn't wake midday reaching for his wife, wondering for a few blissful seconds if she was in the kitchen making them breakfast. No, he wanted to wake clear-headed and ready. He wanted to know who had killed Callista Weathers and—he was sure now—who had killed her employer, Cedarville's one-time sweetheart and full-time recluse, Barbara Lace.

CHAPTER 7

FADE IN:

EXT. A FRONT PORCH - NIGHT

Two sisters, MABEL and JANE, in a porch swing hum
quietly to themselves.

> MABEL
> We could have left him for the crows to
> find, you know. Nobody would suspect.

> JANE
> That's the difference between you and
> me. I know how to work a shovel.

> MABEL
> You saying you don't have blisters?

```
                    JANE
I'm saying I don't care. You always
paraded for our parents in your
pretty dresses and curls. You
always paraded. And I let you.
Because someday I knew we'd be
here. Sweetness?  All it attracts
is teeth, and you let somebody take
a bite out of you. A shovel, Mabel.
A woman needs a shovel.


              from Once Upon a Town (1956)
              Written by Carol Ann Smith
              and Bucky Carruthers
              Directed by Tyson Banks
```

Agent McKinnell didn't buy Samson's story about a double homicide. He ran a hand through his unkempt hair and stared at the man in front of him. Samson stared back, a little dead-eyed but as alert as he could be under the circumstances. They sat in the parlor of Fanny John's pink two-story home. The house was renovated in the late '60s, and Fanny was partial to sheep figurines and handmade doilies. The antimacassar shifted when either guest moved on the ancient couch. It was the only place to sit in the den, and Samson could tell McKinnell would have preferred a straight-back chair, something with more authority.

"From the beginning again, if you would, sir."

The first thing Samson noticed about McKinnell besides his

boyish face was his complete lack of any accent. It was like talking to a Midwestern newscaster, and Samson found the experience unnerving. He would ask where he was from if the circumstances were different. Instead, he kept his tone polite and repeated himself, doing his level best not to change a single detail.

"The Meeker brothers, Cully Barnes, and I got called to the Barbara Lace house about the body. We're not much for church—"

McKinnell held up a hand, cutting Samson off. "The night of the murder, please. You arrived around what time?"

Samson stuck mostly to the truth, saying he'd gotten there around ten o'clock.

"That's pretty late."

"It is."

Samson let the boy work up to his question, a feeling of resignation washing over him. He wasn't sure why Bishop was putting his neck out for him, but he'd certainly been right. Nobody would second-guess an affair. He and Callista were around the same age, both single. There weren't a lot of warm bodies meeting those two criteria in the vicinity. It wouldn't eliminate him from all suspicion—plenty of romances turn sour—but mutual needs made a pretty good cover. A place to start at least until Samson figured out what was really going on.

"You were seeing Miss Weathers?"

Samson waved at Fanny, who happened to appear at that moment with sliced apple cinnamon bread. She fussed with the plate, moving a little pot of honey to the side and setting down embroidered cloth napkins. Her cheeks were pink, and Samson couldn't be sure if she was embarrassed by what she had overheard or proud of her handiwork.

"Don't mind me," she said, shuffling in place. "I just like to make my guests feel comfortable is all."

Samson smiled at the woman who had arranged her long gray

hair into a braid and put on an "I Love Grandma" apron over her jeans and sweater. She looked straight from central casting, and if she wanted to pretend that it was completely normal for her to have customers, Samson wouldn't put an end to the charade. He didn't even shudder at the sailboat wallpaper, though he wondered briefly if her husband would object if he offered to fix the visible leak in the ceiling. In another year—maybe sooner—the plaster would start to crumble without attention. The roof could be patched, and he could put on a layer of stucco inside.

"Mrs. J., this looks divine," Samson said.

"Well, you know how I like to freeze apples in the fall. These were calling out to be baked. Now I'll leave you men to it."

Fanny took her time exiting, and he let her, knowing it was too much to ask that his business—in this case his lies—be kept. Gossip was Cedarville currency, and she would be flush after this meeting. When he thought that their hostess might be out of earshot, he nodded, and McKinnell cleared his throat.

"You and Miss Weathers."

"It wasn't much to speak of," Samson said.

"I see. And you weren't in her bedroom at the time of the murder?" Part of him wished he had been. He wasn't much of a fighter, but maybe his presence alone would have scared off whoever lurked inside. "You're saying somebody snuck in, hid, then waited for you to wander downstairs for a glass of water."

"I was going home. I don't like to sleep away from my place." That much, at least, was the truth. Samson would drive six hours for a new piece on occasion, a wardrobe or something, then turn around and drive right back. Before, he hated to be away from his wife for even a single evening. Now, it was habit. Sometimes if he was relaxed enough, if the highway was straight enough and empty enough, there would be a few minutes when he'd think she would still be there, leaning against their front porch railing, beaming at him. Or it would feel like she sat next to him, hand lazily resting on his knee.

"Did you hear anything besides the scream?"

Samson glanced away from McKinnell to hide the wave of sadness that had washed over him. He'd been alert to every creak, but there had been no ominous noises the night Callista was shot. No heavy footsteps or unfamiliar voices. Where had the killer gone?

"An old house like that has plenty of crawl spaces. Between the walls, at the top of the closets," said Samson, half to himself and half to McKinnell. "An attic."

"We're searching the premises."

Samson was so tired he couldn't imagine ever being fully awake again. But he fought against the currents, wanting McKinnell to believe him. This one was ambitious, wanted to wrap up the case and deliver it with a bow. "Who's searching the place?" Samson asked. The bread smelled like the holidays, and he leaned forward to reach for a slice.

"We have a team. And I can have backup if I need it."

"And there's Sheriff Bishop."

McKinnell didn't respond to that suggestion, and Samson guessed that the TBI agent thought they were all a bunch of yokels. All the better, he thought. There was no reason to keep him, and Samson thanked Mrs. John for her hospitality and walked out, pausing to take a look at the roof from the yard. It needed more than a patch, but the Johns couldn't afford a full replacement. He'd help with repairs if they let him.

Once outside, he didn't know how best to spend his time. Continuing his Callista Weathers research didn't seem like a smart move. He was frustrated that McKinnell didn't believe Barbara Lace had been murdered. Samson didn't have any doubts, though, and he retreated to his work shed. There was always something there to occupy his hands if not his mind.

It took a few days before he found his new routine, tinkering with his table in the morning, reading through Lace's papers in the afternoon, mostly letters. There were at least a hundred, and the handwriting was hard to decipher. A few were typed, but mostly there was careless cursive running into the margins. He tried to sort them by date and sender, but the timeline was difficult to follow. Her sister had been her most reliable pen pal until she died, but there were plenty from L.A. addresses, even a few from names he'd heard before or seen at the library. A couple of birthday cards from her agent. A love letter or two signed M—. Plenty of postcards from Isadora Alvarez, who seemed to live in five-star hotels. Her friend rarely wrote more than a line or two.

In one inspired moment, he dug out a chalkboard, something he'd picked up at a flea market and promptly forgotten. He started with facts, birth and death dates, movie releases, her mortgage and overdue water bill, then began to fill in what he remembered from his library research. He wished he had a better memory and knew that at some point, he'd have to go back. Lace had left Cedarville at eighteen, at least according to Mrs. Answood, and she'd returned at sixty-two. More than forty years in Hollywood. No husband, no kids, just fifty-five film and television credits to her name. Lace had been a workhorse, reliable and talented, while not talented enough to make the stars sweat. The perfect character and bit-part actor. She'd played a chorus girl and an arsonist's sister, a nun and a schoolteacher. Somebody's mother seven times, a grandmother once. He ordered a dozen VHS tapes from a collector down in Biloxi he trusted, then a projector for the reel he'd stolen.

The photographs interested him the most, small 4x6 prints, curling up around the edges. Ms. Lace was rarely in them herself, presumably behind the camera. Not that Samson was an expert, but she seemed to have a good eye, often catching her subjects unaware, in moments of deep thought or mouth hanging open mid-conversation.

They seemed to be party shots, from intimate gatherings to splashy affairs. He thought he recognized Orson Welles on the patio of a sprawling pink mansion, but his face was in the shadows. There was a snapshot of Ms. Lace and an older man in one, his arm slung possessively around her waist. Isadora was a frequent presence, which wasn't surprising. Dark hair and dark eyes, she carried herself like a ballet dancer, all sharp angles, chin a little lifted. She looked somehow delicate and dangerous at once. If you flipped through the pictures fast enough, they almost became a short film about Isadora, a documentary of sorts. She'd appear in every third or so image, her face imperceptibly older until you compared the first and last shots. She stopped smiling as much along the way, and Samson could relate.

He taped one up onto his chalkboard. Someone had taken the camera from Ms. Lace and captured her and Isadora seated at a small card table, tarot cards laid between them. Isadora had tied a green silk scarf around her hair, exposing her long neck and a gold pendant necklace. She leaned over the table, her gaze unflinching. Ms. Lace's posture was more casual, and she'd clearly noticed their photographer, smirking at him in a sideways glance. Isadora was notoriously mystical, every magazine commenting on her faithful adherence to horoscopes and palm lines. She thought fortune could be found in the right signs, the alignment of planets and the movement of stars. Samson didn't know Ms. Lace's views on such topics, but her expression conveyed amusement rather than true belief. She was having a bit of a lark at a soiree. The friends were at the start of the reading, only a few cards laid out and only one in focus: the tower.

The lone returned letter had never been opened, and Samson felt—despite everything he'd done—that opening it would be a violation of Ms. Lace's privacy. He'd held it up to the brightest light he could find, and while he could see the writing, he couldn't decipher any words. He put it in a plastic bag for safekeeping. At night, he'd store everything in the small, locked fireproof box he kept in his bedroom. He'd moved it into the closet to make it a little less conspicuous, though he supposed if the TBI got a warrant to search the place, it wouldn't matter. A hiding spot in the floorboard would have been safer.

But Agent McKinnell didn't contact him much—a fact check here and there—and Samson didn't go anywhere, preferring to plot Lace's life in white chalk, an erasable and incomplete biography that was more confounding than revealing. One unsigned letter in particular plagued him. On studio letterhead, someone had scrawled "It's your time, love!" And she'd kept it, tucked between notes from her sister and fan mail. He taped the note onto his timeline and waited for it to speak. Samson Delaware had infinite patience for ghosts.

CHAPTER 8

All aboard! Early Sunday afternoon, Isadora
Alvarez said "I do" to the heir of Southern
Ocean Trains, Clark Masterson. Surrounded
by close friends and family, they exchanged
vows before sneaking away to an undisclosed
honeymoon location. Maid of honor Barbara
Lace wished them well, offering her faux
condolences to Masterson on having to foot
her friend's shoe bill "forever and ever
amen."
—Peter Campbell, *Variety*, June 15, 1954

When Samson first arrived in town, dizzy with optimism, he'd
agreed to assist in the restoration of Cedarville's only landmark, a train
depot built in 1903 and abandoned in 1975. Tall stalks of thistle grew
through the cracked floorboards, and rats made nests in every corner.
When he walked inside, he choked on the smell, a rank musk that would
have reminded him of death if he'd had much experience with death at

the time. His regret was immediate because the task seemed impossible, and he knew what a difference first impressions made. He'd be labeled a failure, somebody you couldn't count on when it mattered. It couldn't be helped—the place needed a bulldozer, not an antiques dealer.

And yet there was a light through the panes of original bottle glass—cracked though they were—a light waving and erratic like a winter lake captured somehow indoors. Sharp, beautiful. He'd read about Broadway theaters using similar tricks in the 1920s, turning stages into bodies of water with some silks and shadows. It was hard to say if he was hooked because of that magic trick or by a stubborn streak that wanted to make Cedarville his home. He called an exterminator, getting half-hearted assurances that the critters would be trapped and released rather than killed. Samson didn't dare press for more.

If he were in a self-congratulatory mood, he would admit that the place still looked nice, a symbol of possibility in a town of failed schemes. He paused outside the front door to appreciate the paint color, period appropriate, though he'd met with some resistance over the hue. The memory made him grin, and he pushed open the doors in a good mood despite the grim circumstances.

The assembled crowd didn't surprise him. Everyone had come to hear tittle-tattle as much as to help with the investigation. The matriarchs sat in the front row, Mrs. Answood and Mrs. John among them. Mrs. John had taken to her role in affairs, considering herself something of a town liaison. The TBI agent was staying at her abode after all. He hadn't left even when the auction house team cleared out of the real bed and breakfast. Samson was less satisfied with his position, the presumed lover of Callista Weathers, and his mood soured. He ducked his head, not bothering to make eye contact with anyone, and found a spot of wall in the back that he could hold up. There was a photograph of the depot from its grand opening at the turn of the century, a mustachioed man staring solidly into the camera beside a woman, slightly blurry, in a high-necked white dress. The effect was eerie, as if the pair watched the proceedings disapprovingly.

Crossing his arms in front of him, Samson finally looked out to see a few heads turned in his direction. He hadn't seen Brigit since the auction and when he nodded at her, she jerked to face forward, making a knot form in his stomach. God, why had he let himself flirt with the woman? She didn't deserve the disappointment. He watched Brigit smooth her long brown ponytail and tried not to imagine what the strands might feel like between his fingers.

Somebody had located a podium, probably from the high school, and sat it at the front of the room. Samson assumed the microphone belonged to Cane Crawley, who sometimes played in a cover band up in Nashville. The whole setup looked surprisingly official, and if he wasn't mistaken, Bishop had ironed his uniform. He could see Bishop's ex-wife scowling from the third row, and he wondered if bringing a toddler to a murder briefing was appropriate. Maybe he was too young to follow along. Agent McKinnell had slicked his hair back, which made his ears stick out slightly, emphasizing his boyishness. Nobody snickered, though, as the man shuffled his papers and cleared his throat.

"Ladies and gentlemen," he began, taking a moment to make eye contact with a few members of the crowd. Samson wondered if speech class was required wherever young Agent McKinnell matriculated. He looked confident, a bit like a student council president.

"Speak up, son," called Tommy Meeker Sr. from the back, and a few folks laughed. Tommy refused to wear hearing aids, claiming the government could spy on you that way, and made similar demands of the preacher to "speak up" every Sunday at First Baptist.

"Right then," Agent McKinnell continued. "While I can't share any particulars about an ongoing investigation, I did want to assure everyone that we have prioritized everyone's safety. You may have noticed the increased police presence, and we will have someone parked downtown twenty-four/seven. We are taking the necessary steps in regards to the death of Callista Weathers. We are following protocol. *The Smithtown Bee* got a few details wrong, namely that we suspect cult involvement. We have no evidence of any group activities in the immediate vicinity."

A few heads nodded. The residents of Cedarville would know if there were goings-on nearby, and they hadn't appreciated the negative publicity. Samson noticed *the Hollywood Sun* writer Kit Forrester looking skeptical, clearly unimpressed by the local paper. But *The Smithtown Bee* wasn't exactly local. It belonged to a nearby county and was staffed by a couple of feisty blue-hairs long past retirement age who fancied themselves revolutionaries. He was surprised that Kit had stuck around, but supposed a murder closely following Ms. Lace's death was too juicy to pass up. Samson briefly wondered if she was on assignment or working on her own before his attention was drawn back to the podium.

"A botched robbery attempt," Agent McKinnell continued, "is more likely. Somebody who read Barbara Lace's obituary and assumed the place would be empty. Nonetheless, please be sure to secure all doors and windows. I've been told this is a community that doesn't lock up. I appreciate the charm there, but those are days gone by now. Circumstances have changed. If your neighbor wants to borrow some sugar, well, she'll just have to knock."

Samson guessed that McKinnell wanted to seem attuned to the life of a rural community, but he came across as condescending. The agent was fast on his way to losing the room. McKinnell looked down at his notes and frowned as if he didn't like what he had written there. He scanned the faces in front of him before he spoke again.

"If you have any information that might assist us in our pursuits, I invite you to speak with Sheriff Bishop. He'll be handling matters onsite."

Bishop stood up and straightened his belt, his black shirt straining against the weight he'd gained since signing up for the force. McKinnell gestured toward Bishop as if anyone in the room didn't know him and his whole life story.

At least his son gets to see him like this, Samson thought as Bishop approached the microphone. He wiped his forehead before speaking, and Tommy called out again for him to speak up.

"You bet, Mr. Meeker. And I can speak to you directly after, if you miss anything." It was the right response, and a few approving murmurs circulated. "Um, let's see now. I reckon I don't have anything to add except that we will catch this killer."

"Fat chance," his ex-wife called out, and Samson cringed while others around him shifted uncomfortably. Bishop blushed and stepped back from the microphone, then up, visibly more nervous than before.

"We don't—well, we don't tolerate that sort of thing here. Let's leave violence to the cities. They can keep it. Thank you."

It was a good speech for Bishop. Nothing to broadcast on the national news maybe, but a decent attempt at reminding the attendees that they were a community. McKinnell took questions next, but all his answers consisted of a variation on "too early to tell" or "classified." Kit had her hand raised, and McKinnell called on her reluctantly.

"Ms. Forrester, this isn't a gossip item."

"Good thing I'm not a gossip columnist then." Kit's clipped accent matched McKinnell's, but Samson liked it more on her. He found himself nodding at her response, even though she made him uneasy. She was a professional, and they weren't exactly practiced at speaking with reporters around there. "It strikes me as odd that Ms. Weathers wasn't better known in such a small town. Do you have any theories?"

Samson had been thinking the same thing and hoped McKinnell

wouldn't respond with something vague. The agent paused long enough that it seemed possible he wasn't going to answer at all.

"She didn't live at 53 Chritton Lane, and it's unclear how much work she did for Ms. Lace. Again, it seems like an unhappy accident that the woman was at the house."

Nobody else raised their hands, and Samson, sensing the proceedings were wrapping up, wandered over to the refreshments. Cane Crawley handed him a bottle of water and asked if the Barbara Lace house might be turned into a museum of some sort.

"Finally get some tourists here on the weekends, you know?"

Cane probably had visions of playing his guitar in the lobby every Saturday, but Samson knew how quickly these kinds of plans died in Cedarville. Nobody was driving an hour to stare at some film stills and once-worn costumes.

"Maybe so," Samson said, grabbing a handful of mixed nuts. He wasn't overly enthusiastic, but Cane seemed satisfied, moving toward the exit. He wasn't the only one. Agent McKinnell finished taking questions, and Mrs. John cornered him. Samson intended to stay until the end, a statement of sorts, knowing that if he fled, the rumors would spread even more quickly. Bishop caught his eye and made his way toward him. The two men stood silently until Bishop muttered "fucking Rachel" under his breath.

"He's too young to remember," Samson said, hoping it was true that Bishop's son wouldn't understand.

"Sure, now. But what about in a year? Three?"

"It'll get better with time."

Bishop grunted in response, and Samson slapped him awkwardly on the back. He'd seen men make similar gestures, but it felt forced when he tried it. If Bishop minded, he didn't say anything. Instead, the officer watched his ex-wife pull his son's arms into a sweatshirt.

When the boy looked over, Bishop waved.

"What I got to do is solve this case," Bishop said. "Then she'll have to respect me."

Samson nodded, trying to remember if there had ever been a real case in Cedarville while he lived there. He recalled some fishing equipment going missing once, but not if anyone had been caught. There'd been a barn fire caused by careless kids. A couple of domestic violence incidents that everyone knew about. A few more they suspected.

"What about this being an outsider matter for outsiders?"

"You're gonna help," Bishop said. Samson started to laugh, but the officer wasn't joking. "I mean it. You owe me."

"For starting talk that I was messing around with the victim?"

"For vouching for your scrawny ass."

Samson took his time before responding. He doubted Bishop meant the kind of help that involved a chalkboard full of Hollywood connections. At first he felt trapped, outmaneuvered or at least strong-armed, and yet—a sliver somewhere inside of him felt freed. If he was going to keep digging around anyway, might as well have the blessing of law enforcement. He took a long drink of his water to disguise his growing excitement. He almost didn't recognize the emotion, but there it was, waiting on him like an obedient hound. Samson nodded once, then headed toward the exit before he had to fully reckon with his decision.

The drive home was too short, and when he pulled into his driveway, the old sorrow returned. Samson wished rather than believed his house was haunted. On the brightest nights, he let the moon swim across his floors and slide into every corner as he hoped for the outline of a figure. Over the summer, he'd slept with the windows open, imagining each gust of honeysuckle was his wife come back. He lit candles so she could find her way home. He prayed for a miracle, cursing God when none came, then he talked to nobody in the dark. His monologues consisted of small talk mostly, how a chair was turning out or whether the Townsends' baby would grow out of that overbite. He wondered if a creak from the old staircase or a hum from the radiator was her way of saying hello.

After the town hall meeting, he lay fully awake, trying to conjure up an unfamiliar noise so that he could pretend for a spell. When he first heard the footsteps below, he relaxed, impressed by how real they seemed, his imagination outdoing itself. It wasn't until the boots got closer that he bolted upright, aware that there was someone—a real, living body—inside. He tried to remember if he'd locked the front door as he scrambled out of bed and reached for the copper bookend he kept on his nightstand. While not quite a weapon, it was sturdy enough to do some damage, and he let his eyes adjust to the darkness, hoping he could surprise the intruder.

Then the footsteps stopped altogether, and Samson swallowed, trying to stay as still as possible. His hands shook as he watched the small hand of the clock tick off a minute, then two. After five, he crept toward the door, peering into the empty hallway. He flipped on a lamp, and seeing no one there, he leapt down the stairs. He raced through the rooms, turning on every light until his home blazed. Empty. It was an old place with plenty of hiding places, but Samson knew them all, and they were all empty. Methodically he retraced his steps, pulling back shower curtains and rifling through closets. Empty.

His heart pounded as he picked up the phone, and he couldn't speak at first when Bishop answered his call.

"Who's this?" Bishop asked, gruff and tired.

"Bishop, sorry. Somebody was in my house."

"Gone now?"

"Gone."

"Hang tight."

Samson sat on his front steps as he'd been instructed, staring at every tree and every bush, considering if someone could lurk there unseen. He left the lights on, not caring if his neighbors a mile off thought he'd lost his mind. Hell, maybe he had. They hadn't thought much of him to begin with, so what did it matter? The patrol car arrived without sirens, a small blessing on an otherwise terrible night. When Bishop emerged, Samson guessed that he had woken him. The officer wore his gun holster over gym shorts and a Braves T-shirt.

"Anything taken?" Bishop asked as he approached. "Electronics? Some of that art you've got?"

The word "art" sounded like "porn" in Bishop's mouth—spat out—but Samson didn't take the bait.

"I didn't notice anything. I didn't really look."

"Want to take a look now?"

As Samson surveyed his belongings, Bishop searched the house again and looked for signs of forced entry. There were faint scratches on the front door lock, but Samson couldn't say if they'd been there before. When Bishop was downstairs, Samson checked his fireproof box to make sure it was still locked, the emergency cash he kept alongside an expired passport and Ms. Lace's things still safely hidden away. He felt more confident that nothing had been taken, but his whole body had gone numb as he counted the possible reasons for an intrusion.

"We can look over everything again in the morning. You got some place to stay?"

Samson waited for Bishop to offer him his couch. When it was clear that no offer was forthcoming, Samson nodded, glad that it was nearly dawn anyway. By the time Bishop pulled out of his driveway, the sky had turned a light gray. The frozen dew crackled as Samson walked toward his shed, hoping the space heater still worked. He put his key in the lock, but there was no point—the door swung open when he touched the knob. What looked like a giant ink spill moved in the dark, and Samson shuddered, reaching for the lamp. An orange glow illuminated the small room, and Samson jumped back. Four sleek black snakes writhed against each other on the floor, hissing in anger that they'd been disturbed.

CHAPTER 9

EXT. PARK AVENUE - DAY

BLUE stops to buy a newspaper next to a shoeshine stand. The boot polisher, HAROLD, shakes his head while his customer ignores them both.

> HAROLD
>
> You won't find anything you want in there, Blue. The world's ending, and there's a sale on laundry detergent.

> BLUE
>
> Maybe I got a whole mess a shirts that need a good wash.

> HAROLD
>
> Rumor has it you've got a big mess all right, but it has more to do with politics than clothes. You tell me next week if you need a job.

BLUE

I might need a lesson or two.

HAROLD

I'm serious now, child. This city's got layers of dirt, and down at the very bottom—below the trains and the sewers—those monsters need fresh blood to survive. Money's not enough, though they could stack it into bricks and build skyscrapers. No, they like it down in the dark. You know I'd never tell a smart lady like you what to do, but you watch your step.

The customer looks at both of them curiously, and Blue winks at him.

BLUE

A barrel of laughs with you this morning, but be easy. I've never met a monster who didn't have a taste for bait.

from *The Loud Return* (1965)
Written by Bucky Carruthers
Directed by Tyson Banks

Eastern rat snakes aren't venomous, but everybody knows they're mean. Aggressive, ornery, and fast. And there they were, invading the only room in all the land where Samson felt free. He closed the door and leaned against it, watching the sun rise and ignoring the wildlife problem for a spell. His breath made clouds in the crisp morning air, and he waved at a red pickup truck passing on the two-lane road. Sometimes folks cut through when there was an accident on Highway 64, someone driving too fast and nailing a deer. Lonely. That's how he felt. Four snakes and nobody to call.

Samson rubbed his eyes, sighing and thinking maybe he could just burn the shed down. The table was worth a few grand, though, and he could imagine Agent McKinnell's fake Midwestern accent droning on about "tampering with evidence." When he opened the door, he knew what the trouble would be: finding the bastards. Two sat where he'd left them, wrapping their long bodies around each other like Romeo and Juliet ignoring the morning lark. The other two—or had there been three?— were unimpressed by the star-crossed lovers and had disappeared in the small space, hidden somewhere amongst the shelves of stains and stacks of knickknacks. He was unsurprised to see that his blackboard had been wiped clean, Barbara Lace's timeline erased, her photograph stolen. Samson jumped when something touched his neck, but it was only a towel he'd hung up to dry. "God bless," he murmured, reaching for his leather work gloves.

He tried to keep his movements unhurried, even humming to himself as he removed a blue tarp from the highest shelf and spread it on his lawn. The results of his excavation made a bleak picnic. Item by item, he emptied the shed, maneuvering around the snakes that he could see and hoping to find the others. He spotted his first missing intruder coiled around a watering can. With a mumbled prayer, he grabbed the back of its head, then pulled its body toward his chest. The tail wrapped around his free wrist, and Samson carried the snake to the nearest field, terrified and not a little hysterical. When he released the animal, it darted quickly away, and Samson collapsed to the ground, sweating and panting. His wife would have loved this story, her city slicker husband saving the day. Then she would have finished the job for him, bare-handed. Instead there were three more at least, and either they had to go or Samson had to move. He walked back toward his shed, bone tired and spent.

A shower didn't help him feel any more human, but he smelled better. While he was under the stream, he considered the unspoken, dramatic warning he'd received. Somebody clearly didn't think he had any business poking around a murder case or two. A small part of Samson's brain had thought he'd made up the footsteps in his house, so in some ways, he was relieved. At least he wasn't going crazy, and thank God for small favors. He briefly considered calling Bishop and begging off for the day. The sheriff would surely understand, but an untapped bullheaded streak pushed him toward the Cedarville police station downtown even though he hadn't slept a wink the night before. He was tempted to try a cup of coffee, but instead, he fixed himself a green tea with honey and poured it into a thermos.

Helping Bishop turned out to mean making house calls. They divided up the town using the white pages, and Samson took A–M. The day warmed up to almost sixty degrees, but Samson never got warm, blasting his heater as he drove from home to home. Mrs. Answood fussed over him a little, and he let himself be fed biscuits and homemade apricot jam. She didn't believe the rumors for a minute, she let him know. A fine Cedarville resident like him getting involved with some strange girl from who knows where.

"Rubbish," she said. "I know exactly what you were doing at Barbara's home that night, and if I were thirty years younger, I would have been right there with you. That girl was up to no good, and she got herself killed."

Samson hoped she didn't share her all-too-accurate theory with Agent McKinnell.

"You didn't much care for her."

"No, I most certainly did not. Who goes around bragging about being someone's personal assistant? That title and a dollar will get you a can of soup."

"You never saw her before?"

Mrs. Answood shifted her cardigan so it lay flat against her shoulders and took her time in responding. Samson thought she might be keeping something from him, but it was hard to tell. She could just as easily have been tired of the conversation. Or she might have been embarrassed that she'd encouraged Samson to look into the affairs of Callista Weathers. Samson tried to make his expression neutral, though he knew his bloodshot eyes were giving him away. He was troubled.

"I looked into her life, but there's not much out there," Samson said when Mrs. Answood didn't answer.

"One of these Hollywood types. Probably swaps her face and name on a whim."

The next few people on his list were less eager to chat. Catfish Cullers made lewd jokes. Sarah Donnell remembered seeing Callista a year before at the Barbara Lace estate. Sarah was trying to get residents to sign a petition for recycling bins, and Callista had said that her employer was not to be disturbed "under any circumstances." Deena Gilbert and her husband didn't say anything about Callista or Barbara but wanted to ask Samson about his yard sale. By noon, everyone knew that he had hauled his possessions onto his lawn, and everyone thought they knew why. Nobody, on the other hand, seemed to know much about Barbara Lace or her murdered assistant. How could that be? How could a whole town know the color of his dining room table, but not know even the tiniest bit of dirt related to their most interesting neighbor? It was as if the whole town was in on a conspiracy. Willful ignorance, Samson decided. Stubbornness outweighing the allure of rumors.

"We can keep things to ourselves," Bishop said, pouring himself a cup of coffee.

The two men had met at the station to eat fried bologna sandwiches and compare theories. They had set up a folding table in the lobby, and Samson took notes for them. There wasn't much.

"Any chance you have some tea?" Samson asked. He'd drained his thermos hours earlier and couldn't remember the last time he'd eaten. The bologna sat untouched on a paper plate, but he picked at the bread. His body was used to deprivation, though, and didn't complain much. Even the lack of sleep wasn't that uncommon. He could easily stay up thirty-six hours or even forty-eight. A couple of naps, and he'd once made it to three days.

Samson shivered, still cold, and Bishop rolled his eyes. Bishop didn't much like snakes either and had been sufficiently horrified by Samson's story. But he still didn't believe that Barbara Lace's death was unusual. An old lady dying in her sleep? It was the dream. No prolonged battle with cancer. No painful fall or fading memory. You slip into your own comfortable bed and wake up some place far better than we could ever imagine. Still, Bishop let Samson use the copier to make a few spare timelines of the woman's life. The work seemed incomplete, but Samson had added everything he remembered from the chalkboard, then he'd checked Ms. Lace's letters again, tempted more than ever to open the returned one, but clinging to some sense of honor. He hoped the tapes he'd ordered would arrive soon. He wanted to at least see her alive again onscreen.

"No tea. We don't arrest a lot of quilters," Bishop said, pleased with himself.

Bishop had gotten through names N–T on his list without learning anything useful. He'd been hoping that Callista had a friend in town or at least a friendly acquaintance, but she'd been almost as reclusive as her boss. It was unclear when she'd been hired, though Agent McKinnell said her story checked out. She was Ms. Lace's assistant, mostly paid under the table. Part time as far as he could tell. Samson wondered why she'd give up her MGM career for ten bucks an hour, give or take. She had her own apartment in Murfreesboro, a thirty-minute drive away, and Agent McKinnell was interviewing her landlord, tracking down friends. There weren't many.

"The thing is, I don't believe this town could keep some sort of grand secret. Nobody here can keep a secret to save their life. Not even a surprise party," Samson said, standing and walking toward the coffee pot then changing his mind. "Decaf?"

Bishop grunted in response, then disappeared inside a back room as Samson stared at the town square through a dirty window. There was the patrol car Agent McKinnell had promised. He watched as Colby Evers crept into the utilities office, shuffling with each step. The old man had ignored him when he stopped by in the morning, refusing to open the door even though Samson could see him inside. Samson waved anyway, and Colby waved back as if nothing had happened. His gray hair curled close to his head and caught the light. It could almost be mistaken for spring outside, and in a couple more weeks, daffodils would pop up. If he lasted that long. Samson tried to suppress the thought, but it was obvious someone meant to scare him or worse. He'd ignored that conclusion for as long as possible, moving through his checklist for the day. But if he wasn't at least a little frightened, he was a fool.

Bishop returned carrying a ziplock bag full of coffee grounds and set to making a new pot.

"You sure that's decaf?"

"Guess you'll just have to trust somebody for once."

Thermos filled with bitter brown liquid, Samson went back out to work on his assigned interviews. Squinting at his list, he made out the names Bob Lichter, John and Candy Look, Jamie Meeker, Leejon Meeker, Tommy Sr. and Leasette Meeker, Tommy Jr. and Trudy Meeker, Brigit Mills. Shit. He glanced back at the jail, wondering if Bishop would trade Brigit with him. He didn't think he could handle her disappointed eyes, the downward tug of her lips when she saw him walk into her office. But no—he couldn't switch without a good reason, and what reason did he have? That he'd gotten the woman's hopes up by comparing her great-aunt to a dragon? Bishop would think he'd gone full loon if he mentioned that Brigit had a crush on him. Samson took a slow drink of his coffee, grimacing, then turned toward the utilities building. It was a short walk, and he opened the door for Mr. Evers, who was exiting.

"Afternoon, sir."

"Say what? Oh. Afternoon, afternoon."

Mr. Evers ducked his head to navigate the curb, then climbed behind the wheel of a 1988 Lincoln Town Car, big as a boat. Before he could settle in, Samson knocked on the window, which Mr. Evers slowly lowered.

"Forget something?"

"Sure enough," said Samson. "I was hoping I could stop by this afternoon, ask you a few questions about Callista Weathers."

"Who?"

"The girl that was killed up at Barbara Lace's place."

"Oh, I don't know nothing about that. Hadn't seen Barbara in years. Already told that to the feds."

Samson didn't bother correcting him, that the state, not the Federal Bureau of Investigation, was handling the case. Samson wondered if it made sense for him and Bishop to be covering the same ground as the TBI, but it was true that locals would be more likely to talk to someone they knew. Not Mr. Evers, though. He started to roll the window back up, and Samson scrambled to get in a question.

"You were friends with Ms. Lace?"

"Days gone by. Best to leave well enough alone. Her life weren't here with us."

Mr. Evers ignored Samson as he put his car in gear and crept out of his spot. The man could barely see over the dashboard, but he'd be safe enough on the mile drive to his home. For a moment, Samson considered following him, but he didn't think he'd be met with much good will. Instead, he turned his attention to the task he wanted to avoid and slipped inside the utilities office.

"They should take away his license," Brigit said as Samson approached. She looked down at her hands with a small sigh, then met his eyes as if daring herself not to blink. She wore a form-fitting black turtleneck and gray slacks. All in all, her appearance couldn't have been more at odds with the fluorescent lights and worn carpet. She looked more like a spy than a secretary, and Samson wished again that she would leave Cedarville and never look back.

"Then how would he get to Smithson's to bet on ponies?" Samson replied after an awkward pause. He was trying too hard to be clever and knew it.

"That old lie. You'd slander a sweet old man like that?" She grinned before continuing, seeming to reach some unspoken conclusion.

"What can I help you with today? Tell me you've changed your mind about that pup I mentioned. She'd be sweet on you."

"Not much use for a dog, I'm afraid."

"Who says dogs have to be useful? She'd keep you company."

Brigit flushed slightly as if she'd said something she regretted. Samson wanted to lean over her desk and say she could keep him company. It was the natural retort, and there was something about Brigit that surprised him every time he saw her. Instead, he sat down across from her, stacking his long legs and considering where to start. He'd been questioning folks all morning, but hadn't gotten any better at it. If anything, he was more filled with self-doubt now than when he began. He tried to think of a transition, but he needn't have worried.

"You want to know if I know anything else about Callista Weathers."

"Or Barbara Lace. But how'd you guess that?"

"You and Bishop have been knocking on doors all morning. Like Girl Scouts without cookies. And look, we're all rooting for y'all over that slick kid from wherever, but there were rules about Barbara Lace."

Samson watched her mouth curve down, just as he'd imagined. But the gesture had nothing to do with him, and everything to do with the mysterious actress.

"How's that?" he prompted when it seemed like Brigit wasn't going to continue.

"Rules," Brigit said, making a dismissive wave with her arm. Two silver bangles knocked against each other and make a small chime as if emphasizing her point. "A silent code of conduct. My parents told me about it more than once. I'm surprised my great-aunt never said anything to you, now that I think on it. Colleen knows, maybe made them up herself. No family left now, but Ms. Lace's mom and dad were our people. Her sister lived up the road until the cancer. No talking to strangers, especially not the press."

"I'm not a reporter."

"No, but you're not exactly unbiased either."

Her voice had softened, and Samson looked at the clock on the wall, anywhere but at Brigit's hazel eyes. The hands had stopped moving at 8:13. Who knows when.

"About Callista—"

"Stop." Brigit held up a hand. "I don't care about what happened between you two. What I care about is a single woman killed behind locked doors. Poor thing. I can't imagine the horror, the fear in her last moments, I mean. You think I'm sleeping well at night? You think anyone's easy about this? Agent Slickhair or you and that sheriff who—bless his heart—can't even get a speeding ticket right. Whose ex-wife mocks him in front of everyone. We'd rather it be you, but don't much care is what I'm saying. What we know won't help you, so just find the bastard. And let Cedarville be Cedarville again."

CHAPTER 10

EXT. BUCKY'S JAZZ CLUB - NIGHT

Four men stumble outside, singing and holding each other up. A well-dressed couple brushes past them. One of the men untangles himself from the group and shouts.

> DRUNK
> Watch your woman. Watch your damn woman!

He growls, and the others laugh as the couple hurries out of sight.

> FADE TO THE CLUB'S INTERIOR

It's last call at Bucky's, and the place is half empty. A tired waitress picks up glasses from a table while the band eases into a quiet, gentle rendition of "A Night in Tunisia." SAL SR., the owner, checks the cash register as his son, SAL JR., watches.

                    SAL JR.
              An okay night?

                    SAL SR.
They're all okay. Not soaring like
we used to, but the mortgage gets
paid. And the boys sound good, don't
they?

                    SAL JR.
They sound real good, Pop. Better
than ever.

                    SAL SR.
That's right they do. You got that
interview tomorrow?

                    SAL JR.
You keep calling it an interview.
It's just a conversation. Men like
Crawley don't do interviews. They
have a conversation.

                    SAL SR.
They let out rope is what they do.
They let you think you need that
rope. What could it hurt?

              CLOSEUP TO SAL JR.'S RIGHT HAND

His fingers tighten around his highball glass until his knuckles turn white.

from *Another Late Fight* (1968)
Written by Seth Horowitz
Directed by Jonathan S. Ferguson

It was an odd feeling to suddenly understand that you're alive. Samson had known, of course, but he hadn't understood. Each time he pushed down on the brakes rather than letting his truck careen into a ditch, each time he made himself a sandwich or accepted a job, he made a choice to live. For a moment, the power of simple decisions intoxicated him. He hummed with the possibilities, the nearness of death and how he outwitted the reaper or at least outran him for a while. Samson's confidence in himself swelled as he pushed open the door to the utilities office and made his way back outside. Once behind the wheel of his truck, his confidence wavered. That's how it went these days. A seesaw of emotion after months of depression. Alive, sure, but was he up to the task he'd been assigned? That seemed less likely.

Her life weren't here. Mr. Evers meant to get rid of him, but he might have been onto something, too. Samson pulled out of the parking lot and turned toward home, leaving all the Meekers for another day. The key had to be Barbara Lace, and he was the only one working that angle. What had she been hiding? Callista Weathers was a nobody, just like him and the rest of them. Lace, though, she was something else. She escaped, built a life rather than let one happen to her. It was as if she'd gotten her script in advance, given herself the meatiest role.

Samson's lawn had been invaded, and he wasn't surprised to see a

93

few of his neighbors circling the blue tarp, deciding if he was selling off his possessions or if he'd finally and unequivocally gone crazy. The table he'd been working on shone in the daylight, a rich honey hue, and he was grateful that it hadn't rained. Maybe he had lost his mind after all. Why would he leave such an expensive piece unprotected? He wasn't quite finished with repairs, but it would be a beauty in the end.

"Afternoon," he said, approaching the group with more swagger than he felt. If anyone had been curious about what he'd done with his life in the past year, here was the inventory. An erased chalkboard, seven different stains, thirty-two paint brushes, a hacksaw, a small chest, two embroidered pillows, a workbench, folding chairs, and the table. Not much to show for himself, but it wasn't nothing either, he told himself. Not one but two fine embroidered pillows? A man could do worse.

"Nice to see you again, Mr. Delaware," Mrs. Answood said. "A barn burner?"

"A misunderstanding."

"I'd say." Mrs. Answood sat on the edge of his workbench, surveying his belongings. "We didn't come to tease you, believe it or not. We came to support you. Whatever you need in your investigation."

Samson looked at the face in front of him, Mrs. Answood's deep-set eyes and mottled, babyish cheeks. Self-elected town spokeswoman. Age came with its privileges. People deferred to you out of respect, at least around here. And many still thought of her as the mayor's wife and right hand.

"You know I appreciate that," Samson said, choosing his words carefully. And he did. He'd been viewed with everything from suspicion to hostility to pity since arriving in Cedarville. Never mind acceptance. And he could easily imagine their views on an affair with the victim, although—he'd be the first to admit—they'd forgive a lot, these people, in the name of loneliness. "But you know you should talk to someone in the law, McKinnell or Bishop. I'm just pitching in."

"And yet, here we are. Tulips amongst the treasures," Mrs. Answood said. Would the others speak about the murder at all? He recognized Jimmy Peters and Karen Xi, who'd faced her own scrutiny when she refused to take her husband's last name. Pumpkin was a middle-aged woman who never outgrew her second-grade nickname. And Cole, who owned a cattle farm a few miles down the road.

"Postman bring this," said Pumpkin, as if the matter were settled, handing him a brown cardboard box. Samson's whole body froze when he didn't recognize the return address. He parted from his uninvited guests as politely as possible, promising to clean up the mess he'd made, anything to be left alone. Cole waited around after the others had gone, and Samson again swore that the lawn would be cleared soon, thinking the man disapproved of his clutter.

"You're a smart man," Cole began, and Samson couldn't tell if it was a compliment or an insult. "I went to school with someone smart like you. We had big hopes for him. A doctor maybe. The teachers coddled him, but we didn't care. He was different, you know?"

Samson nodded, though he didn't fully understand. Was Cole coddling him now?

"Car crash, the summer after graduation. Killed in an instant," Cole continued, shaking his head. "You don't forget something like that."

"No, you surely don't."

Samson waited for Cole to explain himself, but his neighbor climbed into his truck and drove away. When his taillights slipped around a bend and disappeared, Samson laid his package on the grass, reluctant to look inside. Instead, he retreated to his home's downstairs bathroom, watching the box from the window as he peed. Had it moved when he turned his back? He washed his hands methodically, scrubbing under each fingernail, then getting out a clean towel to dry. Finally when he'd stalled long enough, he found some scissors in the kitchen junk drawer and headed back outside. The contents couldn't be worse than what his imagination had conjured up.

Kneeling down beside the package, he ran a blade along the long vertical strip of tape and then slit open the ends. He threw open the flaps, and when no hissing noises followed, he looked inside. An old projector and sixteen VHS tapes greeted him—more than he'd ordered—bundled with rubber bands. "Everything I had on her," the collector's note said. "I'm closing up shop." Samson hoped that meant his contact was retiring not dying, but he didn't let himself dwell on the possibilities. Instead he thumbed through the tapes, some professionally packaged, some recorded from television and labeled with sharpie. Even a couple unmarked. Barbara Lace's résumé, part of it at least, her life's highlight reel. Samson couldn't think of a more fitting end to a long day.

He repacked his shed quickly, not bothering to keep his supplies in their usual neat order. He had a new standard for his workspace—no snakes. Anything else, he could handle. It was dark before he finished his chores, and he double-checked every lock before sitting down on the living room couch. He'd insisted on an Eastlake because it was period appropriate for the house, which meant that he never used the room, preferring the comfy sofa in the den his wife had picked out. Who wanted a backache from trying to relax? God, he'd been humored. The entertainment center had never been updated because they never used it either, and unless it had been hit by lightning, the VCR and television should work.

Samson didn't mean to hold his breath as he slid in the first tape, something called *The Loud Return*, but he was lightheaded by the time Barbara Lace's name blinked in the opening sequence. It was another ten minutes before the actress herself appeared onscreen, but there she was, undercover if he was following the plot correctly. A seasoned reporter who knew her way around a story, the juicier the better. She held a cigarette away from her body, swaying her hips from side to side so that her linen dress swung in a hypnotizing rhythm. Her head cocked slightly, she sized up the movie's villain, a playboy who'd gambled with the wrong men before becoming one of those wrong men. The sad sack hadn't noticed her yet, but he would. He'd notice her brown curls coming loose from a long braid or her new red shoes contrasting with the city's dirty sidewalk. He'd notice her presence, how she took up space, and God bless, why wasn't she the star of the picture? Why wasn't she on coffee mugs and dorm room posters? Why wasn't her name synonymous with glamour, the way you'd say "Oh, she's a Marilyn or a Rita"? Luck made no sense and never had, but Samson kept asking himself the questions anyway in a sort of haze. "You need a light," Barbara murmured before—Samson was almost convinced—she winked at him. "You need a light, and I've got one."

The puppy rolled in dead grass, pausing to consider a dried oak leaf before bounding toward the front porch. She managed the first two steps before tripping on the third and sprawling onto the chipped wood. She yelped and, apparently unharmed, continued her adventure. After a few laps of sniffing around the landing, she collapsed at Brigit's feet, rolling over to have her belly scratched. The woman seemed content to watch her gift bring life to the forlorn surroundings. This had once been a place of joy, but a chill had descended, a chill that had nothing to do with the season. Even in broad daylight, the house seemed haunted, each crow's call a warning to all who lingered. Brigit stroked the dog's ears, then straightened back up and tucked a quilt around her legs.

Samson had felt a jolt when he saw her sitting on his porch swing. He'd watched her from his truck, waiting for the protective urge to pass.

But it wasn't safe at his place, and he had to stop himself from scolding her as he approached. She was a grown woman and hardly a wilting flower. Moreover, whoever invaded his house had been looking for him, not a guest. Instead, he forced a casual expression, not going so far as to smile, but nodding.

"You've come to tempt me, I see," Samson said gently, rocking to a stop at the edge of the steps.

"I've come to insist," Brigit replied, pulling the puppy into her lap. "Let me introduce you."

Had her great-aunt mentioned that he might need a guard dog? The small, furry face peering at him didn't look intimidating. Still, Samson admitted that he was impressed. He was no mind reader, but he thought Brigit had brought him the dog in lieu of sympathy flowers. The town thought he'd lost a lover in addition to a wife and instead of balking, Brigit wanted to help. Her hair was loose around her shoulders, thick and chestnut. It matched the animal's soft coat, and he approached them both cautiously, afraid of himself. His hesitation grew into awkwardness, but he finally settled down beside Brigit, conscious of her legs under the blanket she must have brought, always prepared.

Samson swallowed and cleared his throat, wondering if he should try to explain about Callista again and what he believed about Barbara Lace. He had spent the last few days interviewing Cedarville residents during the day and watching old tapes at night. A few seemed familiar, and he was starting to piece together her career in his mind. He would flip through her letters at the same time, taking notes on any names that reappeared. Her agent, a few friends. A few mentioned a beau, which piqued Samson's interest the most. From what he could tell, an older man that her circle didn't seem to like very much.

"River for now, but she'd answer to something else in a week or so," Brigit said. Samson leaned down and reached out his hands. Instead of sniffing, River leapt into his lap, turning circles and pushing her nose against Samson's chin. She smelled sweet and clean. "See there? A perfect fit."

Samson chuckled, a soft murmur that turned louder as the puppy attacked his ears. "Active. That's for sure."

"Now don't tell me you don't got time for a pet. All you've got is time. Too much, if you ask me."

"It's not that—" Samson began.

A grown dog, maybe. One not scared of snakes. One that would bark if somebody returned to his house in the middle of the night. But this slip of a thing? So fragile. He'd be lucky if it caught a cricket. When he glanced up at Brigit, her eyes were wide, a look of surprise in them, and she stood suddenly. Without thinking, he reached for her hand and pulled her toward him. He ran his thumb along her palm, and she shivered.

"I'm going," she said, moving away. She grabbed her quilt and walked quickly toward her red car. The color stood out against the dull, late winter landscape. The sound, too, of the engine starting sounded like something new, and Samson sighed. What had he done?

Once inside, River found the kitchen and started whining. They'd had pets in the past, but Samson was unprepared and put out a bowl of water before rifling through the refrigerator for something that would work for both of them. Sometimes he forgot to eat, and with the nearest grocery store twenty minutes away, it was a small miracle that he even had bread and peanut butter. He fixed them both sandwiches and retreated to his living room—an explosion of cups and plates, tissues, and unopened mail. Despite his meticulous approach to his work, he'd let everything else slide, assuming that when the dishes ran out, he wouldn't have to go on anymore. Who would expect such feats of strength from him? Then he'd run out of dishes and still had to eat. It hardly seemed fair.

A knock at the door made him jump, and he darted to the side of a window so he could look out without being seen. River followed him, wagging her tail and jumping at his legs. His heartbeat sped up when he saw Brigit's retreating form, and he rushed to the door just as she was climbing back into the car.

"Food," she called, gesturing toward the bag of kibble she'd left on his welcome mat.

"Thanks," he said in response, wanting to add something, but she had already slammed her door and was driving away again. Samson glanced at his feet where River looked up at him expectedly. He hoisted the twenty-pound bag onto a shoulder and turned back inside.

"Come on then."

As he poured food into a bowl for River, he tried not to regret his recent life choices. They'd been made, and he had to live with them. Back in the living room, he pushed bills and ads onto the floor, uninterested in the sandwiches he'd made but taking a couple of bites anyway. Somewhere underneath all the junk, there was a steamer trunk he'd turned into a coffee table. Not exactly period appropriate, but his wife had liked the extra storage. River pushed against his legs, and Samson lifted her onto the couch, only caring a little that her dirty paws marked up the upholstery. Samson offered the dog a bite of sandwich, which she gulped down before turning in a circle and falling asleep.

"No guilty conscience, I guess," Samson said, watching River's legs twitch in a dream. Samson wanted to follow her lead, but he knew that if he fell asleep now, he would wake at 3 a.m. panicked and lonely. What had he done? He finally let himself consider Brigit, how she looked at him with more than pity. How he felt a little like himself around her. But she wouldn't want him after the rumors. Everything about him must offend her, and still she was kind. He'd have to return the dog—he was in no shape to care for an animal—but River could stay the night at least.

He had laid out the letters that referenced a boyfriend, trying to piece together what had happened between them. Ms. Lace's pen pals had mostly referred to everyone with nicknames or single letters—M, I, H, etc. It was if they knew that somebody would be snooping into Ms. Lace's private life someday, and they didn't want to divulge anything. An industry habit perhaps. A smart one. Still, it was possible to identify a few of the major players. No wonder the letters had been hidden in the floor. They contained a few choice words about celebrities from the '50s and '60s eras. Drunk leading men. Promiscuous married ingenues. If the Music City Auction House had found these, they would have gone for a pretty penny. There were only five mentions of "M," the love interest, but they seemed significant. Otherwise cheerful letters would take on a warning edge, one going so far as to say that if she didn't leave him, their friendship was finished. Samson tried to make out the signature on that one and gave up. It was dated July 9th, 1980.

He shuffled through the Barbara Lace VHS tapes, selecting a 1957 sleeper called *Baby in Chicago*, starring Sterling Bryce and Liam Thornton. Barbara Lace wasn't in the front credits, and Samson hoped he didn't miss her. The story involved a kidnapping and mobsters and was a bit difficult to follow. There was a reason this one didn't play on AMC very often. He felt his attention drift until—about thirty minutes into the running time—Barbara appeared onscreen. In an olive pencil skirt and matching satin blouse, she'd been dressed as a foil to the star. She was crisp but bland, adjusting her reading glasses and handing over a stack of newspapers to the detective. Barbara looked tall, sturdy. When she started to leave without speaking, Samson felt disappointed, but then she turned.

"By the by," she began, taking a pencil from behind her ear and leaning over the desk. "Majesty makes a third win for the Nebula Corporation. Three's a charm, you know." She paused to circle something on one of the pages, then straightened, satisfied. "Or a wheel."

Her smirk filled the screen, and Samson reached for the remote, hitting the pause button. Magnetic. Alluring. Mischievous. It was the last that drew him to the still frame. How could anyone miss that potential? She was, what was the word? Interesting. More than a pretty face, though yes, with better hair and makeup, she could be a pinup. But more than that, Barbara Lace could act. She was talented. It had been there all along, but nobody had noticed. Or, Samson corrected himself, they had noticed. She had worked steadily into her sixties, but the small parts got even smaller. Paychecks rather than performances.

Samson felt a familiar thrill, the kind of joy he only felt when stumbling across some jadeite at a yard sale. Or an Eero Saarinen mid-century chair in the dusty back corner of a glass barn. Barbara Lace was a find. But now that he had found her, what was he supposed to do?

CHAPTER 11

Barbara Lace (b. 1920)

Lace is remembered primarily for her five-episode arc on the CBS television show *All the Good Ones* (1971-1977). Her performance as Jo's mother, Cecily Barge, earned her an Emmy nomination. Before those years, she played small parts in a variety of films, including All the Guests (1941), The Neighbors (1946), Once Upon a Town (1956)...

Born: June 5, 1920 in Cedarville, Tennessee

Filmography

Actress (Fifty-Five Credits)

Isadora Alvarez: The Untold Story (Documentary)		1985
Self		
Made for Montana (TV Movie)		1982
Teacher #3		
Blast Out! (Movie)		1982
ER Nurse		
The Plowman (Movie)		1979
Judith		

Mr. Rochester (TV Movie)   1979

Mrs. Reed

All the Good Ones (TV Series)   1971-1977

-The Example (1976) … Cecily Barge

-Always Leaving, Always Learning (1976) … Cecily Barge

-Wait for the Kid (1976) … Cecily Barge

-Stand Up for Yourself (1976) … Cecily Barge

-The Farewell Tour (1976) … Cecily Barge

The Example (TV Series)   1975-1976

-In the Distance (1975) … Dr. Smithsonian

Firebreathers (Movie)   1974

Onlooker (uncredited)

from *Who's Who in America*, 1990

      Samson always sat through movie credits, considering it a sign of respect to read the names as they scrolled. The job titles alone delighted him: camera pilot, boom operator, grip. The lives he imagined for each one appealed to him more than the glamour. Who had built those sets, and who had moved the equipment? One scene from *Clouds Through Sunday* showed Lace leaning out of a Manhattan skyscraper, her hair blowing above pedestrians and taxis. A construction crew on the scaffolding nearby shouted at her, and she pursed her lips, slamming the window shut. She was young in that particular picture, twenty-one or twenty-two, and didn't have any lines.

The projector he ordered was in bad shape. He'd figured that at fifty bucks it wouldn't be perfect, but the machine had been listed in "Good" condition. Several screws were missing, and the base was rusted in a couple of spots. It needed repairs before it would stay together long enough to watch the reel he'd stolen from Ms. Lace. He carted it out to his shed, happy to see the new deadbolt on the door untouched. He set the projector on the table he'd been refinishing, pausing for a moment to run his hands along the mahogany. A handsome piece for the right buyer. He didn't care that the restoration was taking longer than he expected.

Samson decided to start with the guts. He loosened the remaining bolts and carefully laid out the pieces in front of him, blowing dust off the various parts. There were a few he'd never seen before, but it didn't look that complicated. The motor still worked at least. He massaged grease into the cracks and along the metal edges, losing himself in the work. It gave him time to think back over the interviews he'd conducted and letters he'd read. Mrs. John knew Ms. Lace when she was young, as well. She wasn't forthcoming at first, but after Samson climbed onto her roof to patch the leak he'd noticed from her living room, she warmed to him. Her words had mirrored Mrs. Answood's: Baby was too wild for Cedarville, and her real life was in California.

Mrs. John recalled a time that the three of them went to the movies by themselves when they were sixteen, a girls' night out. *Showboat*, she thought it was. Some sort of musical, at least, and they'd gotten dressed up, put on rouge and lipstick. Their parents had indulged them, probably glad to have the giddy girls out of the house for an evening. It was a good drive to the theater, and they laughed the whole way, comparing crushes. Baby had been out a time or two with Hank Answood, but she mentioned liking someone else. She refused to give her friends any details, though, and they delighted in guessing and teasing her about the possibilities.

"All harmless fun," Mrs. John insisted, and Samson didn't judge. Things took a turn when they got to the ticket booth, though. Baby flirted with the boy behind the counter, insisting that it would "mean the world to her" if he'd let her sit in the projection booth. Fanny and Colleen had no intention of joining her, wanting to relax in the plush velvet seats with popcorn and sodas, wanting to relish their freedom and their time together.

Even so many years later, it was clear that Mrs. John considered the night a little betrayal, the first crack in those childhood friendships you assume will last forever. Baby got her way, staying in the projection booth until the credits rolled, then—in an even bigger blow to her companions—insisting she'd find her own way home. She did, of course, but Fanny and Colleen got in trouble anyway, leaving a defenseless girl like that on her own. Who knows how Barbara's parents reacted. They must have known that their child was willful, determined to get what she wanted. A little selfish even. And wouldn't you have to be a little selfish to leave your whole life behind, to start anew?

After indulging Samson's questions, Mrs. John wanted to gossip about Agent McKinnell, reveling in details about his breakfast preferences and phone calls. The man stayed busy.

"But between you, me, and the wall," she had said, "I don't think he's making much progress."

If Samson'd never been to Cedarville before, the glee in her voice would have surprised him. Wouldn't she want a killer to be caught? But McKinnell was an outsider, a city slicker to boot, and they'd rather not see his name praised in the papers. And they certainly didn't want lurid stories about their town. There was always the city council—such as it was—dreaming up a way to bring back more prosperous times. A spring festival or an annual charity race.

After Samson reassembled the projector, he hung up a tarp

alongside one wall, not worried too much about the blue color. He'd be able to see well enough. He pulled the blinds and loaded the film onto the feed spool. There was a take-up spool in the box, and he popped that into a place, a thrill of anticipation lingering on his spine. He flipped on the power, and the contraption whirled into life, bright and loud.

It was rough-cut film, sequential but with obvious breaks between filmed sections. Ms. Lace was hardly even in it, almost an extra. She played some sort of store clerk and sold a woman in oversized sunglasses a newspaper and some vise grips. Ms. Lace suggested the customer take advantage of their two-for-one sale on gloves, and the woman declined. The camera cut to a handsome young man waiting by the door, then the man and woman walked out together into a gray afternoon, letting the screen door bang closed behind them.

The blue tarp made everything look like it was filmed underwater, the trees resembling seaweed or algae. Even so, the young actor looked familiar, but Samson couldn't quite place him. Samson watched until the end, but that was it. About two minutes of footage. A strange bit of memorabilia to hide under your floorboards. Disappointed, he clicked off the projector and raised the blinds. A figure in the distance caught his attention, and he squinted toward the field. Somebody seemed to be staring right at him, and he froze. When the person headed toward him, Samson's body moved again, and he raced outside, shouting. But there was nobody around. They'd either disappeared into the copse of cedar trees at the edge of his property or never been there at all.

Samson sat on the grass to catch his breath, and who would blame him for not noticing the reporter approach from the more traditional gravel driveway? Kit took a moment to observe Samson, mistaking his fear for despair. When she was just starting out, she probably would have left him alone, pitied him. But she was a few decades into her career now, and she merely paused before speaking. She kept her tone low, but still Samson bolted to his feet like he'd been shot.

"Excuse me," Kit said. "I didn't mean to startle you."

But of course she did. That was always how you got the most honest responses. Even Samson knew that much.

Samson hadn't heard her pull up, and he quickly spotted the reason. A blue bicycle leaned up against his ancient oak, and Samson wondered what she had been thinking, riding that thing around so many blind curves. It was the country, sure, but most of the roads lacked shoulders, and drivers didn't expect to encounter a bike.

"You got a helmet at least, I hope," he said after a moment, his heart still pounding.

"Wouldn't leave home without it."

Samson wondered again what Kit was doing in town, not to mention where she was staying. Ms. Lace had been dead for two weeks now, and her editors surely wouldn't be interested in such an old news item. To be honest, Kit made him nervous, but he invited her inside, apologizing for the mess. River greeted them both at the door, leaping onto their legs and wagging her tail.

"A new puppy. That's a lot of responsibility," Kit said, but she was smiling as she scratched the pet under his chin.

"She's a guest. Temporary," Samson said, more curtly than he intended.

"An animal in the house does a person good. I was sorry to hear about your wife, Mr. Delaware."

Samson ignored the comment and walked them toward his kitchen, where he tried to find a couple of mugs.

"I hope tea's okay," he said. He'd thrown away his coffeemaker when it wasn't needed anymore.

"Tea's fine. Great. Thank you." Samson rinsed off the cups and put water in the kettle. He'd insisted on a gas stove when they moved in. Nobody else had one, and it had been a minor scandal for a few days, everyone exclaiming that it must have cost a fortune. But his wife liked his cooking, and that was all that mattered to him.

"And now Ms. Weathers," Kit continued. "That's bad luck, I'm sorry."

Samson knew that Kit was trying to get a rise out of him, but he didn't understand why. He waited for her to ask an actual question before responding. He'd rather an explanation, but suspected he wouldn't get one.

"Why did Sheriff Bishop ask you to help with interviews?"

Samson shrugged, trying to stay calm. The woman unsettled him, and he took his time fixing their tea before sitting down across from her. She looked the same as she had at the auction, maybe even wearing the same clothes, though they were clean. A neat, relaxed appearance. She wasn't losing sleep, worried she'd be the next victim. Maybe the country suited her. Samson knew he looked like shit.

"I reckon there aren't that many volunteers around here. I keep my own hours."

Kit's brow was furrowed, and she looked at him carefully.

"It seems a little heartless."

"We're not a sentimental lot."

"And you think Barbara Lace's death is connected to the murder of Callista Weathers."

Samson didn't know much about Kit Forrester, but she struck him as bright and persistent. Not exactly eager anymore, but she must have been when she started. Dogged now, you might say.

"That's not technically a question, Ms. Forrester."

"And you're not technically an investigator, Mr. Delaware."

"You got me there. But you know how it goes around here. We don't discuss Ms. Lace with reporters."

Kit hadn't been taking notes, but she pulled out a pen and a piece of paper, jotting down her number. She slid it purposely across the table and didn't let go when Samson reached for it. He met her brown eyes and held her stare while she answered.

"Oh, people talk. More than you'd think."

Samson wasn't sure if he was more unnerved by the figure he'd maybe seen in his field or by the reporter. One could have been an apparition; the other had shaken his hand. Kit Forrester acted like she knew him, and he resented it. Maybe he should have left well enough alone, but that didn't sit right with him either. Something Mrs. Answood and Mrs. John had mentioned about Barbara's friends being in L.A. and not Cedarville had stuck in his mind. The two towns seemed worlds apart, but there was only, what? A five-hour plane ride between them?

Barbara's agent was a man named Herman Stein, and amazingly, he still operated an office out of West Hollywood. Even better, he answered on the first ring. His crabbiness couldn't completely disguise his relief that someone had called, giving his phone something to do. And when Samson mentioned Lace, he thawed even more, praising his former client in such glowing terms that even the most narcissistic among us would blush.

"A saint, I say, and I'd tell that to God himself. I will soon enough, I suppose."

Herman coughed, a wet and unhealthy noise that made Samson cringe.

"I didn't know her well—" Samson began, only to be cut off.

"Well, you should. You'd be better for it. A saint by proxy or something."

Samson suspected that Hollywood's definition of a saint differed from Cedarville's version, but he didn't correct the man. Stretching the phone cord as far as it would go, he could sit at the kitchen table and look through the newspaper clippings he'd collected. He'd made it back to the library, and nobody had taken his papers this time. River chased a bug that had gotten through the screen door, and Samson flipped through his findings. A few faces in the photos he recognized, but most were simply young and fit Californians, squinting at the sun or smiling through dark sunglasses. Their names and titles were sometimes printed underneath, and he jotted a few down: screenwriters Bucky Carruthers and Hope Lancaster, producer Mick O'Hara. Samson speculated that Mick was the mysterious "M" of the letters, but couldn't be sure. Some characters appeared more than once, including the legendary Isadora Alvarez. Alvarez hit the fame jackpot early and was the "it girl" for a good decade. Paparazzi no longer hounded her, but she still got invited to the occasional awards show, got paraded about so that the elite could feel pedigreed and altruistic. See? They cared about their elders. Samson thought there might be one photo of Barbara with Herman, but he was only identified as an agent in the caption, no name. Samson had decided to paperclip the newspaper articles to the letters he'd stolen, fill in the timeline like a biographer. It wasn't a bad idea really. Maybe when everything was said and done, he could write about her life. It would give him something to do.

Without waiting for Samson to speak, Herman started telling a story about when his kids were little and their Halloween costumes went missing—Cinderella and Pinocchio. How the damn things seemed to have vanished, the whole house crying. His kids, his wife, his maid. They were all looking for fake glass slippers and short pants, wondering if they could make them last-minute cowboys or something. Herman mentioned a doorbell ringing as if a fairy godmother were arriving in the nick of time, and then he stopped talking abruptly. Samson waited for him to continue, but it was as if the phone line had gone dead.

"Mr. Stein?"

"Oh, Christ."

Samson waited for Herman to finish the anecdote, then tried prompting him. "And Ms. Lace had found the costumes? Or brought new ones?"

Silence returned his questions, and Samson stood up, a few of the papers fluttering to the floor.

"Didn't know her? Didn't know?" Herman paused again, blowing his nose and coughing. Another pause followed, and Samson waited for the inevitable question. "How did she die?"

Samson crossed to the kitchen sink for a glass of water, his spirits sinking. Why had nobody called him? Barbara had worked with the same representation for forty years. That was more than most marriages, and Herman Stein deserved a little more respect.

"I'm sorry," Samson said sincerely. "I thought you already knew. I never would have bothered you."

"Well—" Herman began then stopped. Samson tried to summon a chipper voice, describe how important Barbara was to Cedarville, but he found that he couldn't quite muster the energy.

"She was special," he said instead.

"Well, I'm glad somebody bothered me. I can at least send flowers. There should at least be more flowers. What's the funeral home?"

Herman's voice faded and came back as if he were looking for a pen and paper. River whimpered at Samson's feet, and he picked her up, amazed at how well she'd done the night before. No yowling. She slept at the foot of the bed until she needed to go out and let Samson know. Brigit had trained her well, but Samson knew he couldn't keep her. At least not yet.

"There was no service, as stipulated in her will. Maybe you know her relatives?" He didn't mention that she'd been cremated, too, thinking that might be too much for Herman to handle. Samson hoped for a list of contacts, but either Herman didn't hear the question or didn't care. It struck him as odd that the woman had requested no funeral, but she didn't have many loved ones at the end of her life. The place would have been packed, of course. Every busybody claiming a connection. But would Isadora have flown in? Would Herman have made the trip? She was independent and singular, even in death.

"How'd she go?" Herman asked, and Samson sighed, rubbing his hand along River's soft fur. There were a few different answers that he could give, but he decided to go with the truth.

"To be frank, sir, that's what I'm trying to figure out."

Brigit lived outside of the city limits up a one-lane road that dead-ended at a pond. The scene should have been pretty, but scum covered the water, and nobody had picked up the fallen branches since the previous storm. Her ranch-style home was neat and tidy with a bright green wreath on the front door, but leaves covered her roof and would start to cause damage if she didn't take care of them soon. When Samson got out of his truck, crows greeted him, aggressive as watchdogs. River darted at them, and they flew up briefly, then landed again, taunting their small visitor. Samson considered turning back, but he was sure that he'd already caused enough racket. He couldn't run now.

Other women would make him ring the bell, but Brigit preferred directness. She opened the front door, stepping out onto the small porch and letting her Irish setters follow gently behind. The dogs wagged their tails when they spotted River, and Samson nodded, happy that he'd made the right decision for once.

"I thought I said no returns," Brigit called.

"You did, yes, ma'am." Samson walked closer, digging his hands into his pockets and trying not to stare too much at the ground. When he climbed the steps, he could smell Brigit's soap, a crisp lemon mixed with something he couldn't identify. He liked the combination and took a deep breath. "The thing is, I may be going away, and I wondered if you might hold onto her for me."

"Away?" Brigit's face fell, then reassembled itself, making Samson think that he may have been mistaken. That it was a trick of light that made her look so sad for a moment. She wasn't wearing any makeup, and her bare face looked young and a little wan. She had freckles he'd never noticed before at the corner of her right eye. "That's a fine idea. You deserve a break after everything."

Samson looked at the ground, then made himself look up again before responding. "I don't know about that, but I don't think Cedarville grew its own killer, do you?"

"There's some vicious types," she said, crossing her arms in front of her body.

Samson agreed. He hadn't imagined the snakes in his shed or the boots in his house, but he needed to know more about Barbara Lace in order to know who had killed her, and he'd convinced himself that couldn't be accomplished staying put.

"All the same. I'm not sure the answers are here."

Brigit stared hard at him, her hazel eyes trying to see past his defenses. How had he never noticed her, that stubborn streak of independence? He stepped closer to her, and she didn't back away. His heart thudded against his ribcage, but he didn't lean toward her. They stood for a moment without speaking, the dogs yipping happily a few yards away.

"Guess you'll be needing someone to check on your place. Pick up the mail and such."

"You wouldn't mind?"

Brigit looked at him—or through him. He couldn't be sure.

"As long as you hurry back. You do what's best, but hurry back all the same."

Samson left reluctantly, Brigit watching him from her porch. Her sweater was too thin for the weather, and he wished she would turn away from him, go back inside. He put his truck into drive as quickly as he could. It felt like running away, but maybe he'd get another chance if he were lucky. He hadn't been lucky in some time.

It was a short drive to complete his next errand. Neither Agent McKinnell nor Sheriff Bishop shared Brigit's generous assessment of his plan. Bishop seemed particularly put out, as if Samson's trip to Los Angeles were a personal affront, a way of escaping responsibility. Samson considered his intentions, wondering if Bishop could be right, that he sought a vacation rather than a solution. He'd started to itch, that was true enough. It was as if his whole body had been asleep and now feeling returned prick by painful prick. There's a good reason why some freeze survivors resent their rescuers. It's easy to drift into oblivion. It's much harder to claw your way out of a snowdrift, risk frostbite and amputation.

"Frostbite? You got a ticket to California, not Alaska," Bishop said, spitting a wad of chaw toward his property line. The two men stood outside his trailer, sure to be watched by anyone who lived nearby. Samson didn't care anymore. He had something like a plan. There was something about Barbara Lace's life that would help, he was sure. Something he couldn't get from newspaper clippings and internet searches. And he'd be back in a few days. A week at most.

Samson realized that he had been rambling and stood up straighter, trying to take an interest in Bishop's more orthodox approach to the investigation.

"Nobody heard anything that night?"

"You mean did anybody notice you acting like a lunatic? If they did, they're not saying."

Samson pushed back his hair, which he'd neglected for months. His beard, too, was more convenience than choice. He looked feral, but his head felt clearer. Like he could put two thoughts together.

"No, not that. You talk to everybody? What about the auction folks, Gabriel Correa and his staff? They were in town for a few days."

Samson hadn't thought about Callista's argument with Gabriel, not since she was killed actually. Her frustration with the man was clear, and Samson wondered how far she had pushed him. Gabriel was a successful businessman, not one to take kindly to interference. On the other hand, what did he have to gain from bumping off an assistant, even one left in charge of a lucrative estate? He'd get his checks either way.

"Yeah, one of them said something about seeing a gold Lexus the day of the auction. Only son of a bitch in a Lexus around here is a lost son of a bitch."

Samson thought back to the auction day, how distracted he'd been. He hadn't bid on a single item, though Mrs. Answood had picked up some nice table settings. Magic tricks work best with misdirection. While he'd been focused on Callista Weathers, had somebody been focused on him? Were they still toying with him?

"It wasn't a normal day around here. Could have been some collector type. What's Agent McKinnell think?"

"Agent McKinnell thinks he's hot shit. Is tight-lipped about the whole thing despite his talk about cooperation. Co-operation. But I'll tell you this—he's not spending much time here. He's crawling all over the victim's friends and family, looking for a loose thread to pull. Still, he's pissed you're skipping town, even if you're not technically a suspect."

"I'm not fleeing the country."

Bishop grunted then reached for his keys. "I better drive you then. It's an hour to the airport, and a last-minute ticket must have cost you. Listen, though, you tell me if you find something. This Lace angle? I don't buy it. But I'll be damned if I let McKinnell pull one over on me. Facts don't care who finds them."

"When you get so wise, Bishop?"

"Shut the hell up and get in the car."

CHAPTER 12

A besotted teenager stalks the owner of a local nightclub. His wife goes to great lengths to dissuade the crush, but when the girl mysteriously goes missing, she's the only one who seems to care.

> pitch for *No Escape* (1970)
> Written by Barbara Lace
> Never filmed

Samson had flown before, but not in years. He'd once had everything he needed in a thirty-mile radius. Now, though, he admitted that he didn't have anything he wanted, near or far. With his knees pressed against the blue fabric of the seat in front of him, he took an inventory of his life. A sister-in-law who checked on him occasionally. A few friends who called at first then stopped when he never picked up. A shed full of unfinished projects. There were a lot of Bellport dining chairs with nobody to sit in them. Maybe that's what bothered him most about the snakes. The whole point of being lonely was that nobody bothered you. Maybe the trade wasn't fair, but that was the trade nonetheless. An ache in your soul for some privacy.

Out the window, the sun set, making the clouds grow red as if angry or embarrassed at the world. Samson shut his eyes but the color still pulsed in his vision, desperate to be seen. He thought of Callista's blood, her shocked face and Ms. Lace's grimacing one. He thought of choices and consequences and how in the morning the wheels of this plane would slam into a tarmac, and no matter what, he wouldn't return to Cedarville the same man who had left. The jolt came more quickly than he expected because—unexpectedly, gratefully—he fell asleep before the meal was served. He didn't particularly regret missing the overcooked chicken and syrupy peaches, but his neck and shoulders felt like they'd been held in a vise. The walk through LAX didn't help his stiff body, and then he had to wait for the rental car kiosk to open. By the time he was cruising toward downtown Los Angeles, he was hungry and tired again. Worn out, and he was only getting started.

After parallel parking between an Acura Integra and a Buick Grand National that had seen better days, Samson stepped out into the bright day. Spring Street wasn't as busy as he expected, but there were still plenty of pedestrians. A few brushed passed him, one in an ill-fitting suit, but most in casual, hip clothes. Tank tops tucked into their jeans. Men and women alike as if an L.A. uniform could be picked up at the welcome booth. Samson squinted up at the art deco buildings, easily seeing their potential underneath years of neglect. One was already being restored, new permits on the windows and what looked like an art gallery next door if your taste ran toward airbrushed canvases.

His feet hurt from the dress shoes he'd bought at the Nashville airport, and he realized belatedly that nobody would have given his boots a second glance. Nobody was looking at anybody, heads down or facing forward. Samson longed to be indoors, separated from the fray. A thin man began shouting at himself, angry about a missed opportunity and gesticulating wildly. Samson couldn't tell if he was homeless, and besides the new shoes, Samson figured he didn't look much better himself. Samson kept his eyes on the concrete as he passed, then searched again for a building number. Sweat dripped down his back, though the weather would be described in guidebooks as "temperate." His jacket had been too light for Tennessee, but was now stifling. A low, steady headache reminded him that he was a long way from home, and he doubted his impulsiveness. What did he hope to find behind door 1315?

When he finally found the building, it was wedged between two functional mid-rises. While in need of a good power-washing, they had their lights on. 1315 looked like it would have collapsed if not braced on either side. Three stories of painted, beige stucco that had been peeling for years, decades maybe. The glass on the front door was covered in a thick film, and Samson couldn't see inside. Some primal instinct told him to run, save his own neck and forget the rest. Instead, he found Herman Stein's name on a buzzer. When the door clicked in response, he let himself in. A light flickered over the stairwell, and he climbed up quickly, then walked a dim, desolate hallway to Stein's office. It was hard to believe that he was still in Los Angeles, not an abandoned Soviet nuclear site. Samson tried to imagine the place in better times, fresh paint and photographs on the wall. A few high-backed chairs, perhaps, for visitors smoking Parliaments and flipping through the latest issue of *Variety*. Now only the honking and shouting from the street disturbed the feeling of desolation. What sort of Hollywood was this?

Herman answered his own door, leaning heavily on a hospital-issued cane. He hunched, too, but when he spoke, there was still something left of the carnival barker.

"You'll excuse the informality," he began, gripping Samson's hand

and gesturing with his cane toward a brocade settee. "My secretary's been out to lunch since 1977."

Herman circled his metal desk and collapsed into a chair. His office was cluttered, to say the least. Bookshelves overflowing, plants all but dead. There was a souvenir Oscar like you'd find at a Universal Studios gift shop next to a stuffed teddy bear. Herman was flipping through a large black binder and stopped when he got to the page he wanted. He pulled out an 8x10 photo and handed it to Samson, who had sat down and started running his hands over the couch's pale blue material. The fabric was ripped, but it would take less than a week's work to make the settee a showpiece again.

"A Kittinger? Some new upholstery, and this would be a beauty," Samson mumbled, half to himself.

"Son, we could all use some new upholstery."

The photo was Barbara Lace's final headshot and showed a handsome woman of sixty or so, makeup heavy and dyed auburn hair meticulously pinned. She looked ready to play somebody's slightly foreboding mother, though she'd never had any children herself. She had no family left at all as far as Samson could discover. Her parents and sister long dead. No nieces and nephews.

"Foreboding, that's the word," Herman replied to his visitor's suggestion. "She rolled into my office a pup of eighteen, as wide-eyed and eager as the rest of them. But surviving thirty, forty years in this town? She was one of the toughest around, bless her."

His voice boomed, then dipped low as he remembered his client. He couldn't have been much older than her when she'd signed with him. A decade between them maybe. Samson could almost imagine the pair, full of energy and ambition, ready to take on the world.

"She did well for herself," Samson said, and Herman focused on him, looking carefully—some might say rudely—at his face.

"Damn straight, she did. Damn straight."

Samson flipped over the headshot to read her résumé. He'd found something similar in microfiche form at his library. This one was more of a highlights reel, focusing on her major accomplishments rather than a full timeline. The movies he'd seen and many he'd missed blended together, stopping in 1981, a year before Barbara moved back to Cedarville. What had happened? That was the million-dollar question.

"Was she still getting work?" Samson asked.

"Oh sure, not every week or anything, but she still got calls. A pro like Babs? A one-take queen? If somebody on set was wasting time, it wasn't her."

"Why give it up then?"

Herman swiveled his chair so he was staring out the window. Samson couldn't help but think that the gesture seemed posed, preparation for a flashback. And used before. Herman was sad about Barbara, but he was also enjoying himself.

"You seem like a good kid. This story's not for you. And my client has rights to privacy."

The response surprised Samson. He hadn't really been expecting an answer other than burnout or simply retirement. Hollywood's always been a notoriously hard place for women, roles disappearing as wrinkles appear. What were the options besides drastic procedures with questionable results? He couldn't help but feel a tinge of guilt over not appreciating furniture in its natural state, always having to sand and polish, make everything look new. Samson sat quietly in reflection, and Herman didn't interrupt him. The agent probably hadn't received guests in a while. As if rousing from a dream, Samson shook himself. He hadn't felt charming in a good long while, but he could at least make an effort. He hadn't flown 700 miles to brood.

"Gotta respect a man who respects privacy," he said, forcing himself to act relaxed. "That's how you got ahead, right? But let me at least stand you lunch. I just rolled into town, and you must know the best places."

If a slight twang snuck into Samson's vowels, Herman didn't seem to notice the change, nodding in agreement and reaching for his gray fedora. "Secrets are fuel in this town, and I've had a full tank most of my life. But I suppose there's no harm in a little chatter. You like a nice pastrami on rye? Of course you do. You look like a man who'd appreciate a decent sandwich." Herman paused, looking again at Samson's face. "You look like a man who needs one, to be honest."

Romance. According to Samson's new inside source, Barbara Lace was running away from romance gone wrong.

The diner bustled with activity, waiters and waitresses practically flinging down food to keep up with demand. The low din of conversations competed with sizzles from the grill, and the noise created a screen for anything the old-time Hollywood agent might reveal. The staff treated Herman like they would their own grandfathers, giving the men a large table even though a sign clearly stated that they were reserved for groups of four. They fussed over Herman, bringing him extra pickles and scolding him when he didn't finish his milkshake.

"Calories, Herman. When you gonna learn? The chocolate not working for you today? We've got strawberry." The waitress stood with a hand on her hip, refusing to take his glass. It was true that Herman looked more bird than man from certain angles, his thin wrists mere bones as they picked at onion rings, but Samson was one to talk. "Pie, on the house," the woman said, shooting both men a reproving look. "You too, sugar. They don't feed you in the South no more?"

She turned before Samson could respond, and how would he defend himself anyway? Food hadn't exactly been at the forefront of his mind lately. The grilled cheese on his plate was good, though, and he took another bite, aware of the irony of trying to fatten up in a city that expected everyone to be as thin as wet laundry. A few of the glam New York supermodels had figures in common with iconic celebrities of the '30s and '40s, but the hot new things in Hollywood were the Winona Ryder and Mary-Louise Parker types, a bit tortured in their beauty, mortal girls rather than goddesses. There was a blockbuster out with a new face and veteran Cassidy Cullers. He'd been a little ethereal in his youth, as well, but had grown into a rugged leading man. Samson had never thought much about the evolution of actors and actresses, of looks as trends, but he'd always been a fan of the movies. He admired the collaboration, how a single work of art required hundreds of hands and different areas of expertise. Everybody playing a part.

"I'm not sure why the waitress is giving you a hard time," Samson said. "The whole town looks malnourished to me."

Samson's eyes fell on a group of teenagers in cut-off jean shorts and sweaters that swallowed their petite frames.

"It wasn't always the case," Herman said, taking a drink of his coffee. Their plates and cups took up most of the Formica surface. "Pretty, sure. Pretty was always a requirement, but the girls had to be healthy, especially the ones in the chorus. You better believe it takes a strong lady to kick and swirl all day in heels. You don't believe it?"

"I believe it."

"You believe it. Look at this kid?" Samson raised a skeptical eyebrow, well aware of his craggy, sun-seared face. Herman was laying it on a bit thick. "A regular Clark Gable."

"You knew Clark Gable?"

"Sure. I knew all the faces. And Gable was a great face. A closeup's dream. Babs, too, though especially those first few years."

Samson wasn't sure how to phrase his next question. By all accounts, Barbara Lace had been successful. She'd worked steadily, supported herself, and saved enough by outside appearances. But had she wanted more? To get so close to fame. Was it harder that way? With hope?

"Will she be honored at the Oscars?" Samson asked, sidestepping the heart of the issue for a moment.

"Working on it. That in memoriam business is a racket. It's all politics. Who we going to bump to get my girl in? Can't be Melvin Spector's wife, though her contributions to costume design were mostly yelling at seamstresses. There's T.L. Hopper, but I know the president's a fan of his early work, those two-bit dramas. You bring the paper?"

Samson had brought the paper. He handed over a copy of *The Tennessean* with Ms. Lace's obituary. Herman had told Samson over the phone that he liked to have them for all his clients and all his friends' old clients, and you could only get the national newspapers in L.A. The agent read silently, his eyes moist and—perhaps Samson was projecting—a little disappointed by the article's length. It was another world, and Samson was out of his depth, not even sure what information he needed. He figured mentioning foul play would leave his lunch date in pieces. He had bluster, sure, but Herman wore his sentimentality right out in the open. And what evidence did he have, really, that Barbara hadn't died peacefully in her sleep? Samson wanted that to be true, of course he did. He just didn't buy it.

"You mentioned romance?"

"Mick O'Hara. A producer sort. Known for running around with twenty-year-old wannabes behind his wife's back. A real peach, rotten to the core. I'm telling you, even at fifty-something, Babs was something else. More than smart. Brilliant. She talked like a Budd

Schulberg script, fast and sharp. Lyrical. And you better believe she turned Mick's head."

Samson thought back to the "M" mentioned in the letters Barbara had kept under her living room floor. Most expressed concern of some sort. A subtle hint here, an outright warning there. Reading between the lines, the man had a temper, and everybody knew it.

"A producer?"

"A producer type. There's a difference. A real producer is an asset on any film, a steady presence and valued opinion. Mick just had loads of cash. Dabbled. Never had a hit, but kept trying."

Herman shifted his gaze to the window, posing again. Samson wondered if he was being played by the old man. Herman had survived a long time in a cutthroat business. His office might not look like much, but the fact that he still had one was a feat in itself. You don't stick around if you're not at least a little cunning. Maybe what Samson saw as sentimentality was a big ol' bluff. He took a bite of his sandwich and tried to think about what Herman might be hiding. Everybody was hiding something.

When Barbara arrived in Los Angeles during World War II, the town was in the midst of a boom. The Golden Age it's called. Stars loomed large, directors flourished, and studios took over the industry. The spirit of independence—the flashes of brilliance only possible in the early days of a new art form—turned into something more money-minded. Fewer risks, more lawsuits, and a sort of mass-produced glitz. The Industrial Revolution meets Hollywood. The Gold-plated Age might have been more fitting. Samson admitted to being susceptible to the varnish. Sure, he knew about the feuds and back stabbings, the actors unable to get out of contracts, all but blackballed from actually appearing in a film. But he still found himself drawn to the bright lies, the carefully crafted stories of your Marilyns alongside the more rebellious Marlenes.

"What went wrong?" Samson asked, pulling Herman's attention—and his own—back to Barbara Lace and her paramour. What about the Barbaras, he wondered. Where did they fit into the pantheon? Had she refused to conform or conformed too well? After decades in the business, somehow a single failed relationship had brought her down. Samson hated Mick O'Hara on principle.

"It's a little fuzzy, to be frank. She didn't confide in me. Just packed her bags and ran."

"Ran?" Samson asked, the hairs on his arms rising.

"Ran."

"And he's still alive?"

Herman paused before answering, taking a drink from his melted milkshake and patting his lips. He took his time as if he knew Samson was on the edge of his seat, waiting for a response. As if he knew Samson wanted something from him. Secrets, as Herman had told him, are fuel, and he wasn't going to burn his all at once.

After the waitress brought their bill and Samson slid a few bills on top, Herman nodded, coming to a conclusion of some sort. Trusting him, maybe.

"Still alive," Herman said and reached for his cane. "But good luck finding him."

CHAPTER 13

INT. AN OFFICE

Thirty stories up, CARL BRASEL and KIP LANGERS drink cognac, toasting the recent acquisition of *Fantasy*, a pornographic magazine said to rival *Playboy* and *Penthouse*. The Manhattan skyline can be seen out of their window. They're interrupted by a secretary, FLORENCE BRENDON, holding takeout containers.

> FLORENCE
>
> If you're going to go down in flames, best have a full stomach.

> KIP
>
> Listen to this. It's a new era, Flor— we've got to move with the times.

> FLORENCE
>
> I don't have to move any way except out of the way.

CARL

You can't leave us. This place would
crumble without you. A sinkhole would
open up and swallow us whole.

FLORENCE

There's a sinkhole all right. Enjoy
your orange chicken.

Carl blocks her way, and she feints to the right.
He puts his arm around her waist and leads her
back into the room.

CARL

One nightcap, old girl. We're all
winners tonight, and I intend to
celebrate.

from *Trespass* (1972)
Written by Bucky Carruthers
Directed by Bucky Carruthers

Mick O'Hara dabbled in mobster business as successfully
as he dabbled in movies. Which is to say, he was convicted of money
laundering in 1983, the year after Barbara moved back to Cedarville. He
served his time, then fell off the grid. Herman had been a bit hazy on that
particular detail but guessed that the man would have fled to Mexico to
make the most of his remaining money. There wasn't a lot of information

to be had about Mick after his release. No more movie making, no more hobnobbing. He disappeared, leaving behind an ex who'd filed for divorce as soon as the judge read his sentence. Mick's grown kids didn't want much to do with him. One newspaper article mentioned a brother, Bill O'Hara, but did Samson really want to two-step with a gangster, even one that was surely well into his twilight years?

For that matter, why was Samson still in Los Angeles a week after meeting with Herman? Sleeping at the cheapest motel he could find, eating out of a gas station, he wasn't exactly taking in the sights. He spent his nights watching Barbara's tapes, not sure what to make of the unmarked ones. Bootlegs recorded with a handheld camera, one was a nearly unwatchable screwball comedy and the other just a brief scene. They both shook slightly and made him nauseous. He rewatched the two movies he thought were best, directed by Jonathan S. Ferguson. No wonder the man had a cult following. His movies didn't follow a traditional three-act structure, didn't follow any structure really. They were original. Even the early ones where the source material veered toward predictable. Then there was *Another Late Fight*, a gangster movie without any gangsters, filmed on only two sets, one inside a bar and one outside. Ferguson kept the cast small, too, no more than six or seven actors even though he had a decent budget. Barbara played the beleaguered wife and mother, doling out good advice that nobody took. Ferguson got a performance out of her, that's for sure. Out of everyone. If the rumors were to be believed, the director terrified everyone with a quiet intensity, an insistence on perfection. A hundred takes was nothing, another try at four in the morning.

Samson had spoken to his only lead and should have moseyed on back home. Sheriff Bishop wasn't exactly pleased with his vacation. But the truth clawed at Samson's brain, something of his old stubbornness that he'd damn near forgotten. He'd been living for months with his wife's spirit, but in an odd way, leaving their home made her seem closer. No, it wasn't that odd. Sitting around and letting himself waste away? That, she would have hated. But now he was on the sort of mission that she would have wholeheartedly endorsed. Doing what's right when nobody cares, that's character. He could hear her low drawl in his head, and he cringed, the sound painful in its familiarity. When he thought about his reasons for leaving town, they didn't seem to have much to do with character.

Samson stared into the bathroom mirror. He didn't look like a man with a mission. He looked like a man who needed a shave, and that much at least, he could accomplish. A donut shop across the street flipped on its neon sign, and Samson's new, reliable companion—a low, mechanical buzz—returned. The neon pulsed into his room, bathing the bed in red light for a moment before retreating and returning in a steady rhythm. It was enough to drive a sane man crazy, and Samson wasn't sure he'd been all that sane to begin with. He'd been mostly locked inside for a few days, watching the tapes that he brought along for the goose chase. Rereading the letters. He'd spread the photos out on the comforter, sure now that Herman appeared in one or two. There may have been two of Mick, but one was taken from an unhelpful angle, the tall, gray-haired man turned away from the camera lens.

One of the bootleg tapes in particular bothered him, mostly because it was a single scene cut off in the middle, then nothing until the tape ran out. The audio was difficult to understand. Barbara Lace was older than he'd ever seen her in previous films, with little or no makeup. There were several close-ups, as if the director delighted in showcasing every wrinkle, every bead of sweat. She almost didn't look like herself. In one part, she talked to an ethereal young man, and Samson could make out a few phrases over the sound of traffic. She "wanted to be left alone" and "put a premium on privacy." Lace approached a cabin, trepidation filling her expression. She disappeared inside, then the film turned white and blank. Perhaps the recorder had been discovered and kicked out?

Samson used the motel's shampoo to lather his face, then pulled a disposable razor across his cheeks and throat, enjoying the sting. He'd have red marks when he finished, but what did it matter? He didn't plan on impressing anyone ever again if he could help it.

Once dressed, he stepped out into the parking lot, looking around for his rental, a compact sedan that smelled like smoke and fake pine. He liked the combination. He hadn't smoked since he was in his twenties, but what the hell, he thought, heading to the nearest gas station. They knew him there, and the owner nodded when he entered. He picked up a pack of Parliaments along with a soda and some chips, congratulating himself on finding the grimiest corner of the country's glitziest city. To be fair, the city was as known for its crime as for its awards shows these days. Crack had transformed once stable neighborhoods, gutting them really. Gangs had taken advantage of the market, thriving despite the best—and just as likely the worst—efforts of the LAPD. It had been less than a year since four officers were acquitted of working over Rodney King and the city responded with riots. The events had seemed distant to Samson, so far away that they seemed historic even as they were happening, unfolding on his small television set. But Samson had driven around some, and the effects couldn't be ignored. It wasn't just the busted windows or concrete barricades. The energy shifted in certain neighborhoods. The expressions changed, defiant or broken.

Samson checked the address, suspecting that he was headed to one of the nicer sections of town. The drive was frustrating for a man who'd become accustomed to country back roads, someone used to traveling for miles without seeing a soul. Bumper to bumper traffic made a twenty-mile trip take more than an hour, but the warm weather meant that he could keep his window rolled down as he took drag after drag, his head light. The nicotine filled his lungs and made him jittery. He remembered why he'd given it all up—booze, coffee, tobacco. His younger self would have mocked him and his sensitive stomach. What kind of grown man has a sensitive stomach? Samson had never really been tough, though, even when he liked a bit more action. He'd only been in one fight, and he'd been thinking about it. The man had split his left eyebrow, but Samson had left him on the ground. He had won. He hoped he wouldn't have to get violent again.

Samson threw the butt out his window, then flipped down the visor to block the sun. He'd called Bishop before he left, filling him in on his plans. Bishop had been distracted, though, as little interested in a retired gangster as he would be in the latest episode of *The Price Is Right*. Back home, Agent McKinnell was still looking outside of Cedarville, harassing Callista's friends. Bishop had made a pretty big discovery, finding the murder weapon in a creek that cut across the Meeker property line. Samson figured one of the Meeker boys had found it, but was giving Bishop the credit. No prints, though, and Bishop had traced the gun to a dead end: a pawnshop sale, paid in cash. Samson's rental crawled forward, and he let his mind wander. He'd chased Barbara Lace through her history. She'd been fortunate to sign with Herman, an agent with a better reputation than most during an era of powerful men who could get away with—if not murder—at least mistreating actresses whose families had rejected them. There were different snakes in Hollywood than Cedarville, but they were plenty dangerous.

Samson put on his blinker when he got close to the exit, sticking his hand out the window and waving at the driver honking behind him. He couldn't see who was behind the wheel, but the aggressiveness bothered him. He took his time changing lanes, ignoring the garbled threats shouted at him as the car jerked past him, accelerating then smashing the brakes to avoid a collision. The traffic off of I-10 wasn't much better, but at least there were stoplights. When one turned red, Samson unfolded the address, hoping the name Sunshine Road was a good sign. He didn't believe in good luck, but he wouldn't kick it out of bed either.

When he pulled onto the right street, the houses were large, but crammed together, not so much gaudy as the same. These homes were for the wealthy who were unburdened by imagination. Beige or white stucco with the occasional column, a seemingly endless monotony, though Samson finally reached a cul-de-sac. He parked at the curb and stared at Bill O'Hara's homestead, lights on in every window. It looked more like a hotel than a mafia lair.

As he approached, Samson could hear raised voices, a woman's high-pitched wail and a man's low growl. The words were indistinguishable at first, then chilling.

"I'll fuck you up, then I'll fucking kill you."

"I'd like to see you try," the woman said as Samson hesitated, finger hovering above the doorbell. When glass shattered, Samson curled his fingers into a fist and pounded on the door. The people inside grew quiet and still. Samson could hear his heart hammering in his ears, but he widened his stance to seem more intimidating. He knocked again and waited, his skin crawling from the smokes. He'd have to give them up again. Soon.

"Christ."

Samson couldn't tell who had spoken, but shortly after, the door swung open to reveal a sweaty old man in slacks and a loose, black T-shirt. He was as tan as a leather boot and stood in his bare feet, sizing Samson up.

"Who the hell are you? You a cop?"

"No, sir. My name is Samson Delaware—"

"Neighbor? Another snitch. Who's got time for this? Delly, you got time for this?"

The man shouted over his shoulder to a woman sitting on a

velour sofa massaging the back of her neck.

"No, baby," she said. "Nobody's got time for this."

The man started to close the door, but Samson put his hand up and stepped closer.

"Is everything all right, ma'am?" he called toward the woman. He could see that she was wearing a tight red dress with cheap high heels, her face blotchy from crying. "Can I call someone for you?"

The woman hesitated, considering, then rose while yanking down her hem, which fell to mid-thigh. Pockmarks covered her arms, and she covered them with a worn Angels sweatshirt before slinging a beaded purse over her shoulder. She was small, but walked with a swagger.

"Sure, honey," she said. "You can call me a cab."

Samson stood with her at the end of the driveway as they waited. She'd called her own car after all, but Samson wanted to at least appear useful. He handed her a twenty, which she considered, then tucked into her pocket. Delly seemed more impressed by the cigarette he pulled out, lighting two then passing one to her. It reminded him of some hazy memory from his youth.

"He get like that a lot?" Samson asked as he took a drag. Delly was older than he would have guessed at first, in her fifties. She rubbed at the mascara on her cheeks and didn't answer.

"Bill and I go way back."

"How far?"

"Far enough."

The day was warm without being balmy, and Samson glanced up at the clear blue above him. Pretty but he preferred the red, night sky. That's how he thought of it—red. The city lights drowned out the stars, leaving a burnt sheen, like poorly exposed film.

"You ever meet his brother Mick?"

Delly inspected her nails until Samson reached into his wallet for another twenty.

"Mick don't come around much. He's too good for us, he thinks."

Samson glanced back at the enormous house, seeing Bill leaning against the doorframe, spying on them. A gangster past his prime, but still dangerous. It should have made him uneasy, but Delly's nonchalant attitude was rubbing off on him. Didn't come around much meant that Mick came around sometimes, suggested he was still in town. A car approaching pulled his attention back, and Samson watched Delly nod at the driver before taking a last drag and crushing the butt under her shoe.

"I don't know where you crawled in from, but take my advice and crawl back."

Delly climbed into the taxi, slamming the door behind her. Samson watched her pull away, exhaust bathing the pavement then disappearing. Reluctantly, he turned back toward the house, his anger at Bill O'Hara sudden and as real as his skin. He could feel his loathing hum across his forearms and up his neck. It sat in his chest, clenching and unclenching like a raptor, and he didn't know what he might do next. He didn't care. A small voice encouraged him to drive away, but he shouted down that thought. Samson had mostly been an even-tempered man, more likely to joke than to fight. But as he got closer, he let his emotions take over and grabbed Bill forcefully by the shoulder, shoving him back inside.

"This is my fucking house," Bill said, turning purple and sputtering. "I do what I want."

"This scum city. Not enough character among the lot of you to fill an ashtray."

Samson kicked the door shut behind him. A table shook enough to knock over the vase on top. It didn't break, but water poured onto the floor and Bill slipped, crashing down onto his back. For a moment,

Samson enjoyed towering over the man, but then shame began to paint the scene in a different light. Bill O'Hara was an old man, and his bare stomach protruded, making him look meek and vulnerable.

"Where's Mick?" Samson asked, quiet and controlled. It wasn't the question he meant to ask, but he couldn't back down now.

"Fuck you." Bill sat up, rubbing his wrist.

"I'm serious. Where's your brother?"

"Mick. Always fucking Mick getting me into hot water. I don't know where he is. At the Standard, maybe? I can't keep up."

"He's in the States then?"

Bill paused, realizing he'd revealed something by accident. He tugged his shirt down and pulled himself up using the table. When he righted the vase, it was clear that he wanted to avoid answering. He held up the ugly yellow container in front of him.

"My dear departed mother bought me this."

Samson resisted the impulse to say the piece was a department store knockoff of a Tiffany design. Worth fifteen bucks, tops. Instead, he brought up Mick again.

"I just want to talk to him."

"That's what they always say. Before you know it, you're cradling your Remington like she's your high school sweetheart, not sure whether to hide or to hunt. How you think I lost my right ear?"

Samson studied the ear in question.

"Looks fine to me."

"A prosthetic. Christ, all right. What do I care? Yeah, he's been back a few years now, but I can't keep up. And good luck to the fool who wants to track him down."

Samson let himself out, guilt making him regret the whole day. The whole trip, if he were being honest with himself. He was no better than the rest of them. A fraud wherever he landed.

CHAPTER 14

An ophthalmologist invents a device that will allow patients to see into other people's minds, receiving a colorful and sometimes shocking series of images. At first, the patients think of DR. MILLER as a hero, but soon their new abilities start to make them insane...and violent. Can the doctor undo what he's done before it's too late?

> pitch for *I See You* (1973)
> Written by Barbara Lace
> Never filmed

At five in the morning, his phone rang and Samson jerked awake, fumbling with the items on his nightstand. The Cedarville area code chilled him. Nobody ever called before dawn with good news. He switched on a lamp, rubbing his eyes. When he answered, his voice was hoarse from lack of sleep and too many cigarettes.

"I'll call back."

Brigit's voice surprised and then warmed him. He was suddenly alert to being alone and almost naked in a seedy motel room. Company sounded nice, even a thousand miles away.

"No, please. I'm awake."

"I don't know any folks out there. I forgot about the time change."

Samson sat up slowly and leaned back against the wall, stretching his legs out in front of him. The room was warm and smelled faintly of mildew, the ancient A/C making noise and condensation but not cooling the small area much. The donut shop hadn't opened yet, and his room was mostly dark. He pictured Brigit in her small but clean kitchen, dogs at her feet, and felt a pang of homesickness.

"I'm glad you called. Everything all right? River all right?"

"River's a right mess, but that's not why I'm calling."

Samson closed his eyes, thinking about her thick hair. He could bury his hands in it, pull her toward him. He should have done that when he had the chance. But her voice had something he didn't recognize, and he reminded himself that she might not welcome his fantasy version of her. He wedged the phone between his ear and shoulder, rubbing his eyes again to wake up. He'd felt better. His mind had been occupied with his quest—or fool's errand—but he'd more than neglected his body.

"I'm listening," he said when it seemed like she was waiting for encouragement.

"It might be nothing, but I picked up your mail yesterday, and there's a letter."

Samson smiled, moving to the side of the bed so that he could find his pants and the last of the smokes. He'd already promised himself he wouldn't buy another pack. He could talk all morning about the mail with Brigit, if that's what she wanted.

"Sure, I don't have a lot of friends, but a letter don't seem so bad."

The long pause punctuated Samson's first good news in days.

"The return address is the Lace house. I thought it was at first, but I wanted to double-check before bothering you. I drove by, and it's the same address." Brigit spoke quickly, the words spilling into one another. "53 Chritton."

"You went there?" The thought of Brigit anywhere near that house made his pulse speed up. There was something wrong about the place. "I'm not telling you what to do, but maybe don't get too close."

If Brigit heard his warning, she ignored it, instead telling him that she didn't feel comfortable opening the letter.

"What if it's evidence?"

"Evidence of what? Cedarville's inefficient postal service? It was probably mailed a while ago, got stuck in the sorter or something."

"Now don't you go badmouthing Clover just because you're tired. She delivers rain or shine."

"You should run for mayor."

"You're not taking this seriously."

Samson appreciated her concern more than he was willing to admit. And while he wasn't much worried about a letter, he disagreed with her assessment. He'd come to L.A., hadn't he? For a moment, he couldn't quite think of why, though. From the outside, it looked a lot like escaping, he admitted. A lot like running away.

"Take it to Bishop. Or Agent McKinnell. Or open it yourself."

"It's your mail."

It was such a small-town response that Samson smiled. He'd had a similar thought when he refused to open Ms. Lace's returned letter. He'd brought it, though, in case he changed his mind. He pulled on his dirty jeans and looked around for the belt he'd need to keep them from falling off. He'd have to find a laundromat soon, or nobody would let him inside a restaurant, not even to pick up takeout.

"Well," he said, pleased with himself and feeling a little reckless, "you better bring it to me yourself then."

Brigit didn't agree, but she didn't say no either. She sort of giggled before hanging up. Samson stumbled into the bathroom and splashed water on his face. Stubble had grown back quickly on his chin and jowls, making him look ragged again. What exactly had he accomplished? He'd met Herman Stein, which seemed like a step in the right direction. Ms. Lace hadn't retired to Cedarville; she'd run there. Samson trusted Bill O'Hara about as far as he could throw him. He thought he was telling the truth about his brother, though. Mick was in L.A. A man like that would still have contacts, would still have a hustle of some sort until his last breath. It didn't seem like such an impossible goal to track him down.

Samson's buzz from inviting Brigit out to California quickly turned to dread. He'd meant it as a joke, hadn't he? At least that's what he told himself. He pushed a thumb into his aching temple, leaving a line of sweat but no relief. His room seemed to be shrinking—not rapidly, no, but a centimeter at a time when he wasn't paying attention. He believed on a gut level that he was in danger, and his body responded with panic. Hands shaking, he stuffed his motel key into his pocket and stumbled toward the door, hoping for a blast of cold air but instead finding no change in the temperature as he stepped outside. It was like living in a climate-controlled diorama, one that had seen better days. He started walking without a destination in mind.

Without a sidewalk, he kept to the shoulder, and a few cars honked as they passed, annoyed by his presence. Another crazed man making their commutes more difficult. Samson walked under the freeway, giving a dollar to the man there with a shopping cart full of clothes. A kind of bridge toll, but honestly, Samson needed the reminder that he wasn't dreaming, that he'd woken up in a rented bed and was choosing what exactly? If he'd once looked for signs of a spiritual world, proof of an afterlife, he now wanted evidence that he hadn't dreamed up his reality, that he wasn't dead already.

"Avoid Westwood," the man said, and Samson tried to focus on his face. His age was hard to guess, but his hair was mostly white. His missing teeth created a whistling noise when he talked, and Samson leaned away from the odor of dirt and piss.

"What about Westwood?"

The man took his time answering, rocking on his heels and biting on a quarter before responding. "The whole road's covered with those damn—what are they called? Piranhas."

"Paparazzi?"

"Vultures. Flesh eaters. You know what kills a demon?"

The man shouted the last question because Samson had moved away, ducking his head and watching his shoes carry him in no particular direction.

"You know what? You know what kills a demon?" the man shouted again, somehow making himself heard above the traffic.

Samson didn't respond because he didn't have to. Nothing kills a demon. Not anything at all.

He remembered a fairytale that his wife used to tell their niece when she stayed over. Those days were long past, his wife's sister sweet but unwilling to trust her child in Samson's care. Fair enough. The girl was going on thirteen now anyway. Probably preferred sleepovers at her friends' houses over her eccentric uncle's place. Samson didn't even have animals anymore. No cats, chickens, or bees. Just a bunch of snakes he hoped would stay far away. Maybe she'd like to meet River when he returned.

The story began as they all began with "Once upon a time," but Samson always suspected that the story was his wife's own creation. When he asked about it, she had laughed and said she couldn't make up such a thing, that she must have read it somewhere. In it, a horse named Cloud wanted to grow wings, so he asked the crows how it was done. The crows promised to tell him in exchange for pieces of his mane. Cloud had a beautiful mane of honey-gold, but he agreed, convinced that he was getting the better end of the deal. They set a date, Cloud's birthday to be exact, and the crows met the horse under the magic tree.

"How did they know it was magic?" his niece had asked.

"Because of the leaves," his wife had answered without missing a beat. They were warm to the touch and couldn't be plucked. Even in winter, they stayed bright green. Birds wanted to make homes there so that they would never have to fly farther south, but the tree always refused, shaking off the pine needles and brush that they brought.

The crows lined the lowest branch, whispering to each other as Cloud approached. The horse galloped toward them, eager to fly. When he arrived, the crows made sure that their agreement was understood, and Cloud stood still as the birds yanked at his beautiful mane. They pulled every last strand, but Cloud wasn't a vain horse and anyway, he knew that the hair would grow back. He let the birds finish their work, watching as they carried their treasures up into the branches to make golden nests.

"The tree will never let you keep them," Cloud said, worried about the crows.

But the horse was wrong. The tree found the golden nests to be so exquisite that it wrapped them in warm, green leaves and let the crows settle there in gratitude.

"And did Cloud grow wings?" his niece had asked.

"Yes, yes!" his wife had answered, surprising them both. The crows did not know how to grow wings themselves, having been born with them—along with lying tongues—but the magic tree was impressed by Cloud's sacrifice, how he didn't complain as the beautiful strands were ripped from him. The tree bent down low and drew two lines over Cloud's ribcage, one on each side. (His wife mimed the action over their niece's pajamas, making her squirm.) Vines grew from the spots, weaving into a pattern too complicated for any mortal beast—or girl—to follow. And at the end Cloud had two big wings, which he could use to hoist himself up into the sky.

"The end," his wife had said.

She never told their niece the real end of the story, though. At the time, the girl wasn't old enough to understand what happens when you fly too close to the sun with wings made of leaves.

At the next street, Samson turned right, glad he'd worn his boots instead of the new dress shoes. His feet ached from the long haul, but at least they wouldn't be blistered. His panic had subsided to a dull ache. He found a pay phone and pulled out a piece of paper from his pocket, ready to make his own a deal. When Kit Forrester had handed him her number, he'd wanted to throw it away, but something stopped him. And now he thought he just might have a story tempting enough to interest the reporter.

CHAPTER 15

EXT. A MONTANA RANCH

Several cowboys herd cattle at dusk, turning their charges away from a mountain range and into an open pen. CARTER TYSON checks to make sure that none have escaped.

                    CLOSEUP OF CARTER'S FACE

                A MAN
            (from outside frame)
        You see something out there? Or you
        seein' smoke again?

                CARTER
        No smoke. Just a feeling.

CARTER turns his horse around and heads back to the group, glancing once over his shoulder.

                    A MAN
A feeling? You just hungry. Tired
and hungry and damn through with
this day.

                    CARTER
You're not wrong about that. Billy
all right?

                    A MAN
He'll live to fight another day.
Doctor will stitch him up, you'll
see. Weren't your fault.

                    CARTER
    My men, my fault.

        from *Wild in Montana* (1972)
        Written by Hope Lancaster
        Directed by Jonathan S. Ferguson

The airport swarmed. There was no other word for it. The staff wasn't exactly unfriendly, more overburdened. Samson asked twice about arrivals before finally deciding to wait at the luggage carousel instead of the gate. He'd calmed down after a day or so, at least enough to recognize that he'd made a mistake inviting Brigit out and that there was no way to rescind the invitation without making the situation worse. And so he waited, watching families embrace and congratulating himself on feeling empty instead of forlorn. Responsibility, that he understood, and Brigit was his responsibility now, at least for awhile. God bless. What had he been thinking.

To make matters worse, he'd made little progress in tracking down Mick O'Hara. What he'd learned about the man hadn't improved his opinion. A lot of families with mob ties had side hustles, a way to seem legitimate in the eyes of society. Often, they helped hide the money, as well. Mick was no different there, but his investment in movies turned into an obsession. After a while, he didn't want to look legit, he wanted to be legit. But Hollywood's the ultimate popularity contest. Money can get you in the door, but it won't get you the best seats. And the more badly you want something, the more you can be manipulated. Mick's name was on a lot of flops—or, if not exactly flops, cheap products for when the blockbusters and Oscar winners were sold out. Theaters had a lot of screens to fill.

As far as Samson could tell, Mick had met Barbara on the set of *Mr. Rochester*, a made-for-television picture that the network hoped would get them some viewers in the wasteland of December reruns. While not exactly a runaway hit, ad sales had been decent, a little holiday bump. Samson wondered if he could get a copy somehow, but he hadn't seen the tape listed in any catalogue.

The first letter addressed to Ms. Lace that mentioned "M" was the same year, 1979. Isadora Alvarez was filming something in Italy and wrote to her friend to say she'd met him once and thought he was a "damn bore." A single sentence, then she switched to the topic of Ms. Lace's latest screenplay, how the writing was progressing. That letter alone would have fetched a few hundred dollars at auction if Samson hadn't stolen it. He thought briefly of Gabriel Correa, wondering if he should hand over his materials to the Music City Auction House. Legally, Correa had a right to sell them. Probably best not to dwell on that. If it was discovered that he'd taken the letters and film reel, he really would be a suspect. Plus, if he were being honest, he wanted to keep everything for himself.

A scream jerked Samson's head up, but it was only a toddler, unhappy to be left with a grandparent while the mother headed into a restroom. Samson and his wife had never discussed kids, never seriously at least. A passing remark about hoping their son had her knack for repairs or his even temper. He'd assumed that she would get pregnant, and when she didn't, he decided that it was all the same to him. He liked his life. When she got sick, the neighbors repeated how lucky they were not to have any children. "How lucky," they said as he stood with his back to her casket. "How lucky."

"Samson."

He hadn't noticed Brigit walk up, and she stood hesitantly in front of him, her arms hovering in front of her body, unsure if she should reach toward him. Samson plastered on a smile, pulling her close with one arm, then pausing when her warmth slid into his body. Dial soap and vanilla-scented shampoo. Almost like home. He put both arms around her for a few seconds.

"You got a bag?"

Brigit pointed out a cheap, black roller board, and Samson hauled it off the conveyor belt, smiling again, this time with more interest.

"River?"

It was enough of an opening. Brigit slid easily into the subject of dogs, her sister looking after them all, her nieces delighted by their furry visitors.

"They didn't mind. This is my first vacation in ten years."

"You should stay somewhere nice. Near the beach, maybe."

"What kind of salary you think Cedarville pays? Besides, I feel relaxed already." She shrugged out of her blue parka. Underneath, her tank top pressed against her body, and Samson wanted to run his hands over the freckles on her shoulders. "It won't be warm for another month at least back home. You know how it is."

"I do."

The ride back was slow, but Brigit never once remarked on the traffic. Samson appreciated her low prattle, then even more how they slipped into a peaceable silence. He watched her in his periphery. He couldn't help himself. She read the billboards and stared at the restaurants and big box stores. L.A.'s charm was difficult to see from inside a moving vehicle. On a whim, he took the wrong exit, trying to pay attention to the road but distracted by Brigit rolling down the window and moving her hand through the air. A mistake, he reminded himself. Inviting her out had been a mistake.

The nearest gas station didn't look like much from the outside and was worse inside. The two rows of snacks and motor oil didn't inspire him, but Samson grabbed a couple of Cokes from the refrigerator and a full-sized bag of chips. He paid in cash, asking about the nearest beach. The question prompted a hard, ugly chuckle from the cashier, but the old man gave him directions anyway, and soon they were creeping down Marine Avenue toward El Porto Beach.

"No motel?" Brigit asked, her steady hazel eyes accessing him. Samson cringed to think what she might see. A man unsure if he was chasing or being chased. And did it matter how he found the monster in the end? In his view, no, nothing could matter less. He'd shaved again at least and washed his jeans and shirts at a laundromat.

"Not yet."

When he had trouble finding a parking space, Samson's head began to hurt again, and he suspected that he had made yet another blunder. Finally he found an overpriced lot, and they walked across a crowded street to the sand teeming with young, tan people in bikinis and wetsuits. The air smelled sweet—almost nauseatingly so—and Samson squinted into the too bright sun. Not too far away, a refinery stood near the shore, its concrete spires rising into the air, and behind that a power plant. But if you ignored those eyesores, the ocean seemed alive with light, dancing in a rhythm all its own, persistent and heavy. Wave after wave cascaded onto the beach, and Samson heard Brigit's sharp intake of breath. In a rush, she peeled off her shoes and socks, heading toward the water. For a moment, he thought he'd been forgotten, deservedly so, but then she turned, her strong body silhouetted in the sun.

"Let's pretend we're the only ones here," she said. And he tried.

Samson felt relieved that Brigit's room didn't adjoin his own. He dreaded analyzing every step and cough. Still, on the ride back from the beach, he'd felt almost content, pleased with himself for thinking about someone else for a change, at least for an afternoon. His neck ached, a physical reminder that he wasn't used to being with other people. He washed down two aspirin with a glass of tap water and sat on the edge of the tub to sort through his mail. He'd taken to hiding in the bathroom when he didn't want to face the red, blinking light from outside. He let a cigarette burn down, taking a drag from time to time, but over the novelty.

Brigit had thoughtfully thrown away all of the ads and unsolicited catalogues, leaving him with an envelope from a client who'd needed a desk refinished, a phone bill, and the letter from 53 Chritton Lane. He opened the client's first, dreading Mrs. Usher's spidery handwriting. The words were variations of the same, all the town matriarchs telling him that his wife had been special. The first note had irritated him, as if Mrs. So-and-So were telling him something that he didn't know. Now that his grief had ebbed, he took the kind words at face value. They no longer made him flinch, but he'd rather they were left unsaid all the same. He folded the woman's check into his wallet and inspected the cream-colored envelope from Chritton.

It had the weight and formality of a wedding invitation, careful calligraphy spelling out his name. The postmark was March 22, two days after Callista Weathers had been murdered. The hairs on his arms stood up, but what had he been expecting? He'd been expecting an error, he realized, a letter sent weeks before that got lost. His hand shook as he hooked a finger under the flap and tore open the paper.

The card was equally formal, personalized stationery with the initials BAS. Samson had to read the message twice before he fully comprehended the meaning, all the implications tumbling into place.

Dear Mr. Delaware,

I regret that our ships so often passed in the night while I lived. *Now, it would seem, our vessels have crashed together, spilling our secrets into the sea.* I always loved the view from the deck of an ocean liner. You would have liked the Stargazer, a beauty of a vessel in 1952. Eighty-two transatlantic crossings. *Her final trip at a record-breaking speed. Not too shabby for an old broad.*

Perhaps her triumph inspired me to take such a gamble. As you may have guessed, I did not die earlier this month, though neither am I living. You and your friends did not carry my body out into a March winter day. I must say, though, an exemplary performance all around! Such somber faces. And one of my best, or so I thought. The poor girl.

I only meant to escape, never to put Miss Weathers in danger. Please believe that I am unmoored by the news. Unmoored. Nonetheless, you must stop your inquiry. You will not reach the other shore safely.

With high regards,
Barbara Sussennox

Samson read and reread the letter, looking for clues in every image. The words were neat and typed while Barbara's signature was gaudy, and he wished that he could compare it to the one she'd sent about his marriage. If that had really come from her. It could all be a fraud, a decoy of some sort. Two inches high and slanted evenly in one direction—forward. Was she really alive? And was she threatening him? He felt cold all over and half-expected to see her reflection when he stood up, legs shaking. The bathroom was empty, though, and he was alone.

CHAPTER 16

FADE IN

A bright but messy kitchen, dishes piled in the sink and crumbs from the night before on the table. CECILY BARGE (56) sits primly, clutching her pocketbook and waiting for her daughter to notice her. JO stares into the refrigerator, lost in thought and not really seeing the contents.

> CECILY
>
> Eggs, dear. You can never go wrong with eggs. Scrambled, over-easy, poached, boiled, deviled. Protein, selenium, Vitamin D.

JO takes out the milk and crosses to retrieve a box of cereal from a cabinet. She places both on the table, then heads to the coffee pot where she refills her mug.

CECILY
(cont.)

You always were so modern, Joanne.

JO
Jo, ma. Nobody's calling me Joanne anymore.

CECILY
I do.

JO
Like I said.

The audience laughs.

CECILY
I only meant to help. How was I to know that man was your boss? I mean, really, he had his shirt unbuttoned. No tie, Joanne!

The audience laughs.

JO
We can't all clutch our pearls. Some of us have water bills and teenagers.

CECILY

You were a teenager once.

JO

I don't believe you.

The audience laughs.

from *All the Good Ones* (1976)

Written by Candy Lattimore

Directed by Scott Feinstein

"Alive?" Brigit's left cheek was creased from her pillow, and she pushed her hair back from her face, sleepy and confused. Samson noticed that her T-shirt barely covered her underwear at the same time that Brigit remembered, pulling at the hem. He didn't want to be left alone under the sickly orange light of the breezeway, but his stomach unclenched a little when she turned back inside to get dressed. She returned in the pants she'd been wearing and sensible white sneakers. "Let's get some food then. I don't do ghosts on an empty stomach," she said.

Samson didn't remember meeting Brigit for the first time, but there had been a bonfire over in the Meekers' field one night, all the drinkers close to the billowing flames, throwing their empty cans into the blaze. He'd met a lot of people, and Brigit could have been one of them, around the outskirts maybe, not that interested in getting blackout drunk. His wife had suggested they go, and Samson said yes to anything she proposed.

Everyone had loved Samson's wife. She was boisterous and kind, would visit every sick bed and bring cards with slightly off-color jokes—or real off-color for the ones who wouldn't mind. She'd been class valedictorian but never went to college, instead taking over the family farm and bringing it out of the red after a few grueling years. A room—or field—seemed to grow larger in her presence, more interesting.

That night, though, all eyes quickly turned from her to the stranger getting out of the passenger's side. As he unfolded his lanky frame, Samson laughed, throwing open his arms as if he were Harold Hill in a touring production of *The Music Man*. He took his new wife into his arms and waltzed her toward the group. They were both terrible dancers and tripped over themselves as the men watched silently and the women whistled. God, they were the happiest couple anybody had ever seen. And Samson Delaware really, truly didn't belong in Cedarville. Nobody ever understood why he'd moved there, but they understood why he stayed.

Brigit said she loved that there was a place to order eggs in the middle of the night. Still, her plate grew cold as she tried to make sense of Samson's ramblings, his insistence that Barbara Lace was still alive. But how? The question hovered above them in the air, undisturbed by the tired waitress refilling their coffee cups. She had left their bill on the table, but they didn't feel rushed. Besides a table of drunk partiers winding down after a night out, the place was deserted. Dangerous even, in its emptiness.

"Help," Samson said, his hands shaking slightly as he reached for more sugar. He'd given up coffee for a reason. "She had help. Accomplices. This isn't the sort of charade somebody pulls off alone."

Brigit nodded, and Samson felt as if he were pleading his case, trying to convince them both. When she spoke, her voice was low, and he asked her to repeat herself as the table nearby shrieked about a pop star they may have seen at the club.

"You touched her, right? She was real?"

Samson thought back to the morning he'd been called, trying to remember if anyone had checked for a pulse. They certainly hadn't seen her chest rise and fall.

"Nobody touched her skin. We wrapped her up and, well, hauled her out."

Brigit considered, her skeptical nature at odds with her affection for Samson. She didn't quite believe him, but she hadn't flown across the country to abandon him either.

"Mr. Pitterson, maybe. He's not that much older than her," she said. "A decade or so. Fifteen years?"

Samson considered the undertaker, his hunched frame and cratered skin, then tried to peel off the years, reveal the steady young man taking over the family business decades in the past. A viable suitor, the town biddies would have deemed him, or, in a teasing mood, a right catch. What would Barbara have seen, though? A trap? A way to get stuck in Cedarville forever, her only claim to fame being married to the owner of a mortuary. A role, maybe, but not a life for her. No more than being the mayor's wife. That role had gone to Mrs. Answood, and she played it well.

"Could be."

"Why did she think you might have guessed?"

Samson considered how to answer. The jewelry box seemed to make the most sense. It had been too much of a coincidence, suddenly appearing on the train tracks. He'd thought perhaps Callista Weathers had thrown it out, messing with him because she didn't like him. But Ms. Lace had left it for him to find herself. Wrapping up unfinished business maybe.

"Could be," Brigit responded to his theory.

Samson didn't tell Brigit about the snakes or the footsteps in his house. He'd rather not scare her. They made sense now, though. They must have come from Barbara Lace herself, afraid that he would discover her secret—or maybe looking for her belongings. If she'd hidden the letters and film reel, they must have mattered to her.

"How wild was she?" Samson asked, looking up. "I mean, does nobody talk about the old days? It's a town that sorely loves to talk."

"You always talk about our town as if it's not yours, too."

"I've never worried much about belonging. We waste a lot of time that way, trying to fit in, find the perfect fit."

Brigit shifted toward the window and put her elbows on the table, taking her time before responding.

"That's good advice, Abby."

Samson leaned forward, too. "I prefer Prudence. More sass."

The door jingled as someone entered the diner, and Brigit glanced away, her cheeks flushed. Herman Stein looked almost chipper, despite the hour. Samson rose in greeting and gestured for Ms. Lace's former agent to sit down in their booth.

"Not a chance. If I make it down there, I'll die on the vinyl. You can send your condolences to this fine establishment."

He hooked his cane over his left arm and looked around. "Sweetheart, darling, love of my life! Could I bother you for a chair? A diamond for a chair!"

The waitress came toward them, hands on her hips.

"Yeah? Let me see what you've got."

Herman mimed a knife through his heart as the woman pulled over a chair and then held his arm as he sat.

"Pastrami on rye. And another round of coffees, on me."

"Big spender," the waitress said as she walked back behind the counter, her tired eyes crinkling at the joke. Samson knew that Herman would pick at his sandwich rather than eat it, but he didn't say anything. If the man wanted a pastrami on rye for breakfast, a pastrami on rye he would get.

Samson thought if he had another cup of coffee his hands might walk away from his body. When he had called Barbara's agent, he hadn't really expected an answer. But Herman had picked up on the first ring as if he'd been waiting to hear from someone.

"And who's this vision?" he asked Brigit, fixing his eyes on her face and adjusting his glasses.

"This vision is right confused," she answered, and Herman grinned.

"Knows her lines, too," he said.

"Brigit Mills, this is Herman Stein, legendary agent to the stars, including our very own Barbara Lace."

Herman winked at Brigit, enjoying the attention.

"I see," she said. "And why would such an important man meet us at the Blue Moon at four in the morning?"

Herman thanked the waitress as she filled his coffee cup and left the pot for them. He took his time adding cream and sugar, clearly enjoying himself, before responding.

"What better time is there to raise the dead?"

The morning sun dipped the whole city in pink, a rose gold that made even the pawnshops look important. The color crept between buildings and up sidewalks, embracing every billboard and radio tower, like a spell slowly touching everything in its path.

"Or a curse," Brigit said. She'd been silent for most of the ride, and Samson had been filling the space with small talk. He thought he'd lost the knack forever, but no, he could still monologue with the best of them.

"Who can tell around these parts? The villains look like queens, and the jesters can't dance."

"You're awfully cheerful."

Samson stopped talking, surprised to find that she was right. He felt light, sure of himself, that he'd made the right decision in coming all this way. Hell, he'd already brought somebody back to life. Anything seemed possible.

"I need you to believe me when I tell you something."

Samson's tone changed. He still sounded hopeful, but a sliver of doubt had crept into his voice. Brigit adjusted her seatbelt and sat up straighter.

"I'm listening," she said.

"I wasn't sleeping with Callista Weathers."

"Okay."

Samson glanced at his passenger, who stared right at him, unintimidated.

"I'm serious. I'd just met the woman. But I was there that night when she was killed. I could have done something if I'd known. I didn't know there was anyone else in the house."

He grew quiet with this confession, and he felt like he was putting his whole life in Brigit's hands. With a single call to Agent McKinnell, he'd be in handcuffs. If he wasn't the lover of Callista Weathers, there was no good reason for him to be in her living room. Brigit didn't answer right away, and Samson kept glancing at her, trying to read her reaction. They passed an amusement park, lights off and rides locked. The place looked desolate, abandoned, though it was clearly operational. Samson wondered aloud how such a small operation competed with the corporate theme parks. He was about to start prattling again when Brigit cut him off.

"I said okay."

Samson whistled, an involuntary noise that seemed

inappropriate given the circumstances.

"I said okay," she continued. "But you got to tell Bishop. I don't care what you keep from that full-of-himself TBI agent, but Bishop's a decent man."

"He knows." Samson pulled up to a red light and turned down the radio. This was a conversation they should have had before he invited her to California, but they were having it now, for better or for worse. At least she couldn't escape unless she decided to bolt from the car.

"Of course he does." Brigit made a strangled, frustrated noise. "You think you don't belong to our town, but you know the language sure enough. Men protecting each other. It's practically our motto."

"You just said that Bishop was a decent man."

"Sure, he's decent. Let me give you some advice, Samson Delaware. You think Cedarville likes to talk because the old ladies like to talk about who's sweet on the Blaire boy or which baby is cross-eyed, bless its heart, but bone-deep? We don't tell nobody nothing. You asked me if Barbara Lace was wild? Really wild? I don't know. But I know that's a secret, and we keep our secrets."

Samson glanced at Brigit again, then checked his blind spot before changing lanes. He wasn't used to the traffic yet, and wanted to be cautious.

"It sounds like you're telling me to give up."

"Then you're not listening. I don't think she's alive. Wait—let me finish. I don't think she's alive, but that letter didn't materialize out of thin air. Something's going on, and somebody's trying awfully hard to make sure you don't find out what."

Outside the windshield, taillights glowed, rows of red eyes waiting for a sucker. They wouldn't have to wait long. Someone would rummage in their glovebox for gum and miss the SUV stopping in front. Or the man begging for change would decide he'd had enough of being ignored for one day and move out into traffic, shouting to be seen. It was a city where getting noticed was a dream, a damn near impossible one with stakes high even to play. Herman had been happy to reminiscence, didn't seem surprised that Barbara Lace was still alive. Had he already known? Or had he just appreciated the plot twist?

They'd stayed at the diner for more than an hour, Herman going off on tangents about mutual friends they'd had. Samson wanted to know where she might be hiding, but Herman had shrugged, rightfully curious about why Samson thought she wasn't still in Cedarville. It was more likely in some ways. But there weren't a lot of places to hide in such a place. And wouldn't she want to get away from the scene of her crime? Faking your own death didn't strike Samson as a major offense, but it was illegal all the same.

Ms. Lace could have been anywhere, of course. And, if she was really alive: wasn't Samson's work done? Couldn't he stop trying to avenge her death? The question nettled him. Callista Weathers was still dead, he had no doubts about that. And this much he'd pieced together—Ms. Lace had been running away from someone when she left Hollywood in 1982. It seemed unlikely that she'd made new enemies since then. She rarely left her house. And you didn't pretend to be dead for kicks. Callista had gotten caught in the middle of a decade-long feud. Samson hadn't much liked the woman while she lived, but she didn't deserve to be collateral damage either. So who would Herman put on the list of suspects? Mick O'Hara was the only name he coughed up, but he promised to think about it.

"I'll ring Bishop this afternoon. Tell him about the letter," Samson said, hoping that would satisfy Brigit. Maybe his gut had known he needed a moral compass when he suggested she join him. Or maybe Samson was good at making excuses for what he wanted.

"Where we headed now?" she asked.

Samson wasn't keen on the idea of introducing Brigit to a gangster, even one well past his prime, but he was sure Bill O'Hara could help. Kit Forrester, the other person he thought might have dirt on Mick, hadn't returned his calls. What was the point of giving someone your number if you didn't want to talk?

Brigit rolled down her window, and the morning air rushed inside, fresh despite the car fumes. There were palm trees and blue skies, but the scenery felt like makeup, disguising the rougher reality underneath. The thing about not quite belonging anywhere was that you could stay anywhere, and Samson figured he could get enough for his house back home to live awhile, at least until he found a job. He glanced at Brigit, his stomach filling with guilt. Maybe she'd stay, too, he told himself, though he knew it was a straight-up lie. Not his first and certainly not his last.

Distracted, the drive to Bill O'Hara's place seemed to take less time than before, and they parked in his cul-de-sac, unconcerned about the neighbors.

"I'd ask you to stay in the car if I thought you might," Samson said.

"And I appreciate that," Brigit said, halfway out.

Bill met them at the door in a red velour bathrobe, one hand gripping a cup of coffee, the other pointing at Samson.

"I told you to stay off my fucking lawn."

"Mr. O'Hara, I don't believe those words were spoken."

"Spoken? You sound like a damn John Wayne wannabe. We got a dozen John Waynes. A thousand. And some of them are sucking cock down on Palmetto. We got no room for you in Hollywood."

"Hollywood? I thought this was Brentwood," Brigit said.

Bill turned his eyes, assessing. Samson didn't care for his suddenly quiet demeanor. It felt more dangerous than the bluster, more calculating.

"This one? She can stay."

Bill turned back inside, and Samson caught the door before

following him. A woman in a jogging suit and headphones was dusting the foyer even though it looked clean. Eavesdropping, but who could blame her. Samson nodded at her, and she pretended not to notice him. Samson was relieved not to see Delly again, hoping the woman had wised up. Bill O'Hara didn't seem like the most stable friend. At that moment, he was pouring Scotch into his coffee. Samson glanced at his watch to see that it was going on 7 a.m. He wished he'd eaten more than toast at the Blue Moon. Bill collapsed onto the couch, not caring that his robe parted and his silk boxers were exposed.

"We just want to find your brother. We're not cops."

Samson didn't trust Bill and wasn't about to tell him that Barbara was still alive. Maybe she was hiding from him. Maybe it was better that both brothers thought she was dead.

"My brother's a son of a bitch, but family's family. You think I'm going to hand you his head on a fig plate? You're digging up bones that want to stay buried."

"What sort of bones, Mr. O'Hara?" Brigit asked, sitting beside him on the couch. He leaned back a little and spread his legs. Samson felt queasy.

"Before, there was glamour. Dinner turned into dancing which led to some basement club where all the best musicians went after hours. All the whiskey you could handle. It was a late-night routine, stars peeling off one by one to make their morning calls. All the rest left to party."

"Sounds nice," Brigit said.

"Everybody wanted to be an A-lister, but me? I thought that looked like a drag. Who wants a curfew past eighteen?"

"And Barbara Lace? Did she want to be an A-lister?"

Samson froze, wishing he'd told her not to mention Barbara.

Bill considered Brigit's question before answering, shifting through his memories or making sure he got his line right.

"Barbara. That what this is all about? You know Barbara? God, I haven't heard that name in a spell. She wanted top billing, sure, but she wasn't ready to play the game."

"What's that mean?"

"You got a voice like a country preacher's daughter, sure enough, but you know what I mean. The girls who come here and drop their pants for every PA? Disposable. But the ones who always say no? They're not going on the marquee either."

Brigit made a disgusted noise and stood up. Samson took a protective step toward her, aware that his anger at Bill was flooding back and not wanted to repeat their previous encounter. He could have killed the man by accident, he was sure.

"Hey, I didn't make the rules," Bill said. "Not my business. What's that buzzword? Not my scene."

"Barbara was successful," Samson said. He believed that, and no amount of dirty laundry was going to change his mind.

"Look at this one," Bill said. "Looking honorable and shit. You'd never know he hit an old man, would you? Some John Wayne."

Brigit turned to look at Samson, and he looked away, afraid to meet her gaze.

"Where's your brother, Mr. O'Hara? You're going to tell us, then we're going to get the hell out of here. He'll never know you told," Brigit said.

Bill chuckled. He wasn't giving them shit, and Samson realized it too late. They never should have come.

"Such language from a child of God," Bill said, rubbing a hand over his exposed belly. Samson grimaced, but Brigit held his gaze. "You better watch who smites you."

167

CHAPTER 17

The biggest surprise of the morning
goes to Barbara Lace for her
Outstanding Supporting Actress in a
Limited Series or Movie nomination.
Lace played the meddling mother of
beloved character Jo Styles on *All the
Good Ones*. Lace's five-episode arc was
memorable in part because it broached
the subject of unwed mothers. Lace is
a veteran of television and film, but
this is her first nomination.
—Kit Forrester,
The Hollywood Sun, July 12, 1977

Samson should have been thinking about what they'd learned
from Bill O'Hara, but he couldn't stop staring at Brigit, half in awe and
half in fear. He was sure he looked like a week-old piece of fried catfish,

but she was fresh-faced, her skin shining as if it had just been scrubbed clean. She had fine lines on her forehead and around her mouth, almost delicate. When had she gotten those? he wondered. When had he finally noticed her?

"I suppose that was a waste of time." He spoke mostly to hide his sudden shyness. The meeting had gone much as he expected. He wasn't some kind of expert interrogator.

"I don't know. Mr. O'Hara seemed awfully determined to hide his brother. That might mean something."

Samson paused, considering her read on the situation. He liked the way her mind worked. "Could be," he said. He felt himself getting distracted by Brigit again, so he turned on the radio, letting songs he'd never heard before push themselves into his head. So much teen heartache and posturing. He'd been surprisingly popular in high school despite his awkward looks. Quick to make a joke in class and just as quick to stay late and straighten chairs. Not really an athlete, but tall, so he'd signed up for basketball and played a few minutes each game to give the first stringers a rest. And girls liked him. Not in a hot and heavy sort of way. They wanted him at their lunch tables to make them laugh, to harmlessly flirt with them. He hadn't seen them in years, but could still recall the black sweater with tiny blue stars that Sylvie wore once a week in the spring of senior year. Those memories stayed with you. Being a teenager was so raw and bright, everything in technicolor.

"Mrs. Answood."

"A fine lady," Brigit said, not following his train of thought.

"She'll talk to me. Or Bishop even."

Samson noticed he was almost on empty again and pulled over into a gas station parking lot. He couldn't remember when in his life he'd spent so much time at gas stations. Brigit reminded him to call Bishop before Mrs. Answood and volunteered to pump their fuel. When she got out of the car, Samson felt deflated but relieved. It was hard to concentrate with her so close. His feelings were wrong, he knew that much. But he wasn't sure who he was hurting—himself or her.

Samson leaned up against the building's brick exterior to use the pay phone, wishing he didn't have the sheriff's number memorized. Bishop picked up on the fourth ring, sounding tired and angry. "There's more of them now. Assistant agents or some crap. A forensics team."

"They find anything?"

"Nothing they weren't expecting, but you know they need to talk to you again."

"I'll be back in a day or two. A week tops."

It might have been a lie, but Samson wasn't sure.

"I ain't the kind of man to tell another man what to do."

"Hell, Bishop, you're a cop. That's what the whole job is."

The pause on the other end of the line made Samson uncomfortable, and he was about to apologize when Bishop mumbled something then spoke up.

"Nobody's listening to me. Kids maybe. Folks passing through that pay their speeding tickets 'cause they don't want to come back to Macotte County for a court date."

"I'm listening to you right now, Bishop. Who do you think killed that woman?"

Brigit started cleaning their windshield, and he smiled at her. She smiled back, making his stomach twist. Her skin had turned golden brown in only a few days, and the freckles made her arms look flecked in bronze from a distance. With her casual T-shirt and shorts, she looked comfortable in California.

"I don't think it was a break-in. No signs of forced entry. I figure the Weathers woman kept something valuable for herself. Maybe Lace was keeping a golden egg somewhere, hell I don't know. If I could figure out what she was hiding, I'd crack this wide open, I'm sure."

Samson made an affirmative noise in his throat, torn between sharing Barbara Lace's letter or not. If he told Bishop, he'd have to answer questions about why she'd written to him and not somebody else on the ever-expanding investigation crew. He'd have to fly home and be questioned by Agent McKinnell or his lackeys. He wanted a cigarette, but didn't dare light up in front of Brigit.

"You seen Mrs. Answood?" Samson asked.

"Should I have?"

"She might talk to you about what Barbara was like when she was young. What does it mean to be out of control in Cedarville?"

"Not much. Those ladies call Bingo night down at the community center a ruckus. I'll ask her, though. Thanks."

Samson could picture Sheriff Bishop in his uniform pants and an old white undershirt, one bought by his wife when they'd been married. But then again, when was the last time Samson had replaced his own T-shirts? He couldn't rightly say. The sheriff's kitchen stayed clean because he never used it. The flowerbeds were empty, too. Few folks noticed, of course. They only saw the patrol car in the driveway. But the rhododendron died months ago, and Bishop had torn it out one weekend by hand. Samson had noticed.

"There's a name that keeps popping up: Mick O'Hara. I think he'll have some answers if I can find him."

"Find him then and get on back. I'll send you an address if I can rustle one up."

Samson hung up as Brigit stepped out of the convenience store, arms full of sodas and snacks. She grinned at Samson again as if she couldn't help herself. Two years. It had been two years since his wife had taken him into town, and they'd bought T-shirts and socks. He'd picked out a bowtie with tiny, dignified flamingos, and she'd indulged him even though they never dressed up. She must have known that she was sick at the time, but she hadn't told anyone yet, not even him. A pact between her and her doctor. Part of his brain knew that he was being stubborn, refusing to let go of the dream that she might come back. It was why he was so eager to believe that Barbara Lace's letter was real while anyone else would be skeptical. They'd carried her body into a hearse, for God's sake. Or somebody's body at least.

He headed back to the pumps and talked to Brigit over the roof of the rental. "What we need is a handwriting expert."

"We could mosey on back to Cedarville then. Bet those hotshot TBI folks could find one." Samson's expression must have changed because Brigit nodded. "But what fun would that be? Let's find Mick O'Hara. I've always been partial to a love story anyway."

Kit Forrester knocked on his door around midnight, and Samson pulled her into his room before anybody spotted her. Not that the desk clerk would bat an eye, but he might say something to Brigit.

"I left my number," he said, closing the blinds and flipping on the desk lamp. He jerked a shirt from the closet and pulled it over his head as Kit watched him, looking bemused by his modesty. As if she'd be turned on by his pale, concave stomach.

"People lie over the phone. They think it doesn't count."

Samson had been so confident when he'd called her, sure she would be able to help. It couldn't be a coincidence that so many of her Hollywood Sun bylines were about Barbara Lace. He'd counted fifteen in total, ranging from 1965–1980. He'd thought that if anyone knew Ms. Lace's Los Angeles enemies it would be Kit. When he hadn't heard back for days, then a week, he'd given up.

"A story for some information. Seems like a fair swap to me," Samson said, trying to find a way to buy some time. He hadn't been asleep, but his mind was foggy all the same.

"You're pretty good at lying in person, though, aren't you, Delaware?"

Samson didn't like her tone and stepped away from her. The reporter wore dark clothing that blended into the shadows. Her short hair was slicked against her head, and she kept her right hand in her jacket pocket. Samson didn't like the look of that pocket.

"I don't want any trouble," he said. The red sign light outside his window pulsed into the room. He'd gotten used to it, but now it made him feel disoriented. What had he wanted from her again?

"Nobody wants trouble. I've been working in this town for twenty-five years now. When I got here, I thought what could be more sparkling—more fun—than awards shows and movie premieres. But what the readers really want? It's all behind closed doors with men who end careers for sport. Vicious, but you know that already. The stories would turn your stomach."

Samson had never been an ambitious man himself, but he knew the dance all the same. It was coming back. When he'd called her, his plan had been to sell her on the idea that Barbara Lace had been murdered in exchange for anything she knew about Mick O'Hara, preferably his whereabouts. Now, though, he had a better story, and he reached for the letter. Sure, he felt guilty about telling a reporter rather than Bishop, but if he wasn't mistaken, the woman was threatening him. He noticed her flinch when he moved, and she could easily pull the trigger on the gun she so poorly hid. He didn't blame her for bringing it along. A woman visiting a motel room in a bad neighborhood? Still, he'd rather not have any holes blown into his body.

"A deal's a deal, but you talk first," she said.

Samson unfolded the note, hands shaking, and started to read in a low voice. The motel's walls were paper thin, and he didn't want to risk being overheard.

"I regret that our ships so often passed in the night…" he began. He glanced at Kit while he was reading, watching her face go from cynical to shocked. Her jaw hung open slightly, and she finally removed her hand from her pocket to take the letter from Samson. He let her have it, sinking down onto the bed, adrenaline flooding out of his body and making him feel sick.

"Can you verify this?" Kit asked, starting to pace a little, agitated or excited, Samson couldn't tell which.

"You mean do I got a fact-checking team calling sources? No, ma'am, but it's something."

"But you touched her body."

Samson had gone back through that morning a million times, and he was sure now. Nobody had so much as placed a pinky on Barbara Lace's skin. They'd wrapped her up in that quilt and carried her out.

"She wasn't breathing. I'm sure of that."

"Self-induced overdose?"

Samson shook his head, not exactly disagreeing. It could be possible to reverse an overdose, but why go to such a risk when there was another, simpler, albeit morbid solution? A decoy body. The undertaker had called them for help, and they'd never second-guessed his intentions. In a big city, there would be some sort of protocol. A medical examiner or some such. But Cedarville didn't have the funds for rules. Mr. Pitterson could have planted the corpse, then waited for a neighbor to ask questions. Samson recalled that the body didn't smell as bad as he expected, already preserved perhaps. And Barbara's grimacing face? She'd looked older than she should have. Ancient rather than a mere seventy-three. It wasn't her. Probably someone from a neighboring town who'd had the misfortune to kick the bucket around the same time Barbara asked an old sweetheart for help. Not that Samson was about to share his theory with a reporter. To be honest, he wasn't much interested in who might have helped Ms. Lace fake her own death. He was much more interested in why she'd done it.

"The letter could be real, or it could be some sort of scam, but here's the thing. I don't think Ms. Lace retired peacefully to Cedarville. Do you? I think she was running from something. Running from someone to be more specific, and I think you might know where he is."

Kit considered Samson, unimpressed by his quivering hands. He looked like he needed an IV, not a lead, but he'd held up his end of the bargain and then some. Maybe it was just the kind of story she needed to resuscitate her career. Samson didn't quite know that, but his gut told him she needed something. You don't fly across the country for an obituary.

"Her death didn't make sense. No diseases. No prior health scares. I wondered if the assistant had killed her."

"The possibility crossed my mind."

"They overlapped at MGM, you know. This Weathers person gives up her career for some speck on a map? No offense. Gives up a salary, friends, prospects. To fetch coffee? Bullshit."

Samson felt sorry for Callista, but he wasn't going to rewrite her history. He hadn't bought the woman's story either. He waited for Kit to share her theories with him, but she processed the new information she'd received before coming to a conclusion, holding up her end of the bargain.

"It's an open secret," Kit said. "Illegal, but not so illegal that cops are going to bust the place. This isn't Prohibition. If a club wants to break curfew—a club with certain protections—who's got time for the arrests?"

Kit scrawled down an address on a piece of paper, and Samson thought back to when Kit had been in his kitchen. She'd made him uneasy then and now his skin crawled. He hoped he never saw her again, but he thanked her all the same.

The lights from nearby condo buildings made the alley look even darker than it was. The glow from above didn't reach the wet, sticky pavement, and Samson resisted the urge to put out a hand in front of him, wary of making himself look more vulnerable than he already was. He was lost and alone, sneaking out and hoping Brigit was fast asleep. His plan seemed safer this way, and he'd hurried past her door, gripping the address Kit had given him.

He'd tried the entrance to the building to no avail. A furniture store, but not the ones he liked to browse. A mishmash of pieces, from a 1970s-style futon to a wire bookcase. The lamp could have been handmade because the base was a pink umbrella and the shade was a sheer, silver slip strung over six wires, each one easily seen through the fabric. Doing a quick mental calculation, Samson guessed the entire inventory was less than $4,000 and most of it would never sell. A front, and a conspicuous one at that. Kit wasn't lying about the place having protections. Sure, the mob had lost some of its strongholds on the city, replaced by younger gangs, the ones popular in the gritty pseudo-documentaries, demonized and glorified in equal measure. But the old connections—favors bought and favors sold—ran deep.

About midway down the alley, he found a steel-plated, handleless door that belonged more to a prison than a club. He knocked because there was no other option, then waited because he didn't have any other ideas. This was the address Kit had for Mick O'Hara, and to be honest, it looked like the sort of spot you'd find a man like him. Samson expected a hulk to answer, a former wrestling star maybe or paramilitary. Instead, a tall woman in a platinum bob wig scowled at him when she cracked the door. Her dress shimmered despite the dark, and Samson got the impression of a wild animal, a jaguar maybe, kept too long in captivity.

"Evening, ma'am."

She rolled her eyes at his slightly exaggerated drawl, but she stepped outside anyway, lighting up a cigarette and taking a drag as if it were her last smoke before execution. Beautiful but exhausted, he thought, finished with life.

"We don't seat latecomers," she said, leaning against the brick wall when she exhaled as if she might collapse.

"I'm not here for the show."

She studied him, evaluating him as predator or prey. In her heels, they were the same height, and Samson didn't like the way his body reacted to the sight of her.

"Everyone's here for it. People like you who say they're not here for the show? They're here for the show."

Samson pulled out his wallet, catching the woman's hesitation when she thought he might be going for a weapon. He was nearly out of cash, and when he handed her a twenty, she didn't seem impressed.

"Tickets are sixty."

"Like I said, I'm not here for the show. Twenty for the kitchen."

The woman uncurled her body and stepped away from him, dropping her cigarette onto the ground and smashing it once under her shoe. The embers still glowed faintly. He could see a dark stain on her shoulder where the damp wall had made a mark. She didn't say anything, but she didn't try to stop him from following her inside.

Music pulsed from the main room, an electronic tango that could be heard over the glasses clinking and silverware dropping onto plates. It was loud, and Samson was surprised he hadn't heard anything from outside. The place must have been soundproofed from top to bottom. His guide disappeared through an unmarked door, and Samson followed the sound of cutlery. Kitchens always felt off-kilter, especially a lively one like this. Everyone with a designated task and too little time to complete it. Mick O'Hara's place was called Saints Lair. It served overpriced shrimp scampi and medium-rare steaks. It was hot and busy near the stove, and nobody had time to question the lanky figure maneuvering his way to the back as if he owned the place.

Samson had spotted the office right away, some forgotten instinct pulling him to the right spot. The best place for an office is far from the floor action unless you want to be interrupted by drunk VIPs every quarter hour. Owners who try to keep up with the patrons? They're wasting their time with girls and coke. The door wasn't even locked, and Samson walked in, excitement mixed with fear for what—or who—he might find.

The two men looked surprised to see him, glancing up at the blueprint spread over the Chippendale pedestal desk, beat-up but still valuable. Five grand, easy. The younger one straightened his collar and cleared his throat, ready to show their unwanted guest the exit. The holster at his waist was empty, but only a fool would think that the gun wasn't nearby. Samson tucked his hands into his pockets and whistled, an appropriate response to the stacks of cash occupying all the available chairs. The older man didn't react much, putting a hand on his colleague's shoulder and circling in front while making a welcoming gesture.

"Samson Delaware. Son of a bitch. I thought you were dead."

Chapter 18

An aging actress decides to abandon Hollywood to make sculptures in a sleepy mountain town near Spokane, Washington. When she arrives, though, she finds herself on the receiving end of increasingly violent threats. When two children are found drowned in the quarry, she tries to convince local authorities that their deaths were not an accident. Will she survive long enough to find their killer?

pitch for *Signs of the Children* (1979)
Written by Barbara Lace
Directed by Jonathan S. Ferguson
Never released

In 1975, there was plenty of work for a man who could make some spray-painted plywood look like a Roman piazza. The first set Samson worked was a Bucky Carruthers flop called *Ocean Sunset*, about a nurse in love with a coma patient. Then there was *All in the Stars*, which needed a ship prow and a ballroom, followed by the greenhouses in *The Heights of Marbury*. B—sometimes C—films, but they needed carpenters who wouldn't complain about unpaid overtime. And there was young Samson, hardworking and easygoing, never one to kiss and tell if an actress needed to relieve some tension. And Los Angeles? Los Angeles flamed with a dirty intensity. You could get Dom Perignon at the Marquis, then score some crack-laced weed on Aerick. Louboutins and Converse on the same block, sometimes in the same closet.

Samson met Barbara Lace just as he was getting burned out and the name of her hometown sounded like a clean, ice-cold creek. He could baptize himself in the waters. Barbara had thought he was crazy, of course, called it a "one-horse town that forgot the horse," but Samson didn't care. He'd had his Hollywood adventure.

Mick hadn't changed that much since Samson had last seen him. More weathered, sure, his face cracked and pouchy. He'd never been a handsome man, though, his features a bit too large, his flab a bit too pronounced. He had the same dead-eyed stare that had once made Samson cringe. But Samson had long since decided that men like O'Hara were small, drunk on power, and like all drunks, likely to go too far, take too much.

"You know me, Mr. O'Hara. I can't resist a reunion tour."

The younger man had stepped between them, tense and ready for a fight. When he reached his hand out, Samson smacked it away, hard. Much harder than he intended. It had already been a long night, and it was only getting started.

"I never knew you, son. You were a piece of dirt, a dime a dozen.

181

There were twenty boys lined up around the block who could take your place. Doesn't seem like much has changed."

Mick meant the words to hurt, was used to everyone around him wanting fame and fortune. Samson had no interest. Take a man who's known real happiness and not much will tempt him anymore.

"I'm just asking for a tour, Mr. O'Hara. For you to show me around the place. What's the harm?"

Mick's dark eyes squinted at him, looking for weakness. "I was sorry to hear about Barbara, too, you know. No sense losing your mind over it, though."

Samson hated hearing her name in his mouth, but he tried not to react. That's why he'd come, right? To see if Mick might be responsible? It'd been more than a decade, but Samson still remembered the fear in Barbara's voice when she had called him to pick her up from Mick's penthouse suite downtown. By the time he'd arrived, Mick was passed out on the bed and Barbara had more or less collected herself. But her false eyelashes were in her handbag, and her blush was streaked from where she'd been crying. Samson knew why she'd call him. They weren't exactly close, but he was as tight-lipped as they came. He was a vault. Mick had woken up when the door closed behind them, and he'd come storming into the hallway, grabbing Samson by the throat and slamming him against the wall. Mick's right fist connected with his temple, splitting the skin. Mick seemed surprised when Samson fought back, landing a decent punch to his jaw, sending Mick to the carpet where Samson somehow resisted the urge to kick him in the teeth, landing a blow to his stomach instead. Still, Mick laughed, calling Barbara a has-been and telling her never to come to him for anything ever again.

"You got some nice-looking girls here," Samson said.

Mick didn't move, but his partner must have picked up on a signal because he stepped even closer to Samson as he gestured toward the door.

"A moment, please," Mick said when Samson didn't budge. "I need to finish some business."

Samson would have preferred a confrontation, something to do with all of his adrenaline, but he stepped back into the kitchen as asked, letting the door close behind him. Nobody from the staff seemed to notice him, their refusal to acknowledge him rehearsed and complete. He wasn't the first to be expelled to the four squares of small linoleum that weren't being used. Still, his body wouldn't relax, seeming to absorb the frenetic energy of cooks and waitresses. Windowless. The whole place was windowless, trapping every bead of sweat and every flash of smoke.

Samson never told Barbara that he returned that night. He hadn't been satisfied by a single punch and kick, and he'd had some time to drink. He remembered the lobby so vividly he could have drawn it. Gaudy, crystal chandeliers and crimson couches. A bank of elevators and a fire exit tucked tastefully behind velvet curtains. The concierge had stepped away when Samson arrived—a happy accident—and he slipped upstairs unseen. There may have been cameras, but Mick never filed a police report, and nobody ever came for him. When he'd knocked on the door— pounded it damn near off the hinges—Mick had sworn from inside, telling him to fuck off. It was lucky, perhaps the luckiest moment of Samson's life, that another door had opened, revealing an older woman wearing silk pajamas and holding a phone, cord stretched inside. She threatened to call the cops, and Samson calmed down. Or, in any event, he left and never came back. Barbara forgave Mick, and that should have been the end of Samson's involvement. Now, he was standing in a hot kitchen, a little afraid of what he might do next.

By the time Mick and his lackey emerged, Samson had watched thirty plates swoop out into the club's main room. He'd identified the server who wouldn't last, the one who'd let pesto sauce dribble over the plate onto his hand and confused a Niçoise salad with a Greek. He'd studied the ambitious sous-chef, the way his hands maneuvered knives like they were calligraphy pens, light and sure of himself. He thought he was better than everyone else, and Samson agreed with him.

Mick indicated that Samson should follow him, an unreadable expression plastered onto his face. The other man turned toward the alley, leaving the two of them. Samson didn't let down his guard, though, knowing age made Mick more dangerous, not less. He'd had a lot of years to practice hurting people, and it had always seemed to come naturally. Mick found his calling early.

The club room bustled, every seat taken and every hand garnished with a drink. If this had been 1953, the men would have worn three-piece suits and the ladies would favor tea-length evening dresses. Instead, the crowd mixed a few blazers and slacks with printed shirts and designer jeans. A few women had on sleeveless tunics, but most were dressed like their dates, androgynous. A lot of loose, white and black fabric. Monotone. Even the hairstyles tended toward unisex, long bangs and shaved on the sides.

The only people who matched the gaudy decor were onstage, women in silver briefs and matching bras suspended from the ceiling by invisible wires hooked to the illuminated wings on their backs. They looked like avenging angels even before they started to fight, an elaborate routine that nonetheless made real bruises and drew real blood. The crowd erupted into cheers as the blonde landed a vicious kick, sending her opponent back several feet, her body swinging momentarily over the audience. When she swung back, she lashed out at the other woman, raking acrylic nails across her exposed stomach.

"All aboveboard," Mick said, pleased by Samson's alarmed expression.

"Sure."

"Licensed even."

"If you say so."

Samson surveyed the place, admittedly impressed if a bit queasy by how it combined elements of old-world glamour with an updated, brutal floor show. Red leather booths lined the perimeter, occupied by attractive groups who wanted to be seen rather than watch. The tables all had flower centerpieces, crisp and bright. And the place smelled good, the kitchen's best efforts mixing with perfumes and colognes. It was late, so most of the patrons were drunk. This was an after-hours place like the kind Mick's brother had described, perhaps unwittingly giving him a clue or having some fun at his expense. Samson had missed it, but he was here now anyway, fate dragging him back into this world he'd left so many years before. Left and never missed, his wife's smile in the morning all the entertainment he needed.

The blonde landed another kick, knocking her fellow angel into a spin that took her head dangerously close to the floor. Samson squinted to see if he recognized either performer, if one had let him inside for twenty bucks, but they were wearing too much makeup. They could have been anybody.

"New Hollywood not your bag?" Samson asked, knowing that Mick's great ambition in life had been to produce an Oscar-winning film like *On the Waterfront* or *Midnight Cowboy*. Mick, more than anything else, had wanted people to take him seriously. Instead, he got mixed up in some universally panned pictures and a couple of cult classics.

"Producing got boring, you know? Writing checks, making recommendations that nobody wanted. Here? This is all mine. A sort of pet project for my twilight years."

The two women onstage were gripping each other with their legs and clawing at one another's face. Feathers from the costumes floated down below them, and ticket holders snatched them up as souvenirs.

185

Samson felt out of his depth, his stomach sinking further as the women reached into their boots and pulled out knives that didn't look much like props.

"Dinner theater, sure," he said. "Sure."

The women didn't kill each other. Barely any blood, to be honest. There seemed to be rules that the audience knew, but Samson did not, expecting at every pass for one women to slit the other's throat. By the end of the fight, Samson's hands were shaking, and he walked toward the bar for a club soda. Part of him wanted to add a shot of whiskey, but he ignored that part.

The bar was a solid piece of mahogany, at least forty feet long, and Samson examined it in genuine admiration, momentarily distracted from the horror show he'd witnessed. It was clean, too, even at 3 a.m., and smelled faintly of wax. The bartender nodded at him as he finished garnishing a martini for another customer. When it was his turn, Samson ordered his club soda and put down a twenty-dollar bill, glad he'd saved it.

"We haven't started lacing the water with gold flakes yet," the bartender said, pulling out a clean glass.

"You worked here long?"

"Depends. Are you a cop?"

"A friend of Mr. O'Hara."

The bartender snorted and pushed the water toward Samson, leaning toward him. The man was young and as attractive as the other employees he'd seen. Los Angeles attractive, even, which was saying something. Bright green eyes, dark skin, even teeth.

"Mr. O'Hara's an okay boss. We don't see him much to be

honest. We deal with the other one, Seven."

"Seven?"

"Yeah, the man who's been watching you from the viewing booth since you walked in." The bartender gestured toward an upper-level glass panel and waved. "We call him Seven because he's missing three fingers."

"Three is a lot of fingers."

The bartender checked around him to make sure nobody needed his attention. "He's got some nice fake ones, but he takes them off when the place is closed. Says they itch. Who knows? Maybe they do."

"He runs the place?"

"He does everything practical. Mr. O'Hara concerns himself with the talent and the guests. Anything that gets seen."

The bartender was being summoned, so Samson let him go, taking a sip of his water and settling in to observe. From his perch, he watched Mick circulate, impressed by how spry he seemed at eighty, give or take a few years. He was in better shape than his brother, but then again, a suit could hide a lot. Bill O'Hara seemed to prefer a life of sweatpants, and at his age, who could blame him? Samson didn't want to relate to either brother, but out of the two, he understood Bill more. A thirst for fame turned his stomach, always had, even though he'd once been surrounded by men and women who'd found a way into that most exclusive of exclusive clubs. You couldn't buy your way in, not fully at least. You could buy yourself a credit, but not a starring role.

His wife had known that Samson built sets and lived in California, but she never asked about Barbara Lace, and he had never said anything. She would have thought it was a lark, would have laughed at the idea of Samson hobnobbing, then kissed him and forgotten about it. But she might have mentioned it to her sister or somebody else in passing, and he didn't want tongues wagging about him. After Barbara moved back, he figured he would run into her at an event someday, a fundraiser for the local park or something, but when he finally saw her, she didn't seem to recognize him, and he left well enough alone.

Mick limped a little on his right side. Samson hadn't noticed at first. Everyone shook his outstretched hand, occasionally thumping him on the back as if he'd told a real good joke. He was the master of the ceremony, the captain of the ship, the Hugh Hefner of the Saints Lair. Samson shuddered at the last thought and wished again for something to mix with his soda. He'd intended to march in and ask Mick if he'd threatened Barbara, but now he was second-guessing himself. If this impresario had a role in her disappearance, did he really want to kick the hornet's nest?

At some point, Seven left the viewing booth and joined Mick on his rounds. It was clear that he made the patrons nervous, though, and he didn't stay long. Seven may have been running the place, but Samson would bet his Georgian cellarette that the man used to be paid muscle. There was something in the way he moved, as if he was carrying a bag of bowling balls under each arm.

When Seven left again, Samson felt some of the tension in his shoulders release. He tried to piece together everything he'd found out so far, adding Mick's verve to the list. Mick was far from feeble. Samson remained convinced that Barbara knew who had killed Callista Weathers, but he hadn't really paused to consider what kind of danger that information brought with it. His head ached a little from the late hour, and he was craving a cigarette again. He didn't dare leave, though, not when so much was at stake. He wanted to talk to Mick at least once more before he lost his chance. He'd wait until morning if he had to. Hell, he'd help them mop the floor if it meant he got some answers.

The place emptied slowly, each new set of girls finding themselves with a smaller and smaller audience. The kitchen stopped serving at three, though the bar stayed open and busy enough. Samson had downed three club sodas before Seven returned, and Samson tried to look alert. His eyes burned from lack of sleep. Seven made a beeline for his boss, showing him an envelope and nodding at the response he received. When both men turned to look at Samson, his heart froze, but after a moment, he held up his glass as if he were in on the plan, as if he were having a ball. He quickly lost sight of Mick, who had disappeared into the crowd. He couldn't have missed Seven if he tried. The hulking man strode toward the bar, customers parting like the Red Sea. Samson wasn't sure if they knew him or simply sensed a threat. Instinctively, Samson stood up taller, expecting a confrontation. Inch for inch, they were around the same height, but there the similarities ended. Samson had more in common with a broom than the muscular figure in front of him.

"Trouble," the man said when close enough to speak over the music. "Mr. O'Hara says you smell like trouble."

"You've got a musk yourself, though I would never dream of saying anything about it. Certainly not to your face."

Seven didn't respond, instead handing over the manila envelope he'd shown to Mick, then turning away. The room grew hotter, and Samson watched Seven retreat through the doorway that led to the kitchen and back office. He wasn't a floor man; he'd never work the crowd with his charm. No, Seven had been hired for a whole other set of skills, one of which became clear as Samson dumped the contents of the envelope onto the bar. Three low-quality photographs fresh from a rush print job. Not exactly museum-quality, but they made Samson jump all the same, his shins connecting with one of the bar stools. He hardly felt the pain.

The first one was the license plate of Samson's rental, the second of his motel sign, and the third of a single room number: 218. Brigit's room.

He had no memory of getting to his car, but Samson drove recklessly, headlights from other cars seeming to explode in his head. He remembered racing this way when his wife had fainted the first time, when she wouldn't wake up. Should he have called an ambulance? The question still kept him up some nights, even though years had passed since that night, even though she opened her eyes halfway to the hospital, insisting that she was fine, hinting even that her symptoms might mean good news. They'd never tried to have a baby, but they'd never not tried either, determined to be content either way. How could they have been so stupid?

That night, the country roads had been deserted, the trees glowing in moonlight, Samson alert to every movement in the distance, worried about hitting a deer at such a high speed. Now, there were other drivers, heading home late or to work early. Once off the highway, Samson slowed to what seemed like a crawl, each stoplight he hit, each apartment complex he passed, increasing his dread. He should never have encouraged Brigit to join him on this foolhardy mission. He should have taken it back. He should have insisted she stay in Cedarville, broken her heart if necessary. What a coward he'd been.

Finally he slid into a parking space and raced toward the building, taking the metal stairs two at a time. His footsteps echoed loudly into the night, a clear warning. He raised his shaking hand to the door, swallowing his impulse to pound and lightly knocking. A light flipped on and spilled underneath the door, filling him with hope. He saw movement through the peephole, and Brigit's murmur of surprise made him want to laugh in relief. They'd leave the city, go back to their lives, forget they'd ever known criminals and low-lifes.

Samson's elation plummeted when Brigit finally opened the door and he saw the fresh blood on her T-shirt, the red vivid and bright as a poppy.

Chapter 19

Filming began this week on *Signs of the Children*, the latest project of eccentric director Jonathan S. Ferguson. On the condition of anonymity, a producer was in high spirits when he spoked to us, being so bold as to claim the Academy would be "daft" to give the Oscar to anyone other than star Isadora Alvarez. Ms. Alvarez declined to comment, unsurprising given the strict rules that Mr. Ferguson expects his cast and crew to follow. While a producer might share a tidbit or two, everyone else must sign a non-disclosure agreement before seeing their contracts. Publicity stunt or not, there's definitely a buzz—and perhaps a chill—in the air surrounding this much-hyped picture.

—Kit Forrester,
The Hollywood Sun, July 12, 1980

"Easy now," Brigit murmured. "Not too fast."

Samson obeyed, letting himself be comforted before finally, reluctantly, sitting up. He'd passed out cold, some hero. The stains on her shirt looked less foreboding in the light, and he could see the streaks underneath her nose that she'd tried to clean, then abandoned because she was more interested in sleep. A nosebleed. She was tired, too. In the silence that followed, Samson began to doubt what he'd seen. The envelope he'd left at the bar in his haste felt like a figment of his imagination. Sweet relief flooded his body even as he knew with a certainty he'd never felt about anything else, that he was in over his head. Already drowning. He'd noticed too late, head already submerged.

They checked out in the middle of the night, the desk attendant seeming unfazed by their decision and more interested in the pre-dawn news program. They drove toward the nearest beach without a plan. Samson wanted to see the water, and Brigit wanted to be with Samson. Their breakfast consisted of hotdogs and canned sodas. Later, Samson wouldn't remember exchanging more than a few words. He wouldn't tell her the truth about his relationship with Barbara Lace and definitely not with Mick O'Hara. He'd never even told his wife, happy with the detente he seemed to reach with the retired actress. Barbara never seemed interested in exposing him, and he left her alone.

Los Angeles was a city of myth, neither as dazzling nor as dark as the media machines wanted everyone to believe. Were there mission-style mansions and members-only clubs? Suburbs with more security than the airport and star-studded film premieres every week? Sure, and not even a desert could stop its sprawl. L.A. grew like a python outside its terrarium, uninhibited and hungry. But for all its magazine-ready success, there was poverty and frustration, whole communities forgotten or intentionally ignored, pushed to the side. There was blight and its twin, violence. It was if the scales had to be balanced at all times.

Samson had lived in the in-between, spending days on pristine studio lots, models of industry, though as cutthroat as any Wall Street trading floor. Then he'd driven through the heart of the city, stopping before the cookie cutter, manufactured communities with their timed sprinklers and imported palm trees. His apartment in Montecito Heights was on the second story of an open-air complex. It looked out over a pool that had been drained for cleaning, then never refilled. A couple of tags and a small octopus had been spray-painted on the bottom as if the graffiti artists were phoning it in after a long night. The lounge chairs stayed occupied by kids getting high. His place was cramped and hot, but he could walk to the nearby lake on a day off, pretend he lived in the country. He hadn't hated his life, but it always felt like a way station, like limbo. Everybody holding their breath, some without knowing why, others tuned into the reality of what happens when the rich and the poor get pulled apart from each other. Eventually, like magnets, the myth and the reality have to crash back together.

Brigit had thrown away her ruined T-shirt and wore a long blue dress that caught between her legs when the wind blew. She smiled every time, even when her arms were covered with goosebumps from the cold. Samson needed her to understand their danger, but couldn't quite bring himself to spoil her mood. When he spoke of Seven, he tried to keep his words foreboding, but he couldn't help himself from joking a little, mentioning that the man looked born to play a goon. Eventually the beach filled up with other people, surfers then sunbathers, breaking the spell.

"What I can't figure is how I was so easily found," Samson said, and it was the truth.

They claimed a free bench as they brainstormed what they should do next, Samson knowing that it would be best if Brigit left, not knowing—or not willing to admit—why he couldn't follow through.

"You're open to the world, Samson Delaware."

He cringed at that characterization, knowing he should tell her he'd been here before, but not willing to sacrifice the faith she had in him. It was all he had left.

"Once I found a 1967 leather-top library table on the side of I-24. I didn't know what it was, caught a glimpse of wood and emerald green fabric and pulled over. She was an absolute wreck. Legs torn off, the whole thing scratched to hell—pardon me. But somehow still solid. Should have been splintered, but somehow was only in a few big, repairable pieces."

"Have I seen that one?"

"No because when I got the girl home, nothing went right. From the beginning, the legs wouldn't reattach, the scratches wouldn't come out. I sanded the whole thing down and still, the stain wouldn't match. It wouldn't even dry for some reason. Two weeks of my life, and nothing to show for it."

Brigit studied Samson in the bright morning light.

"I understand."

"I'm not sure I do." Samson turned toward her more fully, his body tense.

"That table didn't want to go back together. Some things are like that. Beyond repair." Samson nodded, vibrating, but when he opened his mouth to speak, Brigit cut him off.

"But you're not a damn piece of furniture, Samson, not even a 1967 whatever you call it. We're human, and we break all the time. We splinter and crack, lose parts of ourselves. But we're still here. You don't have to be whole to be human."

Samson never told anyone, but he followed Mick for weeks after the hotel room incident with Barbara. Not all the time, of course. He worked, sometimes long shifts. The movie wasn't particularly memorable, a slapstick comedy with multiple scenes in a cornfield. The fake stalks got trampled, and Samson made them right, wondering the whole time why they wouldn't find an actual farm to use. But he kept his head down and his mouth shut when on the clock, then moonlighted as a wannabe private eye. He told himself that his intentions were good, making sure that Barbara was safe. And hadn't she called him? Hadn't she roped him into this position?

Samson's official title on that set was standby carpenter, but he stayed with the overnight crew sometimes, grueling hours that crawled by. A few hands making a general store appear or a record store, the paint still wet at dawn. Mostly he lingered off-camera during filming, giving him time in the evenings for his new pursuit. He was young and didn't need that much sleep. Samson didn't have a particular goal; he watched, waiting for when he might be needed.

1980 and the city pushed and pulled from every direction, the local news filled with reports of children killing each other in the streets. Southcentral became synonymous with gangs, and the LAPD answered to nobody, justified every brutality that couldn't be swept under the rug. A hot city, a city of embers ready to ignite. But the real explosion was a decade off, and if you had the means, Los Angeles was a playground, an amusement park for the rich and famous. Mick O'Hara's generation of gangsters didn't get as many inches in *The Times*, but it was there, and it had the means to distribute whatever new drug needed to make its way from port to customers' pockets.

Samson wasn't surprised to find that Mick spent little time in his suburban desert home near Edwards Air Force Base. The roads stayed busy, and Mick never noticed Samson's car in his rearview. He didn't feel comfortable spying on family time, so he'd wait in a grocery store parking lot, watching for Mick's flashy red convertible. It was hard to miss. Then he'd follow him to Sunset Strip. The Roxy seemed to be Mick's favorite, and he took Barbara to see Patti LaBelle on a cool clear night in May. When alone, he'd hit the burlesque spot down the street. Samson rarely went inside, not having that kind of cash to throw around, but he made an exception when he found out about reservations for Steerson's on a sure-to-be busy Friday night. Samson thought he could disappear in the crowd, not get caught.

A lot of places had adopted an edgier aesthetic, wanting to attract the Debbie Harry and Andy Warhol types, a pseudo-Manhattan crowd. But plenty of spots embraced their glamour, thought money should look like money. That included Steerson's. Samson watched Mick toss his keys to a parking attendant then walk around to help Barbara emerge from the passenger's side. She was wearing the kind of dress that turned heads, a long-sleeved metallic number that fell to her knees, cinched with a red belt. She managed to look both classic and modern. Nobody recognized her, but she looked confident. She looked like somebody you'd want to know. Her Emmy nomination was only a couple of years old, and Samson thought success suited her. He also thought that she could do better than Mick O'Hara, who—to his credit—had worn a tailored pinstripe suit and slicked back his gray hair.

Samson had worn a suit, too, but the pants hem was a little too short, his shoes a little scuffed. He'd thought ahead, though, and had brought a date, the script girl he'd met on set who cleaned up much better than him. They weren't exactly an item, but they got dinner sometimes. Nowhere as fancy as Steerson's before. Carly had a carefree disposition, though, and didn't overthink things, always ready to have a good time whether over tacos or lobster. She was a lot like Samson had been back then, and a part of him wondered how he'd so quickly become a vigilante-in-training. To be honest, he was enjoying himself, too. Carly liked to gossip about their co-workers, and he liked to hear her gossip. A grip with a coke problem. A camera operator with a crush on the assistant director. They didn't talk about the stars, not even the lead, a bland-faced comedian who flirted like the devil with anyone in a skirt.

Once inside, Samson and Carly were seated at a small two-top near the kitchen as he guessed they would be. Mick and Barbara were given their own booth near the entrance, champagne waiting for them in an ice bucket. Mick had his arm slung around Barbara's shoulder when the waiter approached, and she looked comfortable—not overly enthusiastic, but Samson may have been projecting. He didn't spy on them the whole time, and Carly thought it was a fun coincidence to see Ms. Lace in the same restaurant.

"You think it will be a hit?" Carly asked, then laughed before she could stop herself. *The Plowman* was designated to be a flop, dated before it hit VHS and not even a cult classic.

Samson liked Carly's easy laugh, even though he suspected she liked the free meal more than she liked him. A funny-looking man surrounded by actors with broody expressions and blow-dried manes? Samson had liked himself just fine, hadn't wanted to be anyone else.

The meal was delicious and uneventful. Samson started to regret the expense, dipping into his meager savings account, but then they got a free show. Samson and Carly heard the murmurs before they saw her— Isadora Alvarez in the flesh and blood. Even Samson caught his breath. Isadora sauntered in a few steps ahead of her husband, who never cared for having his photo in the paper. He would have ruined the shot anyway. That night, Isadora wore a sequined jumpsuit with a risqué if not quite

197

plunging neckline. She was only a few years younger than Barbara but had aged better—or had paid a team to fight time, and they had won. Long, sleek black hair and bright red lips, impossibly fake eyelashes. Up close, she might have looked garish, but Samson had been in town long enough to know that it was all about the pictures. Like Barbara, she'd survived decades in a business built on disposability. Unlike Barbara, Isadora Alvarez was a legend.

Samson moved his chair to get a better view, but he wasn't the only one, and his maneuvering went unnoticed. His date whispered something about "dining out on this story for ages," and Samson agreed. Barbara greeted her friend enthusiastically, and the two men shook hands formally. A few cameras flashed, then the host quietly urged everyone to enjoy their meals.

While other guests snuck glances at Isadora, Samson kept tabs on Barbara as Carly finished her crème brûlée. He'd had more wine than usual and the restaurant seemed overly warm, the lights overly bright. The dinner became a performance for Isadora and Barbara, a few bits of their tinkling conversation somehow carrying occasionally over the jazz quartet. Mick and Isadora's husband faded into the background, a couple of props with martinis. Samson was much too far away to hear any of their conversation, but he watched Barbara hold her friend's hand for a second or two, an almost private moment in a public arena. Samson would remember that gesture, the flicker of relief he felt that Barbara wasn't all alone in the world.

His thoughts were interrupted by the waiter bringing their check, or rather letting them know that Table Three had taken care of it for them. Carly was delighted, but Samson grew even more flushed, embarrassed that he'd been spotted. He had to own up to the mistake and lead Carly over to express their thanks. The room spun a little, but Samson managed to walk in a straight line and even bow a little when he approached.

"What a sweet dress, dear," Barbara said to Carly. "Have we met before?"

Carly mentioned that she worked on *The Plowman*, and Barbara nodded, pretending to know her.

"Of course, such a well-run set."

It was a non-compliment compliment, but nobody batted an eye. Barbara introduced Isadora as if everyone in the room didn't know her face, a sort of game people liked to play in the movie business. Isadora in turn introduced her husband, Clark, while Samson watched Mick warily, wondering how long he'd known. The man could have seen Samson as soon as he walked in. His plan had been foolish. Mick leaned forward onto the table, the rings on his fingers ready to split somebody's cheek. A camera flashed, and Samson swayed a little, black spots filling his eyes. When Mick stood up, Samson panicked, thinking the man was coming for him. But Mick walked toward the photographer—a tourist rather than a professional—and yanked the camera away. He popped open the back to stunned murmurs, ripping out the film and dropping it into a nearby water glass.

Isadora lightly chastised him while Barbara looked on, her expression hard to read even if Samson had been sober. When Mick passed back by Samson, he paused.

"You don't deserve to share oxygen with that woman, you little fuck. You hear me? Not even the same air."

CHAPTER 20

EXT. COUNTRY - DAY

LUCILLE struggles to remove her suitcase from the trunk of her car. A man walking by stops and stares at her. For a moment, it seems like he might help her, but he shakes his head and moves on. When she finally succeeds in getting her case out, she smooths her hair and surveys her surroundings.

                    PAN TO COTTAGE EXTERIOR

The place is rundown, with cobwebs on the porch and dirty windows. Is a shadow moving inside? LUCILLE climbs the steps and doesn't try to hide her disdain. She takes out keys, but the door is unlocked and swings open.

LUCILLE

Is anyone there?

LUCILLE shrieks when a long, sleek snake slithers past her.

from *Signs of the Children* (1981)
Written by Barbara Lace
Directed by Jonathan S. Ferguson
Never released

Finding Barbara Lace without the O'Hara brothers seemed like a cruel carnival game, not so much Needle in a Haystack as Star in the Cosmos. She could be in any corner of the country or beyond. Her letter should have revealed something useful, but Samson scoured each sentence, finding only frustration for his efforts. Frustration with himself, sure, but also frustration with Barbara, whose actions were effectively hiding a killer. Now, it would seem, our vessels have crashed together, spilling our secrets into the sea. Except Barbara had been wrong. They were both clinging to their secrets with all their might. Her final trip at a record-breaking speed. Not too shabby for an old broad. She hadn't planned to stay in Cedarville, though Samson's haphazard inquires may have changed her mind, at least temporarily.

Herman Stein had stopped returning his calls, which was why Samson was camped out on his street, waiting for the lights to come on in the upstairs office. He hadn't been on a stakeout in a decade plus, and his legs were cramping up. He'd bruised his left arm when he passed out, and the length throbbed periodically. In the backseat, Brigit slept, covered in one of his sweatshirts. She looked peaceful, and Samson worried that she still hadn't processed the risks. Of course, that was more his fault than hers. He'd told her about Mick O'Hara's place, emphasizing the man's uncooperative nature but leaving out some salient details. He hadn't even mentioned the women fighting to entertain the customers, not wanting Brigit to know about how they hurt each other for money.

Samson checked his mirrors frequently, worried about seeing Seven's bulk waiting on him. There had been a Seven when Samson had lived in L.A. before. He had all his fingers, though, and a regular name like Dylan or Darren or something. Mick's muscle. But they'd never spoken, never had a reason to converse. He'd been missing the night Samson returned to teach Mick a lesson, and that was also a lucky break. D would have messed him up.

There was a hierarchy on set, and unless one of the leads decided a gaffer was cute enough for a night, the different classes didn't mingle, and D stayed close to Mick. Samson never saw much filming, but he caught a read-through with Barbara once. The cast had assembled on set even though it wasn't finished yet because the usual office space was being painted. From what Samson had overheard, her role had been a bored, wealthy housewife meddling in the life of her eldest niece. There was a distinct cadence to her speech, a clipped perfection that evoked expensive private tutors and long, lazy afternoons. Not a hint of her Southern upbringing. When he'd caught a glimpse of Barbara between hauling timber and rewiring the fake streetlamp, he'd been surprised by her casual white shirt and black pants. At fifty-seven, she would have been easy to overlook, but then she spoke, and jewels seemed to fall from her mouth. She was an attractive woman, and Samson had been free to admire her. Barbara had liked the young man's admiration.

There had never been anything between them except a spark, a possibility. They'd exchanged banter and then numbers, but Samson had never called, convinced that she wouldn't remember him. And what was he supposed to do with an actress thirty years his senior? He'd taken out Carly instead, her face sweet and forgettable. But he hadn't been that surprised when Barbara called him in hysterics from Mick's hotel room. Maybe he should have been, but even an unambitious man is the leading man in his own story.

The blinds on Herman's office slid up, and Samson sat up taller, smacking his knee against the steering wheel. He grunted in response, relieved that the noise didn't wake Brigit. When he tried to sneak out of the car, though, she opened her eyes, blinking in confusion at her surroundings before settling on Samson's face. Her happy expression sent a jolt through his body, and he mumbled awkwardly about not wanting to disturb her.

"I'll go with you," she said even as Samson shook his head.

"No, this won't take long. Get some more rest. Lock the door behind me."

He left the keys in the ignition and exited before she could object. Following someone into the building didn't raise any suspicions, and he climbed toward Herman's office without having to explain himself to anyone. When he knocked at the door, he wasn't happy with the response he received. Herman shouted that a senior citizen should be left in peace, but when the door swung open, it wasn't Herman Stein but Bill O'Hara who greeted him. Without a bathrobe, the man looked younger and more intimidating. More like his brother. The suit may have been old, but it still fit.

"You've arrived just in time, my friend. Mr. Stein's going to make Delly a star."

If Bill looked younger, the same magic wasn't working on his companion. In the unforgiving morning light, the woman's heavy makeup looked garish, her blank expression doing nothing to hide her boredom.

"Good to see you again, Bill. Delly." Samson made his voice even, as if he ran into gangsters every day, and tried to work out what these two were doing in Herman's office. His late-night visit to Mick's club had not gone unnoticed apparently. God bless, but he was good and truly screwed.

Delly nodded, leaning back into the worn leather couch and crossing her long, bare legs. Her skin was spotted and dry, but Samson admitted to himself that she must have been a looker when she first arrived in Hollywood, before—before what exactly? His thoughts bounced from the woman's circumstances to his own. Clearly, Herman had been trying to warn him away, and even now looked distressed. Had Bill threatened him? Or was he simply waiting for Samson, letting the prey come to him like a helpful little mouse?

"Is it good to see me? Because I was hoping to never see your ugly, smug face again. Can't a man enjoy his retirement without being dragged back into his family's affairs?" Bill's voice had a dangerous note, the sliver of humor a mask for something much darker. He brushed some dandruff from his shoulder and adjusted his outdated tie.

Samson raised his hands to show that he didn't mean any harm, but by the look on Herman's face, that was the wrong move.

"Intentions get too much credit," Bill continued. "I didn't mean to is what? It's nothing. You still got a lost briefcase or a broken fender. A fucking knife in your side."

Samson forced himself not to cross the room and check on Brigit. Maybe they didn't know she was with him. He was glad he'd left the keys in case she needed to escape.

"You should have been a philosopher," Samson said, wishing he had anything at all that could be used as a weapon. He tried to scan the office but Bill watched him with unnerving intensity. It was as if the suit had transformed him. Samson should have roughed him up when he had the chance.

"I should be asleep is what I should be. You know how hard it is to get a cleanup crew at this hour?" Delly laughed, and Bill whipped toward her. "You think that's funny, baby? You got a sick sense of humor."

Samson used the distraction to step closer to Herman, spotting the fake Oscar and hoping it wasn't made of plastic. He put his hand beside it as Bill shook Delly, her skeletal frame somehow withstanding the abuse, like a palm tree bending in a hurricane.

"It is funny, though, jeez," Delly said. She hiccupped before continuing. "Ain't no hard or easy time to get a cleanup crew. You just call them and they come."

Delly stopped laughing but Bill started, straightening up and turning back toward Samson and Herman.

"She may look like a dumb broad, but there's enough going on upstairs to keep the lights on."

Samson put his full force into the swing, the base of the statue connecting with a loud crack against Bill's skull. The man stumbled backward, stunned, and when he touched his head, he came away with blood.

"Son of a bitch," he said. "I will fucking own you, Delaware, before this is through."

Samson grabbed Herman's arm and steered the man toward the door. Before they made it, a shot plowed into the ceiling, covering them all with plaster. Samson glanced behind him to see that Delly had risen and was aiming a gun at them both. If it wasn't an antique, Samson couldn't tell a Glock from a Colt, but it looked deadly enough. They ran the last few feet, Delly laughing again behind them, having a good time.

"You're lucky she's a crap shot, Delaware."

Samson took the stairs quickly, pulling Herman faster than his frail body wanted to go. The old man wheezed, but followed, clutching the Oscar in his left hand and the railing in his right. They fled into daylight where Brigit now sat behind the wheel, engine running, flagging them down.

"Lucky?" Samson said. He'd been called worse.

Herman lived next door to a popular bar in the heart of Encino. It would be raucous later in the day, but at 10 a.m., the place was locked tight as a tomb. The street below them had some late commuters, though, and every car horn made Samson jump. He couldn't help but notice that he was the only one on edge. Brigit boiled water for tea as Herman wiped his statue with a washcloth, singing tunelessly to himself. Samson's hands shook, and he shoved them into his pockets as he checked the window again, sure that they'd been followed.

It was a nice neighborhood with plenty of manicured lawns. Johnny Carson lived there, and Carole Lombard supposedly. But Herman's studio sat in an old condo building on a busy avenue, not on one of the quaint, tree-lined side streets. A few takeout joints were starting to open for the early lunch crowd, and Samson could see somebody moving around inside the synagogue.

Samson watched a patrol car circle the block and wondered if he should call Bishop. Beg forgiveness for keeping Barbara's letter from him. At this point, Bishop would be obligated to tell the TBI, and Samson would find himself on the wrong side of an investigation. How had he botched everything so badly? He'd set out to avenge Barbara's death— and her assistant's as an afterthought—and now he needed to save his own neck. Bishop wouldn't know what to make of this mess anyway. Samson would call when he had a clearer sense of what was going on.

"How'd you end up here, Mr. Stein?" Samson asked, forcing himself to step away from the window.

"Herman, please. We nearly met our maker together." Herman laughed, and Brigit joined, dropping tea bags into the cups she'd found. Samson marveled at the pair of them. He freely admitted that ice did not run in his veins. He felt feverish and uncertain. He wanted to lie down.

"Herman then. You washed off the evidence?"

Herman looked puzzled, then held the Oscar to his chest.

"Evidence? Who cares about evidence? Look around, kid. This is my most valuable possession."

"It can't be real, surely."

"Can't it?"

Brigit handed out the steaming mugs and then sat down on the sofa, tucking her legs underneath her body and leaning back. She looked comfortable in the spartan surroundings, and when she saw that Samson was staring at her, she winked.

"Earned or stolen?" she asked Herman, who placed the gold statue on a shelf and shuffled toward her. They'd forgotten his cane in their rush to escape, but he seemed to be getting around okay. The ring of hair around the base of his skull stood on end, making him look like a pink and gray jellyfish.

"Pawn shop."

Samson didn't laugh, but his shoulders relaxed a little, and when he checked the window again, he didn't expect to see anything. They'd been at Herman's place for an hour or so, and nobody had come for them. How bad had he hurt Bill O'Hara? Not bad enough. It was a cruel thought that felt alien to Samson. He wasn't a cruel man, but his anger pulsed in concert with his fear. The city made him reckless. The O'Hara brothers made him mean.

"The bars," Herman was explaining. "They come and go. I moved to this neighborhood in 1921 and never left. First a home, then when the kids had families of their own and my wife died, this place. Better for a widower than knocking around some four-bedroom mausoleum. 1921. The war missed me by a couple of years, and I let it. I had a neighbor, fourteen years old, who lied to enlist. A couple of other kids around, too. What happened to them? Dead. All dead. So I moved here. I stay, and the bars come and go."

"You could sell it," Brigit said. "Make a pretty penny, I bet."

"I've made enough bets in my lifetime. Where would I go?"

When Herman voiced the question, it was rhetorical, but it was the question that dogged Samson, following him around from life to life. When he moved to Cedarville, he hadn't expected to stay that long, certainly not forever. Then, after getting married, he'd never wanted to leave, even after Barbara Lace returned. Any shame he might have felt in usurping her hometown was masked by love for his wife. Their paths rarely crossed anyway, and Barbara became more myth than memento of his past. Where was she now? Did it even matter? He couldn't rightly say what had brought him to this precipice. It was like walking out of a fog to find yourself at the edge of a cliff.

"We should celebrate," Herman said. "A toast to our getaway driver, a regular Steve McQueen."

He pulled a bottle of bourbon from underneath the kitchen sink and distributed a healthy splash into each of their cups. Samson didn't resist, though the smell made him recoil. He knew a bad idea when he smelled one.

"To Brigit, a marvel among marlins," he said quietly, taking a sip as his companions did the same.

To Brigit. Would she even be here if she knew the truth? Samson wouldn't kid himself. The woman was a straight shooter, someone with enough pride to give him the boot, even if she suffered a little, too. He liked that about her. He liked everything about her.

The morning and afternoon crept by, each hour raising the

volume of the bar below. They'd decided to hole up, make sure they weren't being followed. Being trapped inside made Samson restless and frustrated, but he tried to imitate his friends who seemed to stay busy somehow. Herman wrote a little on his typewriter, pecking at the keys and refilling his bourbon from time to time. Brigit found a jigsaw puzzle that was only missing a few pieces. She convinced them to play Rummy, and they talked about what they should do next. Samson's halfhearted attempt to get Brigit to go home went ignored, and Herman helped them come up with a list of Barbara's friends.

By midnight, Herman had crawled under the blankets on his bed and was softly snoring. Brigit was lying on the couch after Samson insisted that he was fine on the floor. He wasn't. His back ached, and each time he shifted, his bones pushed against the hardwood floor. When he groaned in frustration, Brigit sat up and held out her hand. Samson hesitated, trying to see her eyes in the light seeping in from the street. Then he curled his body around hers, the cushion and her heating comforting him. He kissed her neck, and she stretched, moving her hair out of the way. When his mouth found hers, he shuddered in pleasure, hating himself.

The studio apartment became a base camp. Samson thought Barbara's friends could help them find her if they weren't actively hiding her themselves. She had no reason to stay in Cedarville if she wasn't keeping an eye on Samson, and she hadn't left Hollywood willingly. Getting out of the country would take a passport, but a cross-country flight would be easy enough with a fake driver's license. Nobody would look twice at a grandmother boarding a plane. And why wouldn't she return now that she could? A new name, a new identity. Who would recognize her? As far as the O'Hara brothers knew, she was dead. Brigit still believed she was, but she didn't think talking to Barbara's friends would hurt anything. They could share more incriminating information about Mick, and Sheriff Bishop could take over or—as a last resort—the TBI kid.

They went in pairs to interview Barbara's former colleagues and friends—what was left of them at least. Most of Herman's names turned up obituaries instead of leads. The ones they located expressed regret at her passing, and nobody seemed to be hiding her in a guest room. On one outing, Samson and Brigit thought they might be onto something, but the strange noises from the basement turned out to be a squirrel that had gotten trapped inside. Brigit ushered the creature back into daylight and received a hero's thanks from the old woman who'd resigned herself to cleaning up a carcass when the visitor finally died. They walked back to their car with a tin of cookies and a to-go container of soup.

Samson deemed it their most successful questioning yet, and Brigit pulled him close to press her lips against his cheek. The gesture felt natural and exciting. She smelled like Dial soap and dryer sheets. She smelled a little like Herman. Samson remained grateful for the old man's presence in the apartment, so that they couldn't go farther than they'd regret. To be honest, he remained grateful to Herman in general for insisting that they stay. The old man didn't believe that Barbara was still alive either. He liked the possibility, but he dismissed the letter as another scare tactic, less memorable than snakes perhaps. Still, Herman knew something big was going on if the O'Hara brothers had come out of retirement to terrorize them.

"Who knew we'd get gifts for snooping," Samson said, crawling into the passenger's seat. Brigit had taken over all driving responsibilities, and she navigated L.A. traffic as if she'd been born in the city.

"Who's next?"

Samson looked down at his notes, where twelve names had been whittled to two. He crossed out May Riley and put his finger by

Isadora Alvarez, hesitating. Brigit would know who she was, would maybe enjoy meeting the actress. Isadora's name could still be found on Hollywood Boulevard, though tourists rarely stopped to take their photo with her spot. Her most famous film, *Beyond the Moonlight*, broke box office records in its day, and rumors circulated that she'd been having an affair with the director. When she'd disappeared from public view for a year, tongues wagged even more, and conspiracists claimed that she'd given birth in private and left the child at an Italian orphanage. It was quite a tale, and while Samson didn't believe it, her disappearance piqued his interest. Alvarez knew how to keep secrets, and perhaps she wouldn't have minded an old friend on her doorstep. Alvarez and Lace appeared in three movies together, Alvarez as some sort of glamorous bon vivant, Lace as a sensible secretary or the like.

Isadora Alvarez should have been first on their list of interviewees, but Samson had nudged her down the list, worried that she might remember him from the Steerson's dinner. He comforted himself with the knowledge that she'd seen a lot of faces over the years and probably hadn't paid that much attention. Unless Barbara had spoken of him. His palms began to sweat as he directed Brigit toward her address. Samson thought he might tell Brigit that he had worked with Barbara. He even formed the sentence in his mind. But now his confession would only seem suspicious. His window of opportunity had closed.

More to stall than anything else, he asked Brigit to stop at a pay phone along the way, so that he could at least give Bishop his new number at Herman's. If Agent McKinnell couldn't get in touch with him, he might think Samson was trying to make a run for it.

"Best get it over with anyway," Brigit said, pulling into a strip mall. It was the kind of place where people sold guns out of their trunks, and Samson walked quickly toward the phone. Bishop answered, then put down the receiver to yell at someone in the background.

211

"Damn heathens, Delaware. I swear to God, I will never complain about you again."

"You complain about me?"

"You know you're damn annoying. Ain't no big secret." Samson fought the urge to hang up. "They park wherever they feel like it. One of these agents backed into the fountain, and did he offer to replace it? You know the punchline to that joke."

"Bishop, that fountain hasn't worked right in years. Where do you think we live, Versailles?"

"See. That's what I mean. Damn annoying." Samson watched Brigit climb out of their car to stretch her legs and waited for Bishop to get to his point. "I found something. I've been trying to reach out, but the motel said you'd moved on. Apparently Callista Weathers has got a nasty ex. No domestic violence record, but should have one. Many times over. But she'd change her mind, never press charges."

"They think he killed her?"

"God, I hope so. I'm the one who got somebody to talk. You know how these backcountry offices run. All Xeroxes and Post-it notes. I paid them a visit while Agent McKinnell was waiting for somebody to call him back. You got to look somebody in the eyes."

Bishop sounded pleased with himself, and Samson congratulated him. Could the solution really be that simple? It would make more sense than whatever maze he'd created for himself.

"I suggest you come on home, Delaware. There's nothing out there for you. We've about wrapped this up."

Samson hung up and considered. Could Callista's death really be separate from Barbara's? Had he gotten himself mixed up in something dangerous for no good reason? It seemed like an awfully big coincidence.

He was preoccupied when they finally arrived at Alvarez's

security gates. The system was ancient, and the intercom cracked and popped as they said their names. When they were let through, Brigit pulled the car into a circular drive, admiring the pink mansion that couldn't be seen from the road. At first, it was if they'd stepped into a postcard. Even the weather seemed to agree, the sun twinkling in the palm trees and kissing the white columns. When they walked up the front steps, though, the emptiness on display through the bay windows was startling. The rooms seemed stripped. No lights or furniture in sight. When the door flew open, Samson lurched back, expecting bats or specters—anything but a faded star.

CHAPTER 21

A fire broke out at the Gravel Lane
Post-Production Studio last night,
destroying $100,000 worth of equipment
and dozens of film canisters. The
building has been deemed unsafe for
entry by the LAFD. No neighboring
buildings were damaged, and regular
traffic resumed this morning.
—T.S. Graveson,
The Los Angeles Times, November 11, 1981

Someday he would stop believing in ghosts. He would wake
up to clawing in the attic and think "vermin" like any other owner of an
old house. Wind from an unsealed crack would be wind, not a phantom
hand on his cheek. When exactly had he grown superstitious? He'd
always been sensitive, but crazy was new.

Isadora Alvarez didn't seem to remember Samson, but then

again, she didn't seem to see so well either. The thick lenses of her glasses enlarged her eyes, and they looked like two prize goldfish at a state fair. Her hair—as jet black as it had ever been—was pulled back so tight that the skin around her temple stretched toward the ceiling. She had on thick stage makeup as if she'd been expecting company. She stood ramrod straight and welcomed them with an obvious lie.

"I'm afraid my staff has the day off. Please follow me."

She swept them into the dark interior, the contrast with the bright day making Samson blink. Brigit seemed unfazed, but she glanced into each empty room they passed. It was as if the furniture had vanished, leaving only the wallpaper and light fixtures behind. Ready for a renovation or a new owner. The kitchen was dark, too, but a lamp burned in the corner, illuminating an unoccupied bird cage. A pot of water boiled on the stove, filling the room with steam. Grateful for small favors, Samson took a chair at the table when instructed to sit by their hostess. Although Samson was at a loss, Brigit seemed to know instinctively what to do, noticing the instant coffee on the counter and scooping the dried grounds into three cups. Samson considered for a moment how easily she fell into the role of caretaker, considered in a confusing blur of thoughts how she would have taken better care of his wife than he did. When he felt Isadora staring at him, Samson turned his attention back to the actress, wary.

"You're here about Barbara, I suppose. Another stop on the sympathy tour."

"Sympathy tour?"

"Oh sure, you think an old lady doesn't know how to use the telephone? I've been warned about you."

Samson bristled at the word "warned," wondering if the woman was being dramatic. When Brigit set his cup down, he looked at the weak brown color, and he thought it might be okay. Maybe he could take a few sips without shaking later. He really wanted a cigarette, but he told himself to stop thinking about it.

"Hometown ambassadors, you might call us," Brigit said, taking a chair between Isadora and Samson. "Were you close to Ms. Lace?"

"Like sisters for a time. And you know how sisters can fight. Dresses and boyfriends. Scripts and auditions. She was jealous of me, but we had good days, too. Parties at the Wilshire. Then painful early call times in the morning. You're only young once, though."

She glanced at Brigit on that piece of advice, then looked away. It all seemed rehearsed, a little wooden and premeditated. Brigit nodded, though, encouraging her.

"Had you talked lately?" Brigit asked.

"We kept in touch the old-fashioned way. Carrier pigeons and the post office. Birthday cards and the occasional news clipping." Isadora moved her chair back and removed a blue shoebox from underneath. "As I say, your visit was not wholly unexpected."

Dozens of cards nestled inside along with movie reviews and other newspaper clippings. There was a magazine article from 1989 about a lifetime achievement award that Isadora had received. The writer had summarized decades of films and accolades in a hundred words, and it was accompanied by photos from every era. Samson didn't recognize the byline and was grateful that he hadn't overshared with Kit Forrester. He hoped she wouldn't be able to find him again, but he also worried why he hadn't heard from her. Wouldn't she be shopping her story about Barbara not really being dead? He'd been careless, he realized much too late. The story would put Barbara in danger from the O'Haras again.

"I remember the ceremony," Brigit said as she handed back the paper with a memorable photo of Isadora. "That purple dress."

"Ah yes, LaSalle deigned to make something for a mature woman. We bickered over the décolletage, but I was right in the end. You don't make it to sixty without knowing a little something about your own body."

Isadora's voice had taken on a dreamy quality that still felt forced to Samson, but was he looking for reasons to be suspicious? Perhaps this was how she always behaved with strangers. To be honest, he didn't like the cavernous house. He knew what empty rooms meant, but he was having trouble rustling up sympathy for the woman. A studio darling who married well. What had she done with her fortune? He didn't care for the way she spoke about Barbara either and wanted to object. Barbara had never been a catty sort as far as he could recall.

"I have something to add to your collection," Samson said, pulling out the letter that had been returned to Barbara. The plastic bag made it look like evidence, and he shook it out quickly. It was still unopened, and when he handed it over, Isadora raised a penciled eyebrow at him.

"A gentleman until the end, I see."

Samson usually liked being called a gentleman, but something about Isadora's intention didn't sit well with him. She seemed to be mocking him.

"I have a hard time with the handwriting anyway," he said. "All those loops and curls."

"She always did write like one of those airplanes blowing smoke."

Samson glanced at Brigit, and she nodded at him with encouragement. He'd done the right thing for once. Even better, Isadora took the handle of her spoon and pulled it under the flap, opening the letter from her friend eight years late.

"Dear Dory—" Isadora began reading. "I hated that nickname, and she knew it, you understand. Dear Dory…"

Isadora read the letter as if she were auditioning, and Brigit leaned forwar to enjoy the show. Samson was still wary, but admitted that he liked the sound of her voice. It had a slight rattle from age, but was soothing, familiar.

Dear Dory—

I've picked up my pen and put it down a few hundred times now. If we were on your sweet little velvet loveseat or even out at The Queen, I'd know just what to say. I've been remembering our trip to Montreal, though I can't remember the occasion. One of your events, most likely, where I'd drink all your champagne and open all your gift baskets while you had to work. You never made it look like work, though, and I admired you for it. You knew I admired you, yes? Still, after everything, I admire you.

They interviewed me for the documentary, and I spoke in such glowing terms that it will never make the final cut. They'll look for some throwaway comment that makes us both look bad. The bastards. A betrayal around every corner. At least they're predictable.

I hope that lessens the sting. I was sorry to hear about Clark. I'm not sorry for anything else, but I love you all the same.

Yours forever,
Barbara

Isadora seemed to forget that she had company, staring at the letter in her hands and turning it over to make sure she hadn't missed anything. She ran her thumb across the signature, as if making a wish for her friend. Samson was glad he hadn't opened the letter after all. The words meant nothing to him, but clearly touched Isadora. Her rigid posture relaxed, and she seemed to sink into herself a little.

"Excuse me if this question is impertinent, but did she seem like herself when you last spoke?" Samson asked quietly.

Isadora turned her dark eyes on Samson and made a sweeping gesture. "Last spoke? Oh, that's been a fair number of years gone by. After she fled Hollywood, she went quiet."

"Fled?" Brigit asked.

"Nobody retires from this town by choice, not the ones getting work." Samson started to object when Isadora stood up from the table and paused dramatically, keeping her focus on Samson, suddenly angry in a way that he understood. The letter had made her vulnerable, and he'd brought the letter. The fresh grief was his fault. He should have seen the blow coming. "You know that better than anyone. You were part of our lives once."

Samson's skin grew cold as he met the woman's stare. He could feel Brigit's body shift beside him, but he refused to look at her. Isadora had known him after all. Why was he surprised? She knew his number and wanted him on guard. When he'd imagined Isadora recognizing him, he'd thought of a well-meaning remark, perhaps a question about Carly. Not a calculated signal. Samson didn't know what game she played, but it was clear she made her own rules.

"I don't know about that," he finally said, his tone assertive but as fake as Isadora's had been. The house seemed more malicious than ever, and he pushed back from the table and turned toward the exit without asking what he really wanted—why had Barbara fled? He could hear Brigit thanking Isadora for her hospitality as Samson opened the front door and stepped into the sunlight, hoping the warmth would flood his body, bring him back to life. He felt nothing but cold, the inescapable sensation of his past catching up with him.

The drive back passed silently. Brigit appeared lost in thought, not even bothering with the car radio. Her only display of emotion was the white of her knuckles as she gripped the steering wheel. She didn't speak until they were parked outside of Herman's building. The bright light emphasized the black streaks from years of rain. A few bricks were damaged, especially on the lower level, and most windows above the bar were dark. Herman's windows hadn't been opened in years, painted shut in a different era, fire hazard be damned. Samson concentrated on these details, worried about what Brigit might say. It was worse than he imagined.

"Did you kill that girl? Is that why you left Cedarville?"

Samson felt the question in his throat, a tightening that made it hard to respond. He tried his best to explain, but he couldn't breathe properly.

"No. And I didn't know Barbara better than anyone else there."

"But you did, Samson. I've lived there my whole life and never even seen her. But you, what? Followed her there?"

Brigit leaned away from him, her back against the car door, keys gripped in her hand. The pose made him ache to comfort her.

"Nothing so menacing as that."

He wanted to explain, wanted more than anything to vanquish the hint of fear in Brigit's eyes, but he'd never been able to explain the move to himself. Why had Cedarville captured his imagination?

"Barbara," he started, then hesitated. Brigit shook her head, climbing out of the car and slamming the door behind her. Samson scrambled out after her, ignoring the car horns that blared at him as he stepped briefly into traffic before coming around to Brigit. "Ms. Lace talked about her hometown. It was her go-to interview topic, made her sound charming and relatable. I don't know. She made it sound like the opposite of Los Angeles, and I'd started to hate it here. Hate myself."

He sounded irrational, he knew. His voice was raised, almost yelling, and Brigit didn't seem convinced.

"Charming and relatable," she said, parroting him.

"I thought I'd be long gone by the time she returned. I just meant to visit, rest my legs for a bit. But then—"

Samson couldn't bring himself to say his wife's name out loud. He hadn't said her name since she'd died. When someone expressed their condolences or praised her, he flinched, afraid she might need the name wherever she was, not wanting to take it from her. What right did he have—what right did anyone have to something so personal?

"This is your quest, not mine. I'm some sort of lackey, simpering after you."

"I'm simpering after you, too."

"Don't. Just stop. I'm some sort of what's his name cleaning up windmills after you fight them."

"Sancho Panza."

"Fuck you, Samson. We get it. You're smarter than the rest of us. But where has that gotten you? You tell me that."

Brigit's anger turned her cheeks red, and she pressed a palm against her face. Samson could almost see the scales falling from her eyes, could almost guess her thoughts. The city must have looked different to her than when they'd first arrived. She hadn't minded the motel room and even liked the worn-out quality of Herman's street, as if it couldn't be bothered to spruce itself up, was too important for fresh paint. But where she was from? You cleaned your house. If you didn't have money to replace something, you scrubbed it. Where she was from? Liars got what they deserved, and Samson was a first-rate liar, no question.

Samson touched her arm, and she jerked away, lost to him. The pain spread from his throat, seeming to fill his body with lead.

Once they were both upstairs, Herman watched her pack. The first flight she could get left in two days, but she wanted to be prepared.

221

She wanted to do anything but look at Samson hunched over Herman's old newspapers, seeing which actors were dead and which ones were still alive, hidden in their falling down pink mansions. The words swam in front of him, but he didn't dare stop, afraid that if he did, his mind would simply fall apart once and for all.

"Work," Herman said, making Brigit look up. "I am married to my work. There were dalliances, sure, I don't mind telling you. After my wife died. A few broads over the years. But who'd give up all this?"

He spread his arms wide to show off his small apartment, and Brigit forced herself to smile at his joke. Herman had taken the news in stride, not that bothered by Samson neglecting to mention he had personal reasons for wanting to find Barbara. Everybody had personal reasons.

Samson stopped searching the obituaries, a cold reality gripping him. He was at the end of his list, and he had no idea what to do next. Finding Barbara seemed impossible, and yet also like the only way forward, the only way to save himself. It was painful to admit, but that's what he'd been doing all along, looking out for Samson Delaware. Not Barbara Lace or Callista Weathers or even Brigit Mills. Lovely, steady Brigit with hair like a spring colt and a kick like a full-grown mare. Too good for him. He wasn't sure exactly when he'd decided that he wanted to live, but that was the truth now, a life without love. But not without purpose.

If Brigit's flight left in two days then he had two days. A man could do a lot with forty-eight hours. Especially a man who didn't have anything left to lose.

CHAPTER 22

53 Chritton Lane. $25,000. 4BR, 3BA. 2
acres. A historic classic Victorian on a
quiet stretch of land near Maplewood Creek.
Good bones! Cedarville, TN.
—*The Smithtown Bee*, March 1, 1982

The basement window wasn't locked, and Samson crouched down, then lowered himself into the dark space. He thought he heard something scurry away in the corner, and he froze until his eyes adjusted. Concrete floors and corkboard ceilings made the whole place seem damp. A faucet dripped somewhere in the distance, a waste of water in this uninhabited place. If anyone had been down there in years, Samson would have been surprised. It was completely empty except for a light layer of debris and dead bugs, a couple of folding chairs. The walls smelled of decay as if something had died there a few months back. Only desperation pulled him forward instead of back outside. He'd slept on his plan, but in the end, he had to come back.

Scaling the fence around Isadora's property had been easy enough. He'd stayed in his car for hours, his legs growing painfully stiff, until he was sure nobody was home. Samson had started to suspect that nobody was ever home, that the pink mansion was more set than abode. No furniture in any of the rooms. Isadora didn't really stay there. She had been playing with them, but though an idea tickled at the back of his brain, Samson couldn't say for sure what it meant. Another eccentric being eccentric didn't quite work for him.

The stairs creaked underneath his boots, but he took them two at a time, nearly slamming into the locked door at the top. It was like a mausoleum down below, and he had no intention of staying there long. He'd never tried to pick a lock before and didn't bother to experiment now. Instead, he braced himself against a wall and pulled until the old doorknob popped out of the frame. He'd used the same crude trick when swapping ugly brass ones in his own home for jadeite beauties he'd picked up a yard sale. The bones of these old homes were usually good, but the hardware? He tossed the knob behind him, not caring if anyone knew an intruder had broken in. If his suspicions were correct, nobody would be stopping by for a while. And cops would be more likely to blame squatters than a man who planned to be far from Los Angeles by that time. He'd worn gloves so his prints wouldn't be found anywhere besides where they were expected.

The same empty rooms greeted him above, and he inspected the kitchen first, hoping for some sign. There were coffee grounds from where Brigit had spilled some without noticing. Their three cups lay on the table, his mostly untouched and theirs empty. Isadora's had a ring of dark pink lipstick. Opening the cupboards, he found one more cup but no other dishes. The refrigerator was empty, as well, and—how had he missed this before—unplugged. The place was quiet, his steps echoing off the bare walls. He hoped he couldn't be seen from the road;

fortunately, the yard was overgrown, blocking most of the windows. There was nothing there to tell him anything about the retired actress, and he walked quickly from room to room, each one confirming what he already knew.

When he pushed open the bathroom door, he jumped back. Some primal part of his brain had been expecting them somewhere, and the tub was the logical place. Four small, sleek black snakes stark against the dingy porcelain. A leak from the faucet dripped onto their skin, making them glisten, the only glimmer in the whole house. Samson was less scared than he'd been the first time, and it didn't take him long to notice that they were fake. They were too perfect, no sand color peeking out underneath. Solid and still. Samson picked one up, the rubber flopping down and slapping into his thigh. A child's toy, and not even particularly lifelike. Still, he wanted to leave. He struggled to understand how all the pieces fit together, and he felt outmaneuvered. A man improvising while everyone else had a script. He opened the medicine cabinet to find old, caked bottles of stage foundation along with temporary hair dye. She must have taken the lipstick with her.

He didn't run exactly, but he didn't take his time either, exiting the same way he'd arrived. The basement window wouldn't close all the way behind him, but the crack was barely visible, and he didn't care. Samson stalked back to his rental, which he'd parked a few blocks away. The sun felt hotter than it had before, less postcard-beautiful and more oppressive. His life had turned into a labyrinth, but he didn't just want to find the exit. He wanted to burn the whole thing down. It was as if there were flames in his mind, and he couldn't put them out. He had to release them.

On the way home, he furiously worked through what he knew, lining up the players in his mind, each one hiding something or someone. When he got back to the apartment, Herman had left him a note to say that he was getting his cane and then taking Brigit to lunch. His heart leapt into his throat, and he found himself angry at Herman's recklessness. They could be followed. When the phone rang, he thought it must be them, needing help. But Sheriff Bishop's drawl greeted him instead.

"What do you got for me?" the man said, not interested in Samson's greeting.

"You tell me, Bishop. Last I heard, you had the whole thing tied up."

A heavy sigh greeted him in response, and Samson could picture him in his living room, belt undone and shoes off, on duty but also on the verge of giving up. Bishop had been bone-tired for quite some time. Samson was only now noticing.

"The boyfriend had an airtight alibi. Was in another state."

"Witnesses and such?"

"Fucking witnesses and such."

Samson waited for Bishop to continue, and when he was met with silence, he asked about Agent McKinnell.

"Getting nowhere in this town. You know how it is."

"Maybe they don't know anything."

"You think I'm calling you for kicks, Samson? You think I like the fact you might be right, that there's nothing here?"

Samson pulled the phone over to the window to make sure there was nobody suspicious outside. He watched for Herman and Brigit, anxious for their return. Even if Brigit still wasn't speaking to him, at least they'd be in the same room. He could smell her drugstore shampoo and admire her fury.

"I don't have anything concrete yet, Bishop. But something's not right. Damn snakes."

"Snakes?"

"You heard me. Guess our friends couldn't get their hands on real ones out here, thank God."

Bishop wasn't that interested, mumbling something about coincidences.

"Oh sure. Everybody's keeping toy snakes in their bathrooms nowadays. It's all over *Variety*."

"What the hell's *Variety*?"

Samson couldn't remember if he responded or not, distracted by where to find back issues of the popular magazine. They could help, he realized. They could fill in some of the gaps he had in Barbara's timeline, in her friends' lives. Celebrities seem familiar, like cousins you see a few times a year, asking about their kids or jobs. For all the glitz, that's what keeps fans interested, the illusion of accessibility. They're aspirational, but not out of reach. Samson had never cared, at least that's what he told himself. Actors and actresses might as well have been holograms, programmed into existence, their stories curated and controlled. But Samson knew Barbara was flesh and blood. And he believed that she was still out there, hiding perhaps. From Mick O'Hara, from her past, from Samson even. While he cared about Callista Weathers, while he repeated to himself that he cared who killed her, he also wanted to find Barbara Lace, see for himself that somebody could be raised from the dead.

"She's alive," Samson said, cutting Bishop off. He'd been complaining again about the TBI cars.

"Who is?"

"Barbara Lace."

"Like shit she is. You've lost the thread, Delaware."

Samson didn't really need to convince Bishop, but he wanted to at least try. When Kit Forrester finally got around to selling her story, he wanted to be able to say honestly that he'd tried to tell Bishop.

After the sheriff hung up, disgusted with him, Samson grabbed his keys, heading for the nearest library. Any place in L.A. was bound to have more resources than the one he'd used back home. Serious literature and gossip rags alike. In his rush to leave, he nearly slammed into Brigit opening the door, her groceries tumbling out of the bags she carried. He apologized and knelt down to retrieve cans of soup and oranges. A package of open potato chips spilled onto the floor, and he scooped up the food with his hands as Brigit went for a broom without speaking to him. He wanted to say something clever, something to make her thaw a little, but he couldn't think of anything appropriate. He felt high, jumped up on fear and adrenaline.

"I'll get that, Brigit," he said when she returned.

"Thank you, but it'll go quicker with both of us."

They cleaned up the mess quietly and carried everything into Herman's crowded kitchen. Every inch of counter space was taken up with appliances or newspapers, so they put the grocery bags on the floor before filling the refrigerator and cabinets.

"We'd starve without you," Samson said.

"Oh, I think Herman misses the doting he gets at the diner. You should have seen him today, pretending to be embarrassed by all the attention."

Brigit never looked directly at Samson, but warmed a little when she spoke of Herman. They'd both grown fond of the old agent, settling into a routine in his apartment. In the mornings, they'd pick at toast and butter, try to work the crossword together. Then he and Brigit would see who was left, which of Barbara's friends were still around for a conversation. Neither of the O'Hara brothers had returned, and Samson thought perhaps they were like snakes themselves, not likely to strike unless you stepped on them. And hadn't he been stepping all over their nests, showing up at Bill's home and then Mick's club?

Now that Brigit was there, he wasn't in such a rush to leave, but he needed information that wasn't going to come from the loaf of bread he put on a shelf. She told him that Herman was taking a walk and would be back in a few minutes if he wanted to wait. Samson wanted to wait more than anything, wanted to soak up every minute he had left with Brigit, but he left anyway, making a beeline for a bodega to pick up another pack of smokes. His last, he promised himself.

The first drag burned, and Samson coughed a little. But the second one slid smoothly into his head and nose. He exhaled, enjoying the immediate buzz. He felt a little wild and a lot reckless. The street to Herman's place felt familiar by now, the overgrown palm trees and loud kestrels or maybe swifts above. They were several miles from the beach, but still the occasional cry of seagulls would compete with the sound of car horns. The bar hadn't opened yet, but there were a couple of people inside filling salt shakers and wiping down tables. The smell of stale beer and sweat when he passed made Samson cringe, but he also understood the appeal of a rundown but beloved neighborhood joint.

It was next to impossible to find a parking place nearby, and Samson started the long walk toward his rental. He spotted Herman coming home and called out, but Herman couldn't hear him and disappeared around a corner into a small, desolate alley. Samson had glanced down it before and figured his friend must be taking out the trash. As far as he knew, there was no back entrance to the apartment building, only fire escapes that hadn't been inspected recently. He hoped they didn't have to use them.

Samson took one last drag and ground the butt into the sidewalk. He looked up to see if Brigit might be watching him, but the window was empty. Instead, he followed Herman, hoping that the man could give him better directions to the library. All he had was an address from the phone book and a vague sense that he needed to head west. When Samson turned the corner, Herman was easy to spot, hurrying along with his cane, but not exactly flying. Samson could easily catch up with him and broke into a light jog. He stopped abruptly when he saw Herman approach a chain-link fence and pull at the padlock. If Samson had been thinking clearly, he would have followed the man past the gate, but he was so startled that he called out and Herman turned, dropping the key and taking a few shuffling steps away before changing his mind.

"Samson! Fancy meeting you here," Herman said, crouching low to retrieve his key. Samson was disoriented, but still he stooped down to help the old man, his instincts warring. He felt obligated to offer assistance, but it was clear that his friend was hiding something by his reaction. Something he didn't want Samson to know. Samson was forty-three and had never met a secret that meant good news.

"Need help with something?" he asked, keeping his fingers crossed for a logical explanation.

"No, no. Out for some fresh air."

Samson held out the key, then thought better of it, turning toward the lock to open it himself. The first blow hit him squarely in the back, a dull throb like a muscle spasm, but the second one felt like an explosion, the back of his head flaring with pain. Samson touched his scalp, surprised that there wasn't any blood, and took a staggering step to face his assailant. His vision swam, but he concentrated, expecting to see Seven. Instead, Herman held his cane like a bat in front of him and took another swing, connecting with Samson's right wrist.

Samson screamed, then tried to wrest the cane from Herman's grip. The old man fought him, and Samson stumbled forward, knocking them both down. Samson scrambled to his knees, but Herman stayed put, moaning. For one terrible moment, Samson thought he might hit him, frustration boiling up inside his aching skull. His hand hurt when he balled it into a fist, and the sight of Herman's panicked face made him even angrier. Samson had trusted every word out of his mouth, lapping up stories about Barbara in her youth. Charmed by the agent's quirks. More than charmed, Samson had felt protective, guilty that he'd gotten such a nice fellow wrapped up in his mess.

Samson reared back, intending to connect with Herman's face, but the roaring in his ears slipped to a whisper, and he picked up the cane instead, flinging it away. He slumped down onto the sidewalk, lying down beside Herman and letting the world spin. He panted, trying to catch his breath and make sense of what had happened, what he had to do next. He wanted to stay there forever.

"I thought you were going to hit me," Herman said after a few minutes had passed.

"What the hell, Herman. You could have given me a concussion."

"If I were younger, I could have killed you."

The response didn't endear Herman to him, but both men were spent, and they breathed heavily. The silence was almost companionable, but Samson didn't want the old man to get the upper hand again. He sat up gingerly, checking his head and rotating his sore wrist. He felt like a linebacker after a brutal defeat. He'd feel even worse in the morning, and he didn't have time to waste.

"What's behind the fence, Herman?"

Herman sighed, trying to sit up himself and failing until Samson grabbed an arm and pulled him up. "I've done more than she asked, but it still feels like a betrayal."

"Who? Who's asking you for favors?"

Herman used the fence to haul himself upright, gesturing for Samson to fetch his cane. Samson wasn't crazy about the idea, but he picked up the stick from a puddle and passed it over. Samson checked his head one more time, relieved that the pain was receding. The blow hadn't been as bad as it could have been. Herman grimaced when he saw the state of his cane, wiping off the mud on his pants.

"You can't get these replaced, you know. It's a damn hassle with the insurance company. They'll squeeze every penny from you."

Herman held out his hand, and Samson dropped the key into his palm. He followed Herman inside a small space, hardly big enough for a car. The storage shed at the end had seen better days, its wood splintered and hinges rusted. Samson wasn't eager to discover what hid inside, but Herman went first anyway, his gait even slower than usual. In a different mood, Samson might have felt sorry for him, but he was livid and more than a little disoriented.

The shed itself was unlocked, and Herman pulled open the door and shuffled inside, pulling a thin cord from the ceiling. An orange lightbulb emitted a dull glow and hum. At first, Samson couldn't understand what he was seeing. Some sort of squatters quarters with a twin mattress and sheets in the corner. On the shelf above sat an array of bottles and tonics, murky in the low light. The musty smell of the place competed with rose water, deliberately splashed around.

"She planned to stay with me, but then you got to town and got yourself mixed up with gangsters. You're likable enough, but you might be a damn idiot."

As the dual truths slammed into Samson—he'd been right, he'd been lied to—his heart took slow, painful beats. He couldn't quite imagine Barbara Lace holing up here, especially at her age, but it made a certain sense. She didn't have a lot of allies left. And she'd been around the corner the whole time, not a stone's throw away.

"She's running from Mick," Samson said.

Herman grunted, noncommittally. "If Mick knows she's alive, he wants to find her, sure enough."

Guilt over swapping favors with a reporter filled his gut, but he'd come too far to back down.

"Where's she now?"

"I thought it better not to ask."

"Goddammit, Herman!" Samson surprised himself, the shock

of his own loud voice quelling him for a minute. He reached out a hand toward Herman, wanted to shake him, but swallowed down the violent impulse. Instead he rubbed his head again.

"I swear, son. She said it was safest. That she'd be okay. I'm not so sure now, to tell the truth. But she always had it all figured out. Two steps ahead of me. Ten."

Samson moved away to calm down, inspecting the meager contents of the place, hoping for some little sign. The sheets were pulled tight, crisp and precise. Barbara had folded her blanket into a neat square. Each window had a coating of filth, which obscured the view outside or in. A combination of dust and years of neglect. A few oil cans rested under the sill, and an old elementary school desk rusted in a corner. There was nothing salvageable about the place, no diamond in the rough that could be restored to its former glory. She had always been ten steps ahead of him, too.

"Why'd you come here today then? Take such a risk?"

Herman shrugged and started to strip the bed. "I thought somebody might find it. Start to get suspicious. Nobody uses this place, but it's not mine."

"Somebody like me."

"Sure enough. What's the harm really, Samson? So the woman doesn't want to be found. What's it to you?"

"You hit me."

"You startled me."

Samson didn't disagree with that, but he wasn't happy about the answer. Part of him, he'd admit, was thrilled that Barbara really was alive. The mattress offered incontrovertible proof that wishful thinking hadn't gotten the best of him. He'd have to convince Bishop now, he realized, not just make a lazy attempt. His days of vigilantism were behind him, and wasn't that for the best? He'd be the first to admit that he didn't really know what he was doing, following every impulse, ignoring any information that didn't fit his foregone conclusions. He'd make a crappy full-time investigator, but he didn't have any intentions of changing careers.

"Barbara may not be dead, but the other woman is. Callista Weathers."

"And this is your responsibility somehow. Or perhaps you wanted to escape that little town? Any excuse would do. And if a pretty little thing followed, all the better."

Samson's temper flared again at Herman's casual mention of Brigit.

"Leave it," Herman continued, looking older and more tired than before. "Who's going to care?"

Samson slid back outside, grateful for the fresh air. It seemed unfair that Barbara had fallen so low. But Herman was right about him, too. What sort of mission did he think he was on? Trying to save someone who didn't want to be saved. Barbara wasn't the ghost he wanted brought back to life. She was just the ghost he got.

CHAPTER 23

Video	Audio Lyrics / Narration / Music
1. A young woman sits in front of her vanity applying mascara. She hums along to the intro music, carefree and excited about her night out. When the face of a man appears in the mirror, she screams (silently) and jumps up, knocking over her chair. The camera cuts to a **close up** of her terrified face.	No lyrics. No narration. Intro music, from 0:01-0:15
2. The man's reflection starts singing along with the song. Slowly, the other band members appear in the background with their instruments.	"The night's got a thousand eyes that watch you when you undress. They don't need any alibis, don't hide your cries of distress." No narration From 0:15-0:35

3. The woman and the band are prowling a city street, arms slung around each other, blocking the sidewalk for all other pedestrians. It's dark and late. Their faces are reflected in the neon signs they pass.	"You're the only one that they want, and you're the only one that they need. You haunt them like you like to bleed." No narration From 0:35-0:50

```
from "All the Eyes" music video (1984)
Written by Jonathan S. Ferguson
Directed by Jonathan S. Ferguson
```

Barbara floated down the staircase, a girl no more than twenty-five with a tiny cinched waist and long tan legs. The costume sparkled from every angle, beaded from knee to neck. Her smile matched the smile of every other chorus girl, bright and lined with red. The sound was off, but that didn't interfere with the impressive choreography, simple but precise. Not a toe out of place as the dancers sashayed up and down a grand staircase. The leads swirled in the middle, a crisp tux and ballgown in contrast to the showgirl surroundings. Barbara disappeared off screen, the square television set missing the edges.

Brigit clicked the pause button and examined the VHS box with a hand-scrawled description: 35m and 1h2m.

"It's when she appears," Samson said, his heart hammering in his chest. He and Herman had walked back to the apartment as if nothing had happened, a kind of truce between them. Brigit had asked why he wasn't at the library, and Samson had mumbled something about not feeling well, which was true at least. His head throbbed. He shut himself in the bathroom to collect his thoughts. He knew he should go back to Cedarville, maybe even catch the same flight as Brigit if he could afford a ticket so last-minute. But he wanted to know how the story ended. He splashed water on his face and emerged to find Herman cleaning his cane and Brigit watching Barbara's tapes.

The sight of Brigit stirred something within that he hoped to forget someday. She had her hair pulled back into a severe ponytail and didn't turn when he spoke. He urged her to respond, to say anything beyond the clipped sentences he'd received since she found him out. How would she react to Herman's betrayal? He couldn't bear to hurt her again, so he said nothing. Herman shuffled into the bathroom after Samson, the thin door doing little to hide any sounds. They could tell when he brushed his teeth and used the toilet. They could tell when he spat phlegm into the sink. The place was too small for three people.

"I may have found something," Brigit said after a moment. Samson moved cautiously toward her, afraid of breaking the spell. When she didn't seem to object, he sat down beside her on the couch, keeping a few inches between them. It was as if an electric current ran between his thigh and hers, but she didn't seem to feel anything. She glanced at him, then handed over an unmarked tape that he'd only watched once.

"I didn't know what to make of that one," Samson said, aware that he sounded strange. It was the one filmed with a handheld recorder, an incomplete bootleg of some sort.

"I didn't know either. The woman struggling with her suitcase for a two full minutes. I timed it. And Ms. Lace isn't even in it, so I didn't know why you'd have it." Brigit grew excited, and Samson recalled the unsettling scene that seemed to be part of a longer film. "I've looked at all the tapes, and the scene doesn't belong to any of the movies. It's something else. And wait—"

She slid off the couch, and Samson tried to concentrate on what she was saying. "I think that's all of the ones I have. I filled my bag with tapes instead of clothes. I never meant to stay out here."

Brigit ignored him, sliding out *Town in Lights* and sliding in the untitled tape. "Watch."

Samson focused his attention on the screen, ready for the brief scene. Barbara began to struggle with her suitcase.

"But that's Barbara right there," Samson said, glancing at Brigit's expectant face.

"No, it's not. It's Isadora Alvarez, I'm sure of it."

Samson hit the pause button to study the woman's face. She didn't much resemble the old woman they'd seen at her pink, empty mansion, but this had been filmed more than a decade in the past. Moreover, her face in the film was bare of any makeup, every line showing, every age spot. Haggard, you might say. The director hadn't softened the lights or zoomed out. The effect was almost cruel, a woman at the end of her rope.

Brigit rummaged through newspaper and magazine clippings to find the one she wanted, a candid photo of Isadora playing with her dogs on the front lawn. Samson recognized the mansion, of course, and yes, there was a resemblance to the woman in the unmarked tape, but he was still disoriented, confused about what Brigit meant.

"Keep going," she said, and he obeyed, hitting the play button again.

A young actor stopped to watch the woman try to extract her case. She said something to him about wanting to left alone—the audio was hard to hear—and he didn't help. He walked away.

Brigit looked at him expectantly, and Samson tried to puzzle through what she was showing him.

"Cassidy Cullers."

Samson looked back at the blank screen. "No. You're sure?"

"It's dark, I know, but watch again." Brigit rewound the tape and played it again, pausing when the moody young man appears. "It's him. It's definitely him."

"I thought all that footage was lost."

"Not all, apparently."

Brigit smiled up at him, and Samson smiled back, pulling her to her feet. She was pleased with herself. Cassidy Cullers was a household name now, a star of action movies that made critics roll their eyes and studios rub their hands together. He might as well have been a walking dollar sign, each chiseled muscle a money-back guarantee. Samson rewound the tape and looked at the skinny young man, his hair slicked back and glasses thick.

"You're brilliant," Samson said, pulling her even closer before she stepped away and folded her arms across her chest. "Brigit—"

She held out a hand to stop him from continuing, making her way into the kitchen. Samson knew better than to follow her, so he replayed the tape, watching Isadora, then Cassidy. Samson remembered this was going to be a breakthrough role for him. He'd gone on to plenty of success, but it had taken a few years. Hollywood moved too fast for anyone to care long about the fire that had destroyed all footage of *Signs of the Children*. And the director, Jonathan S. Ferguson, had taken a few years to recover. Some say that he never did, his later films missing the originality and boldness of his earlier, stranger works. Dreams of awards and accolades slipped away, and he became more of a cult hero than a legend. Still, his fans were rabid and would go crazy for this two-minute footage.

They'd go even crazier for what he had hidden in his closet back home—the uncut film that Samson started to suspect was from the same movie.

"I think there's more," Samson said, not wanting to keep anything from Brigit. "I stole a reel from Barbara's house—"

"Of course you did."

Brigit pulled soap out from under the sink and rinsed out the sponge. She attacked their leftover mugs and plates from the day before, her frustration apparent in every move.

"Wrong, yes, I know, but listen. I think it might be from *Signs of the Children*. Cassidy Cullers is in it, as well, I think. Hell—pardon me—I wish I had brought it. There's definitely a young man. Barbara's playing some sort of store clerk, serving a woman dressed to the nines. Isadora maybe. In a later scene?"

Brigit whistled.

"That would be worth some money. Much more than a bootleg clip."

"That would be worth some money," Samson agreed.

Brigit turned her attention back to the dishes, and Samson knew better than to ask if he could help. She needed the distraction and as much space as he could give her. Samson walked over to the window and, out of habit, made sure he didn't see Seven or either O'Hara brother anywhere. He wished the frame weren't sealed shut so he could lift the damn thing and puke his guts out. It was too much. Herman's betrayal of him, his betrayal of Brigit. Barbara was really alive and had been hiding a valuable piece of cinema history in her floorboard. On top of all that, on top of everything, he still needed to find a library.

CHAPTER 24

Barbara Lace: Isadora was ambitious, sure, but God, we all were! Anything seemed possible when you were wearing a Valentino and calling for another round of Aperol spritzes. Isadora's parents disapproved, were devout Catholics and would have preferred she were a nun than an Oscar winner. Not that the Academy ever came calling. There was a rumor once—no, not even a rumor. A whisper, a sliver. [Pause.] A disappointment. You learn not to get your hopes up in that town.

Off-screen: What are your hopes now?

Barbara Lace: At my age? I just want to survive.

from *Isadora Alvarez: The True Story* (1985)
Director: Beatriz Acevedo

Samson hardly slept, alert to every car horn and late-night drug deal. He drifted off for a couple of hours, his hip bones aching from his spot on the floor. He'd been understandably exiled from the couch. Herman gave him directions to the nearest library, and Samson left reluctantly, knowing that Brigit was scheduled to fly home later that day. That didn't give him much time to change his life.

He stopped to call Bishop, and the sheriff sounded genuinely interested in Samson's theory now, such as it was. Barbara had faked her own death to get away from someone dangerous in her past, mostly likely one of the O'Hara brothers. But that past had caught up with her eventually and taken down her assistant with her. Bishop didn't buy all of the speculation, of course. For starters, both O'Haras were still in Los Angeles. Bishop would check flight records to be sure they hadn't left recently. But men like that had connections, Samson reasoned. Bishop admitted that they weren't making a lot of progress in Cedarville.

Samson had time to think in the car. Discovering lost footage from *Signs of the Children* was exciting, but did it help him? The library stood behind a pretty copse of trees, its brick new and clean. The interior, too, smelled like fresh paint, masking any mustiness the books might have given off. They'd moved into their new space recently, and Samson hoped that the magazine collection hadn't gotten tossed along the way.

A young, chipper librarian led him to the racks. Samson saw issues of *Vogue*, *Cosmopolitan*, and *The Economist*, but they only went back a few months. When he mentioned that he needed older issues of *Variety*, the librarian perked up even more, her high-pitched voice rising to a squeal that got a surprised look from the patrons milling through the aisles. Samson guessed her age to be about twenty-five, and she wore a yellow vintage-style dress that accentuated her trim waist. The hem was long, though, nearly to her ankles, and swirled a little when she walked him over to the microfiche. Though wholly appropriate, it looked more like a costume than work attire. Her smooth brow furrowed as she opened drawer after drawer before finding what she wanted.

"This should keep you busy. I love these old ones. All the harmless details. Not like today where every piece seems designed to be hurtful."

"I'm an old-fashioned man myself," Samson said in return. He wasn't sure if that was true, but the librarian seemed to like the response. She flipped on a microfiche reader and showed him how to load the slides. The gentle noise comforted Samson. He'd been chased by gangsters, shot at by a prostitute, and smacked over the head by a man he thought was a friend. The thought of an afternoon spent hunched in research appealed to him, and he realized that he missed his shed and work back home. He'd been kidding himself. He didn't want to stay in California. He wanted his old life back, but it wasn't coming back.

He didn't spot any useful names or images in issues from 1940–1950, but then Isadora started appearing regularly. Her dresses and gowns made the librarian's look like a Halloween throwaway. For a decade, give or take, Isadora Alvarez was the "it" girl. Rumors circulated about clandestine dates and catfights with female co-stars. The articles kept the tone light, though, and admiring. That's what readers wanted back then. They wanted to imagine themselves on yachts and red carpets, every handsome lead a potential husband. And Isadora did wed, in 1954 to some sort of baron, the man Samson had met at Steerson's. That article included the first mention of Barbara Lace as her maid-of-honor, but Samson already knew that detail from her obituary. For a moment, Samson smiled, thinking about how Barbara would react to her own obituary mentioning a more famous actress.

Samson rubbed his eyes, the glare from the machine making them ache. Then he looked back for the photo of the friends together at the wedding. Isadora's white tea-length dress still looked crisp in the grainy image. Barbara had an arm around her friend's shoulders, a drink in the other hand. They looked young and confident in their mid-thirties. Had Barbara been happy for her friend? Always a little more famous, a little more lucky in love.

From what Herman had shared, Barbara was more calculating than sentimental. That spoke to what he remembered, as well. He'd even wondered briefly if she might care for him, the way an idle man of twenty-seven can consider an affair with an older woman. She was still handsome and, for lack of a better word, special. Samson had never known anyone like her. He was embarrassed now to remember this passing idea. It never came to fruition, and he was grateful. It almost made him believe in fate, how his passing fascination with Barbara had led him to Cedarville and to his wife. He'd been lucky in love, too, though he hadn't admitted that to himself in a while. He'd been too angry to appreciate the years they'd had together.

Mick would have killed him if he slept with Barbara. He had no doubts on that score. The man had been obsessed; even a casual observer could see that he was more interested in her than she was in him. And those sorts of imbalances never ended well. Samson kept scanning, finding Mick in a few dozen mentions over the years. There were probably more, but Samson's vision started to swim. He forced himself to read anything related to the fame-hungry O'Hara brother, though. Mick had helped produce a series of bombs. There he was at a premiere, his wife's stout but well-dressed frame beside him. He'd never been handsome, but Samson could relate to that. What he couldn't understand was the man's drive for power and notoriety. It wasn't enough that he was feared by bookies and gamblers. He wanted to be respected by the town's elite. A fool's errand. Damn near impossible.

Samson took a break, nearly ready to give up. He'd been sitting for hours, and his back screamed. His head pounded, and he felt unsettled. Each mention of Barbara had buoyed his spirits. He'd found a nice photo of her from 1960, smoking on the set of a movie he didn't recognize. She faced away from the camera, but it was obvious she knew the photographer was there. Chin lifted, wry expression—she'd somehow combined wistfulness and wisdom in her expression like she was ready to play Queen Elizabeth. It was his favorite image, and he paid three cents to print it before continuing his search. After her Emmy nomination in the '70s, there had been a few more images. The SAG Awards, the Golden Globes. Samson didn't like those as much. The fake eyelashes and curled hair made her look like she was trying too hard. Then nothing for a few years.

He put up the slides from the '70s and reached for the box of '80s, his hands shaking a little. All he'd had to eat that day was a piece of toast and too many cigarettes. As if it had been waiting for him, the first slide had an article by Kit Forrester. It must have been one of her early ones before she was hired full time. She had a lively, light writing style that was at odds with the tough woman who'd shown up unannounced at his motel room. Sure, he'd called her for a favor, but he wasn't eager to form an alliance. He scanned the copy quickly, his ears ringing when he found it: *Signs of the Children*, producer Mick O'Hara. He had the ace he needed.

The club looked much the same in the afternoon as it did at night. There were no windows in the main ballroom, and the tables hadn't been bused from the night before. Mick seemed to be holding auditions of some sort, two young women pirouetting onstage. The silence was unnerving— they danced without any accompaniment, their thin legs whirling. The stage lights were off except for the footlights, so they were partially in shadow, too, almost not there at all despite their best efforts.

Samson took a seat at the back, gathering his thoughts and hoping that the element of surprise might give him a small advantage. He'd waited until he was sure Seven wasn't around. He'd never cottoned to the idea that truth would set you free, and he planned to bluff as much as possible. What did he want? That had seemed so clear when he left Cedarville. He still wanted to find Barbara Lace, but his reasons had shifted. He thought of a small, tidy house along a creek that never ran dry. He thought of a dog in the kitchen, of water boiling for tea, a book and a quilt waiting for him. He could take a deep breath there. He could give up a lot for that life.

Samson pushed away the remains of a gin and tonic, the bitter smell making him nauseous. When his hand touched the table, he jerked away from the sticky film. A laminated menu swam in a puddle of something and steak tartare had never sounded less appetizing. He nodded, at least one suspicion confirmed—the place was understaffed. Mick wasn't as flush as he once was. How much were the dancers paid, he wondered, as he watched the pair of hopefuls stretch during a break. They looked alike, sisters maybe, with their dyed blonde hair cropped short. Two of the veteran performers wandered onto the stage and sized up their competition. In the daylight, the professionals looked like warriors with the bruises to match. Their muscular arms were covered with scar tissue, answering the question of whether or not their fights were fake. Mick seemed not to see them—or was practiced at ignoring them—and focused his attention on the younger girls auditioning.

"Again," Mick shouted. "With more energy. That was fucking flat."

Samson expected the girls to wince, but they nodded. They needed the job. He could relate. He'd taken on some projects he regretted so many years ago. Producers who asked him to lie about safety standards. Directors with impossible demands for a small lot—forests and cathedrals. Even after all these years, the thought still made him sweat. The memories made him grateful to work for himself. He'd forgotten how to be grateful, but he missed his work shed and furniture. An armoire had never given him any lip.

The girls got into position as the performers they might someday replace stalked back offstage. It was if they simply wanted their competition to know they existed, what their future looked like, and it wasn't pretty. It was violent.

"You used to be a powerful man," Samson said, raising his voice, making sure that Mick would hear him. "Now you yell at chorus girls?"

O'Hara didn't whip around as Samson had envisioned. Instead, his body stilled before he began chuckling. "You're a fucking pest, Samson Delaware. Did you know that? I thought we'd swatted you away. My brother must be losing his touch."

Samson stood and walked toward the stage, aware that the dancers watched him warily. They were young, but smart enough to distrust strangers.

"I've been called worse than a pest. And I know we want the same outcome from all this."

"That so? Now this is a tale I want to hear."

"That's the thing about stories, isn't it? We like the familiar ones. Underdogs and lost causes. A knight defeating a dragon or some such nonsense. A horse flying too close to the sun."

"A horse? You mean a boy. Getting himself into trouble for no good reason."

The dancers continued stretching, but kept their eyes on him. Despite their flexibility, they seemed rigid, waiting for danger. Up close, they looked less like sisters, their noses and brows distinct. The one in a pink leotard had brown circles under her eyes. The other had dark roots growing an inch from her scalp. Both had caked on makeup, contouring the skulls visible below their skin. Samson nodded, but they ignored him.

Samson settled into a seat beside Mick, letting his long legs dangling in front of him. He was usually the least intimidating person in a room, but he felt strong beside the older man and the malnourished performers. He wasn't small, and he could throw around a little weight if he needed to. He worried about Seven, but not as much as he had during the past few days. The hired goon's role in this melodrama had become clearer to him. Seven didn't have anything at stake.

"So you've come to tell me about my own life," Mick said.

"Something like that."

"Better start then. It's a long timeline, and I could go any minute. Heart attack. Stroke. There are thousands of ways to die."

Mick wasn't exaggerating, and Samson didn't really know where to start. His suspicions had started with the club really. The old man's need to be in charge. *Signs of the Children* (1981), filmed but never released. Big name director, Jonathan S. Ferguson, big name actress Isadora Alvarez in the twilight of her career and a promising young man. Written by, and here was the part Samson loved, Barbara Lace. After years of trying to get a script produced, she'd succeeded, but what had happened? She'd moved to Cedarville a year later, defeated. What could have prevented the release after the footage was done? Samson didn't know a lot about Mick, but decided to start with the scene he could visualize most clearly.

"On the set of one of those forgettable pictures you kept afloat, you're lurking more than you should as a producer hired for capital not creativity, and a brash woman marches onto the set. I see Barbara in a crisp green suit, maybe, those oversized sunglasses she wore in the seventies. Not one to suffer fools, and you were, forgive me, such a fool. Rich, married, and unsatisfied. It was never enough, was it? You couldn't leave well enough alone."

The dancers had stopped moving entirely, listening to a tale that's been told plenty of times before. Same song, different key. An affair followed by a mess of broken hearts.

"Only ordinary people are satisfied."

"You might be right, Mr. O'Hara. Even so, I'd rather be ordinary."

"Not to worry there, Delaware. You should have been grateful to make the credits, any credits."

"Oh, I was grateful for less than that. All I wanted was a paycheck away from a desk."

As far as he'd figured out, Mick fell in love with Barbara, and Barbara fell in love with opportunity. She was patient, working him for a few years, maybe more. She had steady gigs and success by most people's standards. But she was never going to be a household name unless she got a Margo Channing in *All About Eve*. She'd even written the role for herself. Never mind that she had a drawer full of unmade scripts. This was her golden ticket. Mick was her way out of the chorus, finally in her late fifties. She had momentum from her Emmy nomination and a man who looked at her like she was something special. Never mind his penchant for pain. A tough broad. Barbara Lace had been tough since she was born.

"You hear that, loves? You're not in Hollywood to make photocopies, are you?" The two dancers shook their heads, and Mick chuckled again, enjoying his power over them. Samson felt sick, but continued.

"You were already overspending to be part of the Hollywood scene, but you figured, what's another million or two?"

It wouldn't have happened that quickly. Barbara was clever and would have played the part of hopeless romantic with aplomb. Samson could imagine the late-night meetings in Mick's Cadillac. Drives alone on Ventura Boulevard. A weekend in Napa. Maybe she'd even left the manuscript out for Mick to find. Made it seem like it was his idea. "This old thing," Barbara might have said, trying to put the pages away. If Samson were being honest, he was a little in love with her, as well. He'd been happy when she'd called him, when she needed him to rescue her. He'd flown to Mick's apartment, flaring with pride.

"I was fond of Barbara, sure enough." Mick paused, his eyes watering. "But I'll tell you what. That story was original. Beautiful and terrifying. A man could wait a long time for that sort of project. And once Ferguson got interested—"

Mick cut himself off, but Samson knew a little bit about Jonathan S. Ferguson and his influential career, his unorthodox methods. He'd started his career making romantic comedies and transitioned into thrillers, filming everything in remote locations so that his methods couldn't be questioned. He was said to use butcher's blood for key scenes, and the knives were always sharp. He was still living somewhere, off of royalties presumably. He'd gone into hiding even more successfully than Barbara, unable to recover from his reduced circumstances. His name a joke rather than an honor. Films were Hitchcockian, Kubrick-esque, an Antonioni or a Kurosawa. His name was nowhere to be found.

"Ferguson took over."

Mick looked at Samson for the first time, his eyes again dry and sharp. "What's the phrase? The devil in disguise. Except he didn't wear his disguise very well."

"What'd Barbara think of him?"

Mick considered the question before responding, clearly unhappy with the answer. "Barbara thought he was her savior, come to pull her out of obscurity." He turned his attention back to the women auditioning, seeming to forget that he wasn't finished with them. Or perhaps he pitied them as much as Samson did. "Come back tomorrow morning at eleven for rehearsals. We'll get you started this week."

Samson expected them to squeal or cheer, but instead they simply thanked Mr. O'Hara for his time and walked toward the wings, grabbing their matching duffel bags. The one in the pink leotard paused, then walked closer to the floodlights.

"What happened to the movie?"

She squinted against the lights, trying to make out the two men somewhere down below.

"That's the million-dollar question, honey. Maybe Mr. O'Hara will tell us how this ends."

Mick shifted uncomfortably in his chair as if he'd suddenly remembered that his back was stiff and his knees bad.

"Isadora Alvarez happened. She wanted the part Barbara had written for herself, and she got it. At first, I thought Barbara didn't mind, believed her when she insisted she was thrilled for her friend and wasn't it better to be behind the scenes anyway? A longer career?"

The other dancer returned to hear the rest of the story, too, wrapping an arm about her friend's waist. They looked like they could disintegrate, turn to dust in a storm.

"When did Barbara decide she couldn't stand it?"

"For years, I thought it was a fit of rage, but I've had some time to think about this. Much longer than you, Delaware. And here's what I believe—I'm not saying this more than once, and I'm not testifying anywhere. Barbara waited until the filming had wrapped, wore her best dress to the afterparty, and kissed Jonathan on his perverted cheeks. She posed for the tabloids. I'd never seen her more radiant, age be damned."

Mick stopped talking as if he couldn't bring himself to turn on Barbara, even after a couple of decades, even after she lost him a bundle.

"And then?"

"And then she sauntered into the production studio—nobody thought a thing—and burned every last scrap."

251

"Sabotage."

"Sabotage."

The dancers nodded as if they understood, but did they truly understand how dangerous that act was? She was defying the most powerful people in town, not just the director and producers, but the whole damn studio. Millions of dollars up in flames. Careers gone in a split second, snap.

"And nobody suspected?"

"Oh, MGM suspected that the fire was deliberate, but nobody thought it might be Barbara except for me. It was her script, her baby. I'd been there when she returned, though, her hair wild and smelling of smoke. Why would the screenwriter torch her own work?"

"Isadora Alvarez."

Mick chuckled again, waving the dancers away with his hands. They fled as Seven arrived, sweaty and panting. He'd obviously been signaled in some way. Samson flinched when he saw the imposing figure, but he had gotten what he needed and stood up to leave.

"No point in protecting her now," Samson said, though Mick clearly disagreed. Seven glared at Samson and moved to loom over him.

"Long time," Samson said, trying to lighten the mood, but Seven didn't respond.

"What'll you do?" Mick asked.

"I just want to talk to her. Just talk. As you say, I'm an ordinary soul. And what I want most of all? What I want most of all is to go home."

Mick paused to consider, but didn't stand up. If Samson had been hoping for a handshake and an address, he was going to be disappointed.

"Good news, friend. We've got a body bag your size."

It was the second time he'd been hit in the head recently,

and this time the pain was searing and instantaneous. He doubled over, cradling his skull and staring at Seven's large feet.

"You're never going anywhere with him," Samson said, forcing the words out between his bared teeth. "You hear me, Seven? He's an old, washed-up man. Everything he touches is trash."

The next blow sent him to the floor, spitting out blood onto the sticky wood. A kick to the ribs flipped him over, and he found himself staring up as the stage lights flipped on, blinding.

"You've had this coming for years, Delaware. You think a man like me forgets," Mick said, finally standing so that he could get a better look at Samson on the floor. So that he could tower over him, appreciate the carnage.

Samson struggled to sit up, but another kick slammed him back down. He covered his head as Seven hit him repeatedly, his knuckles getting slick from blood. Samson's skin split in multiple places, and his body shook helplessly when Seven stopped to catch his breath. He didn't bother to sit up this time, hoping that his beating would be enough. When the two professional performers appeared above him beside Mick, they looked like avenging angels, thin but solid blades in each of their capable hands.

CHAPTER 25

"We've got a ship, and we've got an ocean. All we need is someone—and some weather—on our side."

 —Barbara Lace as Joy Morton
 in *Another Bright Horizon* (1961)

"Why is this your story?"

Isadora sat on the edge of a velvet couch, one black kitten heel crossed over the other. Her black, opaque tights shimmered a little in the lamplight then disappeared into a calf-length skirt. She was classic and coiled. There was no other word for it. Her tense body looked ready for an attack despite her absolute stillness.

"Sorry, ma'am?" Even tied up, old habits die hard, and Samson respected the woman's advanced age. He hated himself a little over the politeness, but continued. "I'm not sure I understand the question."

His eyes were swollen, bruised, and bloody. Nobody had bothered to clean him up before presenting him, mouse to cobra. Snakes like a little life in their prey. After a few disoriented minutes, he recognized his surroundings. The filthy basement of Isadora's home had been cleaned up, but not much. Dust filled every corner, and the dim windows didn't let in much light. Somebody had put down a rug and a couple of chairs. The place looked like a student film set, somebody trying her best, but this was never going on the festival circuit.

"Who are you? A man satisfied with his unimpressive lot in life. A house, a truck, a dead wife."

Samson cringed and pulled at his wrists, trying to loosen the rope. He'd been ambivalent about his own death for so long, half-fearing and half-hoping that it would come. Sometimes the easy way out didn't have to mean failure, he'd told himself. Or, if he were in a more honest mood, he used to be all right with failure. The more he squirmed, the more his ribs ached. Broken, most likely.

"Well, I'm still paying off the truck, but I've got a dog," he said. Samson's speech slurred, but the words came out somehow. The woman ignored his joke at first, blinking occasionally but never shifting. She was like a statue slowly turning human.

Then she laughed, an inviting sound that echoed against the low ceiling.

"And a sense of humor, I see. That can get you so far, but it shouldn't get you here."

"Where might that be?"

"By the time I was your age, I could walk into any restaurant in this town and get the best table. Couture dresses arrived by carrier service, and there were half a dozen men ready to escort me to premieres. And did I claw my way to the top? Did I crush other people's dreams under my Steiger heels? No, I most certainly did not. I helped them. I coddled them all. Herman most of all. He stopped getting me auditions by 1975, but by then, I had my own contacts, my own inside scoops. What I'm saying, love, is that this is my story, and you're interfering with the shot."

Samson stopped working at the knots, his mouth hanging slightly open as his mind sorted through the puzzle. A cold March morning with a cold body and a hearse. And he'd opened Pandora's box, hadn't he? What did he expect to find inside?

"Ms. Lace?" Samson asked, though it was hardly a question worth asking.

"I prefer Sussennox, if you please. Lace seemed like such a wise choice at eighteen. Now, it sounds common."

She picked up a bell from the couch, leaning forward in a fluid motion. When she rang, the two performers appeared, their muscular bodies squeezed into cheap, skin-tight suits. Samson pulled more frantically against his restraints, but they were expertly tied. Somebody in the room had experience with kidnapping. Their knives sat almost demurely in their hands. But Samson had seen enough of their performance to know they were deadly. The pieces clicked together slowly, his mind racing to understand. Barbara hadn't been hiding from Mick. He'd been helping her all along, still a lovesick fool—a sick, dangerous, lovesick fool—after all these years.

"Even a bit character has his purpose," Barbara said, giving a signal to the women before standing up. "And it seems that you're the man to take my confession. I'm as dead as I was before, and don't forget that. There's nobody left to see."

"What happened to Isadora?"

"What happens to all of us. There's no cheating death for long."

Samson knew he hadn't missed Isadora's obituary. It would have been a national story. It would have dominated the news cycle, at least for twenty-four hours.

"Where'd you hide the body?"

"You never got this city. You know that? Who asks that kind of question as if there aren't cliffs and ocean water aplenty? You were a rube made for small-town living. And you ruined even that for me. I wanted to forget about my failures, forget I'd ever dreamed of marquees. And there you were, throwing your happiness in my face."

Samson tried to back away from the women as they approached, his arms tense and burning from his continuous efforts at escape. One grabbed his hair, and Samson hollered before the other one brought down a blade on his outstretched neck, pressing but not cutting into his flesh.

"You don't want to kill me," he said, his words muffled and painful.

"Don't I? It gets easier, love. And I don't even have to pull the trigger this time."

Samson tried to look at his executioner, but his neck was twisted at an unnatural angle.

"I thought I was saving you. From Mick."

Barbara made a strangled noise of frustration. "Isn't that my whole life story. Men thinking they know better than me. You didn't get my note, or you chose to ignore it? How could I be sure you didn't plan to sell the reel?"

Samson thought back to the projector footage, and it made sense that she'd saved a souvenir from the film. Her only scene from *Signs of the Children*, as an unnamed general store clerk. Her last role. The snakes in his shed, the footsteps in his house—she'd been looking for the only existing evidence that she started the fire.

Samson tried to bring up Herman, who must have believed the same—that he was saving her—but Barbara silenced him with the flick of a wrist. The knife went a little deeper, slicing into him. He yelped in pain, then felt the blade slide away. It hovered close, though, as Barbara studied him. If anything, she seemed tranquil. But then again, if you're dead, what do you have left to lose?

"Callista found out about you. That you destroyed the footage. You weren't afraid of Mick. You were afraid of that director, Ferguson."

"Auteur, I believe he prefers. Stupid girl thought she could blackmail me. As if I were a dragon sitting on some reserves of gold."

"And the police could hardly suspect you if you were dead."

Barbara touched a red fingernail to the side of her nose. He focused on the gesture, thinking that the truth would be more satisfying if he wasn't about to die. He pulled again at the ropes, but they seemed to grow tighter in spite of his efforts.

"Not just Ferguson," Barbara said. "Though he was barbaric enough. Who knows what he could do in a fury. Nobody's seen him for years. But my whole career, my whole reputation shattered. I was never a star, but at least I wouldn't be a footnote, a scandal."

To be honest, it was the only part of Barbara's monologue that made sense to him. He knew the worth of an honorable life now. Barbara's legacy, such as it was, would be one of a talented actress, an artist really, who worked for decades in an unforgiving business. He nodded to himself, and Barbara seemed satisfied by that response, signaling to her accomplices that the time had come. The knife reappeared at his neck, and Samson closed his eyes. Every part of his body hurt, and a small part of him felt satisfied that he'd tried to live, that he hadn't given up. If he saw his wife again beyond the veil, he would tell her, and she would approve. Her face swam into his mind, the joyful expression she'd been wearing the first time they met, as if amused by the whole world, ready to love bees and stings alike. Samson felt the blade slip into his skin, and he winced, but squeezed his eyes even tighter. Ready.

The sound of glass breaking brought him back to reality, and the brick from outside whizzed past his head. Brigit landed soon after, her boots making a satisfying thump against the concrete. She held another brick in her outstretched hand, hurling it at the woman standing shocked beside Samson. It hit her squarely in the shoulder, making her stagger backward.

"I called the police," she said. "That crazy bitch paying you enough for prison?"

The women's faces flushed in anger, and one took a step toward Brigit, knife held expertly in front of her body. It felt like time had frozen, Samson seeing all the different ways this scene could end, none of them easy. Then he threw his whole body toward the woman closest to him, the attempt awkward and painful in his chair. But he fell into her, sending them both to the ground. Samson's head hit the concrete hard, and when the woman staggered to her feet, she was bleeding, too. But her attention was focused on Brigit, not Samson, who sprawled helplessly at her feet. His panic didn't help him, and he strained to see what was going on around him. He was facing the steps and could see Barbara's kitten heels disappearing upstairs, leaving before the finale.

Brigit sensed hesitation in the second bodyguard, who hovered uncertainly in the background.

"I'm not bluffing. You wait around here, you're waiting for prison."

The woman stayed in place while her friend ran at Brigit, who dodged her and brought the brick down onto the back of her neck. She growled in response, and Brigit kicked out with her cowboy boots, landing a brutal blow to the woman's left knee. The pop echoed in the small space and sent the woman down, shrieking in pain. The other one fled. Samson watched her thump up the stairs, the same way Barbara had left. Then he felt the blade again, this time at his wrists, sawing at the ropes. Brigit righted him, staring intently in his face, and the rush of feeling Samson felt nearly knocked him back to the ground. He could have lived in that moment forever, but Brigit quickly turned from him to make sure their attacker wasn't going anywhere. Samson untied his own feet, relief and pain flooding his body as he stood up. He could still stand, and that was something. That was more than he deserved for being such an idiot for so long.

"Barbara," he said, and Brigit nodded.

"I didn't believe you."

"If you didn't believe me, you wouldn't be here."

Brigit didn't respond, turning her attention to the other woman's injured knee. The fight had gone out of her, and she was babbling, incoherent. Brigit didn't get close to her, but she told her that she would call an ambulance if she wanted. Or somebody to pick her up. Samson would have left the lady on the ground and hoped she never got up. He didn't feel guilty about it either.

Samson headed toward the stairs, his progress slow, and when he reached them, he wasn't sure that he could haul himself up. But the thought of Barbara getting away propelled him. When he got to the landing, he breathed hard, squinting into the familiar kitchen. The furniture had been removed, leaving only the unplugged appliances. He thought Barbara must have gone out the front door, so he headed that way, step by labored step.

But the sound of a gun being cocked whipped his attention around, and there was Barbara Lace née Sussennox, at the second-floor railing, a sort of vision. She looked taller somehow, her skirt pushing through the wooden beams, her posture ramrod straight. The air danced around her, dust disturbed after months of neglect, but it looked like electricity. And she was aiming right at him, a 1910s-era Winchester rifle that looked eerily similar to the one Callista Weathers had used when they'd met. Samson's first unhelpful thought was how she'd gotten the rifle on a plane, but his mind cleared as he started to think that she really might shoot him.

"You're an uncredited role, Delaware. An extra maybe that ends up on the cutting room floor. You are disposable." Barbara raised the weapon a little higher, lining up Samson in her sights. "Nobody will miss you when you're gone."

She pulled the trigger as Samson moved toward the front door, and the bullet ripped through the wooden frame to the right of his head. A crash from upstairs made him turn around to see that Barbara had been thrown back by the recoil. She flailed on the floor, whimpering a little as she crawled. Samson made a quick decision, heading for the stairs instead of the exit. He moved with more speed than he thought he could manage, reaching the upstairs as Barbara pulled herself back up and moved toward the gun. Her neat bun had come undone, and her dyed, lanky locks clung to her cheeks. Her lipstick was smeared, and she didn't look elegant anymore. Frail and lost. Samson hesitated, and Barbara, seeing his weakness, hoisted the gun and took aim at him again from three feet away.

Samson lunged at her, grabbing the rifle barrel with his left hand and shoving it away. A bullet crashed the ceiling, and his palm burned. He didn't let go, though, not even as plaster fell into his eyes. He towered over Barbara, but she looked at him defiantly. She even smiled a little, and Samson felt uneasy, quickly checking over his shoulder to make sure they were alone. They were the only two people on the landing, and his heart pumped blood into his swollen mouth. Every inch of his body hurt, and when he smelled piss, he thought it was probably him. He wasn't giving up, though, and he yanked the weapon free, watching as Barbara stumbled away from him. Then she staggered backward into the railing. Before Samson could react, she tipped over, screaming, and fell toward the ground. There was nothing to break her fall, and she crashed into the floor below. Brigit came rushing into the room a few seconds later and stood over the twisted body while blood pooled and surrounded her boots.

Samson clutched the gun to his chest and looked at them, stared at the macabre tableau, shocking in its finality. The young woman bent toward the older one, checking for a pulse that would never come again.

They interred Barbara's body at her Tennessee plot, a few reporters hovering nearby to capture the real burial, including Kit Forrester, who cornered Samson at the cemetery. He'd given her an interview—his only interview—and called them even, her favor repaid in full. Kit planned to write a book about Barbara Lace and had already secured an agent. It was still hard for Samson to believe, how many men were helping Barbara. Herman, Mick, Bill, and even Mr. Pitterson the undertaker. Not even counting the men who'd hauled the wrong body out of the right house so many weeks before. Hadn't he wanted to help, too? Hadn't he been taken in, kept like a doll in a box until needed? It was easier to believe that she needed help, that he could help someone.

Barbara's fake death had created a stir, and it was a late-show punchline for a few days before being overshadowed by the next story. It wasn't a joke to Samson, but by that time, he had already been acquitted, his explanation of self-defense resonating quickly with the arresting officers once they saw the extent of his injuries. He'd been worked over pretty bad, and his hand would be bandaged for a while from the rifle burns. His ribs were healing slowly—he could almost take a full breath again—and the deep bruises on his face had turned from black to yellow.

Brigit had avoided Samson for weeks, and he felt her absence keenly. He'd finished the table as well as an armoire for Mrs. Answood, who considered his victory her victory. After all, she'd set him on his path. Samson was in desperate need of a new project. He'd taken to sitting up late with Bishop at the station, drinking coffee and smoking cigarettes. They were quite a pair, grateful to have the mess of a murder behind them, but at a loss with what to do with their time.

"Pitterson get out yet?"

The police a town over had arrested the mortuary owner for aiding and abetting a crime, but they'd believed him when he told them he was only trying to help Barbara escape from a mobster. His sentence was lenient, the county unsurprisingly sympathetic when they saw the man in court, tired and defeated. Herman, too, was distraught to learn of Barbara's real character. He'd been deceived for years, and he wasn't taking the blow well. He'd stopped returning Samson's calls. Samson wished him well and hoped he found some peace. She'd wrecked a lot of lives and ended at least two, but if he were being honest—and he was trying to be honest with himself these days—she'd saved his. How much longer could he have gone on moping around his house, picking at his food and waiting for a reunion beyond the grave?

"Any day now," Bishop said, shaking his head. They were satisfied with Mr. Pitterson's light sentence, no matter the damage it had caused. Bishop was dressed in a clean, pressed uniform, and Samson didn't dare draw attention to the fact that the officer seemed to be taking his job more seriously. The town treated Samson with wary respect and seemed pleased that a local had succeeded where the TBI had failed. Samson didn't think what he'd done could rightly be called a success. He'd killed a woman. He'd killed a dead woman, but still.

It was going on ten o'clock, but Samson kept looking out the window, hoping to see Brigit. Perhaps she'd forgotten something at the utilities office and needed to return. The parking lot stayed deserted.

"You know what you got to do," Bishop said. Samson couldn't rightly say how long he'd been staring silently into his coffee cup. Bishop kept decaf for him now and even let it brew long enough. But it didn't taste like he remembered coffee should taste, and he thought he'd start bringing his own tea for these late-night vigils. "You got to go to her."

"You an expert on relationships now?"

"Shit no, but Rachel's talking to me again. I tell her she's a good mom, and she lets me see the boys on the weekend. It ain't bad."

"I'm happy for you. Truly." Samson looked at Bishop more closely, his clean-shaven face making him look younger, though not young. Neither of them were getting any prettier. They had to make do with the faces they'd been given.

"You're happy for me, sure, but are you listening to me?"

It wasn't the first time he'd been accused of not listening. He'd been stuck in his own mind for so long that hearing other voices surprised him. The whole world seemed too loud for him almost, but he was satisfied to be back home, and he was satisfied that he could hear again. Barbara Lace was responsible in more ways than one. And the more his body healed, the more he mourned her. Not the killer she'd become, but the woman he'd known, so confident and charismatic. Refusing to accept anyone else's plans for her. He was afraid to hear Brigit, truth be told. But he knew he couldn't put it off forever.

"You think she's up?"

"Delaware, she's too good for you."

"But so was Samantha Jean."

Bishop grunted. "But so was Samantha Jean."

Samson didn't cringe hearing his wife's name. It made him glad almost to think about her. He pushed himself back from the table, thinking it was time to let ghosts be ghosts. The drive over felt unworldly, a giant moon setting on the horizon, making the trees look blue against the dark sky. The sound of his truck wheels turning onto the gravel made him start to shake. Then he saw Brigit on her front porch, a quilt folded over her legs and a familiar dog at her feet, slapping his tail against the wood. They were waiting for him, and he was ready for them both.

Acknowledgments

Cedarville is inspired by my hometown of Wartrace, Tennessee, about an hour south of Nashville. It's nestled among rolling hills and rich in wildlife. At night, the absence of light can make you can feel as if you're living among the stars. I feel that way when I think about the amazing people in my life, as well. How did I get so lucky? Thank you to Ricardo Maldonado, Kristen Linton, Katie Meadows, Toral Doshi, Matthew Pennock, Tayt Harlin, Emily Mitchell, Eric Hupe, Davin Rosborough, and other remarkable humans. Jason Pinter has created something truly special with Polis Books, and it's a privilege to have him as my publisher. Being represented by the Ann Rittenberg Literary Agency is a dream come true. Ann inspires me with her intelligence and passion for this business. I am also delighted to know Rosie Jonker who draws a mean snake. I received invaluable feedback on the manuscript from Radha Vatsal and Alex Segura. Larry and Nancy Edwards (to whom this book is dedicated) were one of the happiest couples I've ever met, and they both passed much too early. I'm grateful to have known them. My parents Kevin and Paula Wright have given me unwavering support, and none of this would be possible without them. Finally, my husband Adam Province makes this journey worthwhile. Thank you all so much.

About the Author

Erica Wright's latest crime novel *The Blue Kingfisher* (Polis Books) is filled with "substance, entertainment, and chills-a-plenty" according to *The Seattle Review of Books*. Her debut, *The Red Chameleon* (Pegasus), was one of *O, The Oprah Magazine*'s Best Books of Summer 2014. She is also the author of the poetry collections *Instructions for Killing the Jackal* (Black Lawrence Press) and *All the Bayou Stories End with Drowned* (Black Lawrence Press). She is the poetry editor and a senior editor at *Guernica Magazine* as well as a former editorial board member for Alice James Books. She grew up in Wartrace, TN and now lives in Washington, DC with her husband and their dog Penny.

Visit her online at ericawright.org and follow her at @EAWright.